ANDERSON'S GOLD

Stephen O'Sullivan

Whimsical Publications, LLC

Florida

To purchase the authorized electronic edition of *Anderson's Gold*, visit
www.whimsicalpublications.com

Cover art by Traci Markou
Editing by Melissa Hosack

Published in the United States by
Whimsical Publications, LLC
Florida

ISBN-13: 978-1-936167-96-8

Printed in the United States of America

"Don't...please don't," I pleaded to him.

He appeared calm, unlike the scared and terrified image that I must have presented to him. He continued to raise his arm and it all seemed to be happening in slow motion. I knew I should shoot, but I was frozen in a state of fear. He could see it. He could read my reluctance to kill and he was willing to test my fear with his life.

I don't know how I did it – I don't remember making a conscious decision to shoot. The gun jerked in my hand. There was a blinding flash and a loud explosion as the gun discharged. The man's face twisted in pain, his body was pushed backwards and his arms were thrown both up and forward. His gun went spinning to the floor. He stumbled back against the wall and his hands came down to his chest in a natural reflex to cover a wound. His wild eyes stared at me in disbelief.

I watched his eyes roll upwards as he turned sideways, his weight pressing hard against the wall. He stayed that way for a moment, his face continuing to contort with the pain. After a few moments, his weight began to shift as he went crashing down to the floor without the normal reaction of reaching out to break one's fall. When his body hit the ground his head and legs bounced off the stone flagged floor before falling back down. He lay still and a red stream of blood began to flow outwards from beneath his body.

I had killed a man, but there was no time to think about or dwell on my actions. Ingrid had gotten to her feet and was stepping out the door. Her arms were waving in confusion and she was wailing with despair, or maybe it was shock.

"Ingrid, no!" I yelled as I ran to stop her.

I reached out to grab her arm, but she was too fast. She ran out into the open and made straight for the body of her husband. As I showed myself in the doorway a volley of gunfire rang out. I fell back and rolled to the side and out of view. Bullets came tearing through the open door, speeding across the room in search of human flesh. The gunfire from the hill ceased as Larsen's covering fire forced them to crouch down again.

I got to my feet and looked out the window. Ingrid's body was slumped across Olaf. She was not moving and I could see two red blotches on her back, the blood standing out sharply against the pale yellow of her dress.

"Tom, come on, Tom, while I have them pinned down!" Larsen was yelling from the barn.

I stumbled out the door and ran in a confused daze back to the barn.

"You alright? You ain't shot, are you?" he said as he looked me up and down.

"No...no, I don't think..." I couldn't get a proper sentence out, I was in shock.

Larsen hurried to the stalls and led our horses out.

"Let's get goin'," he said.

I didn't answer, I couldn't move.

"Come on, Kid."

He lifted my leg, pushing my foot into a stirrup and then heaved me up onto Eclipse. Larsen grabbed his saddle and swung himself up onto his horse in one swift movement. He reached out and held Eclipse by his reins.

"Yehah!" He let out a roar and prodded his horse with the heel of his boots. Eclipse followed, being pulled for the first few feet.

Leaving the barn, we turned and rode around the side, putting the building between us and the hill. We galloped out of the yard and into a wheat field. The horses cut through the sea of sheaves leaving a trampled trail leading away from the house. We emerged from the golden wheat forest into the open, about fifteen strides from the outer fence. Larsen led – he leaned forward, urging his horse on. They rose into the air before me. Every muscle in the black stallion was taut and working in unison as it lifted its giant frame off the ground. Its front legs found purchase on the other side as its back legs curled to clear the top rung of the fence.

I closed my eyes and hunched down, putting my trust in Eclipse. I felt my stomach heave as we went up, seemingly pausing for a moment before the motion of coming down was felt. We landed hard and I was almost thrown off, but I clung on, throwing my arms around his neck. Eclipse instantly regained his balance and quickened his stride to a gallop as he chased Larsen's horse.

ACKNOWLEDGEMENTS

In memory of my father, who gave me the gift of happy memories – a gift that grows more precious with the passing of time.

ONE

Stranger at the Door

Despite my father's incessant wanderings, Mother would never tolerate any unkind talk about him. I never quite understood the unique bond that had existed between them as it had been forged long before my birth. When word from him ceased three years ago, she knew he was dead, even before the news had filtered down from the Canadian border. But when the telegram did eventually arrive, it broke her heart, and something inside her died. From that day onwards, she was never quite the same person again.

My earliest memory of my father is an image of a lean man dressed in a blue uniform. He had just returned home from the war against the Southern states. I was only seven years old and too young to understand the agony of a nation torn apart. He only stayed a short while before leaving us again. A vivid memory of my mother crying and pleading for him to stay is firmly ingrained in my mind. Her pleas obviously fell on deaf ears, because he did leave. He departed for the wilds of the Canadian Rockies in search of gold. He returned several times over the following years, always broke and disheartened, and each time vowing never to leave us again. But as time passed, his wandering nature would rear its head and he would depart again with renewed vigour.

There were letters, but not many, and always from some frontier town or remote mining camp. The words were always the same; explaining to my mother how he was on the verge of striking it rich, and the wonderful things we were going do with the fortune he was sure to bring home.

Throughout my life, Mother's loyalty to him never faltered, but despite her devotion, she rarely talked about him. As a result, I grew up knowing very little about the man that was my father. Less than a year after his death, she also died. Her last words were, "I'm going to be with Johnny again." With that happy and apparently reassuring thought, she closed her eyes and passed peacefully into the afterlife.

I was often told by people who had known both my parents that I had inherited my mother's traits, a view I would not have argued with. For me, there was no great urge to seek adventure or the hardship that inevitably went with it. I was content. I owned a modest but comfortable house on the outskirts of Boston City, and I had a boring but well-paid occupation with the city council as a subordinate to the city's planning manager. I was young and seemed destined to live a long and unexciting life. Perhaps marriage and children before, just like my mother, I would lie down and bid farewell to the world. At least, that is what I presumed. Until on a bitterly cold and dark January evening, I was startled by someone pounding against my front door.

Wary of opening the door to such a heavy rapping, I called out for the visitor to identify himself. There was no reply, but after a few seconds, the door shook in its frame as the stranger pounded his fist upon it again.

"Who is it? What do you want?" I shouted through the door.

"Is this the Anderson place?"

"Yes. What do you want?" I said.

"To talk, Lad, just to talk." His voice was deep and rough, and had an unusual accent. There was a hint of European in it. I recognised the guttural trait from a German or perhaps Dutch origin.

"About what?" I answered.

"Damn it, Lad, open the door. When I talk to a man, I prefer to see his face."

Indecision filled me.

"I was a friend to your father." His voice had lowered, anticipating that his declaration would influence me to grant him access.

I cautiously opened the door.

He was a stocky man of medium stature wearing old and shabby clothes. He had a thick, dirty beard that was unkempt. From under his cap, I could see white hair protruding. His apparent age surprised me as his voice had made me envisage a younger man. Considering his age and that he appeared to be unarmed, I no longer felt threatened.

"Come in," I said, beckoning him forward.

"Good, Lad," he replied. "If I stayed out there any longer, you'd have to thaw me out."

Entering the house, he made for a rocking chair that sat in front of the blazing log fire.

"Ah, that's better," he said to himself as he twisted and squirmed, making himself more comfortable. "Any coffee, Lad? Make it strong and black." His manner was abrupt, but his tone had a friendly way about it, which compensated for his rudeness.

I retired to the kitchen to make coffee, but I kept an eye on the stranger. He sat basking in the warmth of the fire. He pulled off his boots and lifted his feet into the air, holding them close to the crackling flames. His socks were so worn that more toes protruded through holes than were covered.

I brought two mugs of coffee in and handed one to the stranger. He warmed his hands around the vessel, blowing into the mug. He was seemingly pleased with the cloud of steam that rose from it.

He lifted the mug to his lips. "Sacred Mother of God!" he yelled. "That's the worst slop I've ever had the misfortune to taste!"

I was taken aback, but he looked up at me and in a more jovial tone stated, "You must be Johnny's son all right, you make awful coffee just like him." A hearty laugh followed and I thought he was going to fall off the chair.

"So you say you knew my father?" I asked, interrupting his outburst.

"I did, Lad, for many a year. Jenny too, fine gal, it broke me heart to hear about her dyin'."

"Jenny?" I asked, confused.

"Your mother," he said.

"My mother's name was Josephine."

"In the old days, she was Jenny. I cannot bring myself to

think of her as nothin' else."

"I'm sorry; I never got your name. I think you have us mixed up with some other family." I sat up straight before continuing. "My mother's name was Josephine and it always had been. Why on earth would she have reason to change it?" As I spoke, I was picturing her – quiet, petite, and certainly not the type of woman to be changing identities.

He shifted uncomfortably in his seat, and I got the impression that I had insulted him. "The name is Larson, Bill Larson."

"Bill Larson?" I repeated his words. The name sounded familiar, but I could not quite place it.

"That's right, Lad," he said, with a glance that gave me the impression that it would not be wise not to question his identity. "Jenny or Josephine if you prefer, changed her name back in fifty-three when we hightailed it out of Wyoming territory."

"Why would she do that?" I asked.

"Well, if I recall rightly it was back in Dobson's saloon." Bill settled back in his chair while peering into his cup. "Craig Wilson had snuck up on me, Johnny, and two other fellas while we was havin' us a quiet game of cards. He was holdin' a scattergun and was plum set on blastin' us all to hell. Anyways, Jenny pulled a pistol from behind the counter and shot Wilson stone dead. Right between the eyes if I recall right. She sure saved our skins that time. Excellent shot, course she swore it were plum luck cause she never had fired a gun before that day... least, that's what she claimed. After that, what with the deputy and half the town council being kin of one kind or another to Wilson, it seemed like a good idea to make ourselves scarce in those parts. Anyways, wanted-posters began to show up here and there so, I reckon Jenny became Josephine."

I sat in rigid silence. This stranger was not talking about my mother. She was a quiet churchgoing and teetotaller woman, who I doubt ever held a gun, let alone fired one, and she most certainly did not frequent saloons.

"You were friends with my father?" It was not that I was particularly curious about my father, but I became uncomfortable talking about my mother with a stranger and I was anxious to change the subject to some degree.

"How's about some more coffee, Lad? This one's all tuckered out." He peered mournfully into the empty mug.

While I went to get the coffeepot from the stove, I glanced back to see Bill had took it upon himself to stoke up the dwindling fire, and I watched as he threw more wood on the flames. Returning, I handed him his mug and was treated to a repeat performance; the warming of hands around the cup, and the joy he seemed to relish in watching the vapour of boiling steam billow into the air. Content with his brew and the heat from the renewed fire, he leaned back in the chair and began to tell me something about my father.

"Well, me and your pa were pals out west, long time ago. We were no older than you are now. We worked a couple of spreads cowboyin', but when work dried up, we started driftin' from one town to another. That's how Johnny met your mother. She was working in Dobsons. Anyways, Jen got in a bit of bother with Craig Wilson and your Pa stepped in and gave him a good lickin'. That's how come he showed up a few days later with the scatter gun."

"My mother was a saloon girl?" I struggled to get the words out and the look of shock on my face must have been plain to see as I saw his eyes narrowing.

Bill's expression changed to one of distain.

"Get that sanctimonious look off your face, Lad. Jenny was one hell of a gal. Don't think you're so high and mighty that you can judge others. That's somethin' you'll learn as you get older, if you live long enough."

Bill's comment embarrassed and frightened me.

"Like I said," he continued. "We high-tailed it out of Wyoming and just kept on driftin'. Only now your mother was with us. Well it didn't take me long to feel like a spare wheel on a stagecoach, so we parted ways. That was the last time I saw Jenny, but not Johnny. I heard he joined up to fight the Rebs. Well, I joined up too, except on the other side. Sure glad I never ran into him durin' the war, don't think I could have brought myself to shoot him. After the war, we crossed paths up in the Yukon. We became partners and it stayed that way till he took a bullet from Wilson. Things ain't ever been the same since."

"Wilson?" I asked, remembering the man that my mother shot.

"Yep, Blake Wilson, known as Black Wilson. He got the name on account that he has a black smudge across one side of his face. Powder burn from some mishap with a rifle when he was younger." Bill used his fingers to indicate the extent of the mark. "Blake was Craig Wilson's son. He seems to hold me and your pa responsible for the killin' of his father. Be warned, Lad, of all the Wilsons, he's the meanest and cruellest there is. He's likely to shoot you just to watch you bleed to death."

I attempted to ask another question, but Bill put his hand up to stop me.

"Look Kid, I've given you a lot to chew on for one night. There are important matters we need to discuss, but it's late and I'm done talkin'."

He started to pull on his dirty boots.

"Will you come back tomorrow?" I asked.

"Tell you what, Kid. I got me a room down in Harper's Hotel. Why don't you make your way over tomorrow night and we'll talk some more."

"Harper's?" I asked, as the name was unfamiliar.

"It's down near the harbour, don't you know it?"

"Yes, now I remember." I was lying. I knew the harbour area, but I had rarely been there, and certainly not at night. After dark, it was not a fitting place for a gentleman. "These important matters we need to discuss, what are they in connection with?" I wanted to know, as I had no great desire to visit the harbour district after dark. It was an area of well-known disrepute.

"All in good time, Lad. Harper's Hotel, ask for me, we'll talk then."

Bill left the house and walked over to a tree were a large black stallion was tied. Mounting his horse, he turned to me and said, "Remember what I told you about Wilson, you be careful now."

He trotted out the gate and turned his horse towards the city. I watched as his dark figure melted away into the darkness of the night.

TWO

Wilson's Men

I found it difficult to sleep that night. Our conversation and the revelations regarding my mother, coupled with an insight into my father's life played on my mind. I tossed and turned well into the early hours as I listened to the gentle pitter-patter of rain bouncing off the roof. Sleep however, did come eventually, although I could not say that I slept soundly.

The next morning I woke feeling groggy. I relied on my faithful horse, Eclipse, to guide my buggy into town and deliver me to my place of work, while I lay back half-dozing for the entire journey. I had resolved not to call upon Larsen that evening and decided to forget about the previous night's events. My mother's past was her own business and as she was deceased, it mattered little now. As for my father's adventurous exploits, they were of little interest to me. His absence throughout my childhood resulted in my indifference to his memory. I bore no animosity towards him, but in my eyes, he was practically a stranger, and I felt no bond linking us other than a biological one, which seemed of little consequence to me.

For the next few weeks, I carried on with my usual routine. I absorbed myself in work at the Town Hall. I spent my days hidden from the world in a dingy back office. The room was cluttered with filing boxes filled with contracts, deeds, and planning applications. Documents would arrive on my desk, and I would spend my day checking them before passing them on to someone else. The job carried little in the way of personal satisfaction, but the promotional possibilities in the council were good. All I had to do was bide my time and I would undoubtedly climb the ladder of clerical importance, step by step.

It was a regular practice of mine to attend church services on Sundays. My mother had not been overly religious, but every week without fail, she would insist we don our best clothes to receive our weekly dose of religion. Since her death, I upheld the tradition. It was not out of respect for her wishes or for the supposed benefits gained through worship; I had to admit that my reasons were somewhat selfish.

Saint Paul's church was an impressive monument built to serve the growing Catholic community in Boston. Situated one mile from the city's centre, it towered above the double story buildings that surrounded it. Shaped like a cross and built entirely of granite with a sharp slated roof, the height of which was only exceeded by the bell tower, which was among the highest structures of the city. The tower rose effortlessly above the church roof. The building's arch shaped windows were leaded stained glass and individually designed with depictions of religious figures in a glorious array of colours. Inside was no less impressive. Long rows of pews rolled forward like ocean waves towards the church's altar that had been hand-carved from the finest European oak. A large organ dominated the back wall with its wooden pipes extending almost to the ceiling. When the organ did sound, the vibrations filled every fibre of a person's body as they reverberated throughout the entire structure.

The grandeur of Saint Paul's church reflected its affluent congregation. Sunday services were a social occasion with many of Boston's elite gathering for mass dressed in their finest attire. This was my reason for attending. I would be sure to meet some of Boston's most important citizens there and I felt it might pay me good heed in my future. It was also a good chance to catch up on the latest gossip and current scandals that were dominating Boston's social scene. The previous week's main topic of conversation concerned Laura Winthrop and her improper liaisons with a handsome naval lieutenant. Rumour was that he had a wife and child back in his home port of San Francisco. The Winthrop's were a family of high standing among Boston's social refined community, and her alleged shenanigans had caused quite a ruckus among the city's upper class.

While leaving the services, Emma O'Brien engaged me in conversation. Emma was the nineteen-year-old daughter of Thomas O'Brien, an Irish immigrant who arrived in Boston twenty-five years before. He had quickly gained respectability and modest wealth through his shrewd business dealings. I was well aware that Emma was taken with me. She often went out of her way to engage me in conversation, and she would regularly arrive at my office under the pretence of running some errand for her father.

"Hello, Tom, do you know there is a dance at the church hall tonight?" she said.

"Yes," I replied. "I heard some mention of it."

"Will you be going?" she asked, adding, "I hope so."

I felt a twinge of embarrassment. I had no intentions of attending, but felt it would be rude to declare this to her.

"Well, yes, I suppose so," I said with reluctance.

"Are you going alone?" she asked.

I could see where the conversation was going. I was being led straight into a verbal ambush and being the preverbal lamb that was being led to slaughter, I was powerless to prevent it.

"I suppose, yes I am," I answered.

"Me too!" she announced and stood back to stare at me with those great big blue eyes of hers, holding me in a fixed glare.

"Will you do me the honour of accompanying me?" I asked, guessing the answer.

"Oh, I'd love to!" she said, and shifted her weight from one foot to the other. It was the sort of movement one would expect from an excited child. "Collect me, I'll be waiting," she said, before turning to run back to her father, who was in deep discussion with the priest.

I rode the short distance home. While not overjoyed at first, the more I thought about the forthcoming evening, the more I found myself partly looking forward to the dance. I did like Emma. She was pretty, well-educated, and her father was highly regarded in Boston; sadly, her mother died when Emma was very young. I find it hard to explain, because for any young man considering marriage, Emma would have been an ideal candidate. But there was something lacking on my part with regard to my feelings for her. I could not fully understand or explain it, no matter how hard I tried. However, I would endeavour to ensure that she had an enjoyable evening in my company by being the perfect gentleman.

Later that evening, having washed and made myself presentable, I left my home and guided Eclipse in the direction of the O'Brien's house. I laid a fresh bunch of tulips on the seat beside me. I knew Emma was fond of flowers as she had mentioned it several times before.

I arrived at the O'Brien house and made my way along the winding and pebbled drive that led to the main house. The stones crunched beneath the wheels of the buggy. Finely cut lawns stretched out from both sides to meet rows of carefully trimmed hedges that were being tended to by the estate's gardener. The maid granted me access and I stood waiting, tugging at my shirt collar, the stiffness of which was digging uncomfortably into my neck. The hall was spacious, offering almost as much space as my entire house. A wide circular staircase constructed of dark mahogany, its steps covered with a rich red carpet of many layers, rose up and swept gracefully around to meet the landing of the upper floor. Above me, a massive chandelier hung from the ceiling. Its small glass droplets were glistening in the sunlight that shone in through a window above the main door. Decorative coving ran around the walls at the point where they met the ceiling. I studied the small and finely sculptured figures that were carved into the plastered coving. At no point could I see the same image duplicated.

Mr O'Brien appeared from a downstairs room and ushered me into the study. It was an impressive room lined with bookshelves that reached all the way up to the ceiling. There was a dry and musty smell in the room. It was the sort of odour that one would expect during a visit to a library. We sat at his reading desk to talk. He enquired about my job and council business in general. I prayed a question concerning my intentions to his beloved daughter would not arise. I was relieved when the door opened and Emma entered. I was taken aback by her beauty. She wore a long flowing blue dress that was quite tight around her slender waist. Her bosom was prominent, more so than I had ever noticed before. Her hair had a different style, tied up and dominated by a blue bow to match the colour of her dress. She had obliviously spent a good deal of time preparing for the evening, and I felt somewhat guilty over my earlier lack of enthusiasm.

I stood and handed her the flowers – my movements gripped with awkwardness.

"These are for you, from my own garden."

"Oh my, how beautiful! Look, Daddy," she said while taking in the sweet aroma from the multi-coloured tulips.

"Yes, very nice, very nice indeed." Despite his compliment, it was obvious from his bored expression that he was not a floral connoisseur.

"Molly, Molly!" Emma cried out for the maid and she quickly appeared. Emma handed her the flowers and asked her to find a suitable vase to hold them.

"Goodbye, Daddy," Emma said as she ran across the study to kiss her father on the cheek. "Help me with my shawl, Tom," she said, handing it to me.

I draped it over her shoulders and she pulled it tight around her chest.

"There could be a chill later," she announced.

Bidding farewell to Mr O'Brien, we trotted down the driveway, led by Eclipse. We turned out of the gate and travelled up the road.

"Isn't this perfect, Tom?" Emma linked my arm and snuggled into me.

"Yes," I replied, unsure as to what I should add to my answer.

The evening had indeed become colder than I expected, and I reached down to pull out a blanket from beneath the seat. I spread it across our laps. The cold aside, it was a pleasant buggy ride. The sky was clear and the faint glimmerings of distant stars were beginning to gain strength. I began to enjoy Emma's company and I was looking forward to a pleasant evening.

Barely a mile along the road, we rounded a bend only to find our path blocked by two men on horseback. I pulled back on the reins to slow Eclipse and we came to a halt in front of the men who showed no signs of yielding. A feeling of foreboding gripped me and I suspected they were going to rob us. The man closest to us had the dark tanned skin of a Mexican. The second was a filthy looking character, his clothes dirty and worn. He was exceptionally ugly; his face scarred with the marks of previous injuries. Both men wore side-arms and bore the look that goes with such men that would have no hesitation in using them.

They said nothing, so I spoke. "Clear the road there!"

They glanced at each other and exchanged a nod, the meaning of which I was uncertain.

I repeated my demand. "Make way, we wish to pass!"

"Tom Anderson," the second man said, and I was unsure if he was asking a question or making a statement.

"Make way there!" I demanded for the third time.

"Are you Tom Anderson?" he asked again.

"Yes, I am Anderson, what do you want?"

"Someone wants to see you," he declared.

"I have some money, it's not much." I still suspected a hold-up, and reached into my inside pocket searching for my wallet.

With extraordinary speed, the Mexican drew his pistol and aimed it at me. I froze and Emma's grip on my arm tightened. The other man dismounted and walked around to my side of the buggy while the Mexican continued to point his gun directly at me. As the man stood beside me, I could see clearly how horrid his appearance was. While scared horribly, his face was also ravished with the pockmarked evidence gained from a severe case of smallpox, perhaps from when he was a child.

He pulled my jacket open, and then turned his face towards the Mexican. "He ain't armed," he told his accomplice.

The Mexican relaxed his arm and lay the gun sideways across his saddle, but still gripped it. The man returned to his horse and as he remounted, he spoke again. "Wilson wants to see you. You and the little lady come with us."

He grabbed hold of the horse's bridle and began to lead us along the road in the direction we had been travelling.

"Tom, what's going on, who are these men?" Emma's voice trembled as she spoke.

"I don't know, but don't worry." I tried to reassure her while hiding my own fears. "It's some sort of misunderstanding, we'll get it straightened out," I told her before shouting forward at the two riders. "There has been some sort of mistake; I don't know anyone called Wilson." My pleas were ignored.

We turned off the road and onto a narrower trail. Despite the rough ground, the two men began to quicken the pace, pulling us behind them. Emma and I clung on to both each other and the buggy for fear of being thrown out.

Emma was scared and kept asking me what they wanted with us. I continued to reassure her as best I could. I tried not to appear alarmed for her sake, but the truth was, I was in fear for my own life and I felt helpless in preventing her from harm at the hands of these two ruffians.

After several miles, we came upon an old log cabin. Judging by its shabbiness, I thought it to be unused, but as we got closer, a dim light flickering through torn curtains told me different. We came to a halt outside and the two men dismounted.

"Inside," the ugly man ordered.

The Mexican had still not spoken. To no avail, I continued to protest. I got out of the buggy and helped Emma step down after me. I pushed open the cabin's door and its dry hinges creaked from the lack of oil. We were shoved in through the doorway and the two men entered behind us. One of them pushed the door shut. The room was dim and dank. The far wall was lined with old cupboards and crooked shelving, both of which were in a bad state of repair. There was a large stove halfway along the sidewall that was covered in rust and cobwebs. The middle of the room was taken up by a large rectangular table, which was surrounded by six chairs.

At the far end of the table sat a large man. In front of him lay a tobacco pouch and in his hand was a small slip of paper that he was carefully rolling back and forth between his fingers. He reached forward with one hand towards an oil lantern that was centred on the table. He turned the flame up and the room brightened. His hat was dipped low, covering his eyes and preventing me from seeing his face clearly. After a few moments of intense silence, he leaned back in his chair, lifting his head as he did so. I instantly recognised the dark smudge that dominated his left cheek.

"Tom," Emma whispered, tightening her grip on me even more.

"It's all right." I tried to reassure her.

"Sit down," Wilson ordered us. I began to sit and moved the adjoining chair to allow Emma to sit also, but the man with the pockmarked face yanked her away from me. He fell back into a chair and pulled Emma down onto his lap. I tried to intervene, but the Mexican put his hand on my shoulder and pushed me with great force back into my seat. Emma was struggling and protesting, but the brute laughed and wrapped his arm around her waist while using his other hand to rub her cheek.

"Don't worry, little lady, I won't bite," he said to her.

"Hank!" Wilson barked at him. His tone and threatening glare was enough to put the man in his place.

"I don't know who you are or what you want," I said. "But if you release us now, you have my word as a gentleman that no more will be said about tonight's events."

"Gentleman!" he grunted with disdain before continuing. "When I heard that whore died, I thought I was finished with the Andersons, but lo and behold, I learned that she had bred a brat." He held out his hands, palms facing upwards to make sure I knew he meant me.

"How dare you!" I protested.

"Shut up!" he shouted, and an intense glare of anger spread across his face.

Wilson looked at Hank as if asking a question without speaking.

Hank's expression changed to one of nervousness. It seemed he feared Wilson as well. "We searched his house, Boss, turned the place upside down we did. No sign of nothin'." His arm still clutched Emma's waist. She continued to struggle, trying to pry his fingers loose, but his strength far exceeded hers.

"Where is it?" Wilson demanded as he turned back towards me.

"Where is what?" I replied.

"You know what I mean," he said.

"I swear I have no idea what you are talking about."

Wilson took a slow breath. He lit his cigarette, and blew a cloud of smoke down onto the table where it fanned out in several directions. "When Johnny knew he was dying, I reckon he wrote to that whore. A letter, maybe even a map, something to tell her where he hid that gold of his."

Listening to Wilson's demands, I started to make some sense of what was going on. My father had struck it rich after all. Unfortunately, he never made it home to share his wealth with his family. Before he died, he managed to hide it somewhere and Wilson believed I knew where. I remembered back to the stranger at my door and his words came flooding back to me, "There are important matters we need to discuss." Wilson was right. My father did send a message, but not in the form of a letter. He entrusted his good friend, Bill Larsen, to deliver it.

I decided to keep up the pretence that I was ignorant to the whole affair. "I don't know anything. I have not seen or heard from my father since I was a child. There is no letter, no map. I know nothing of these things."

Wilson became frustrated, his agitation clearly visible. He produced a gun and placed it on the table.

"It's quite simple, Anderson, talk or I will kill you here and now."

"Then, you will never find it." The sudden prospect of being shot convinced me that it would be unwise to continue to plead ignorance.

Wilson hesitated. I could see him thinking. His glare turned to Emma and I could almost hear the devious idea forming in his mind.

"But, I could shoot her." He began to lift the gun from the table.

My disgust for him erupted. "You evil bastard—"

"Or," he interrupted me. "I could let Hank have her."

Hank squirmed excitedly in his chair and used his free hand to pull on Emma's dress, threatening to rip it, exposing her breasts.

"No please." Emma begged him, trying to push his hand away.

Hank laughed at her distress.

"No, wait!" I pleaded to Wilson.

He raised his hand to signal Hank to stop and the disappointment on Hank's face was obvious.

"Where is it?"

"It's hidden."

"Where?"

"My office, there's a safe, it's there." I was lying, playing for time, but it was all I could think of to protect Emma.

Wilson leaned forward with a confident look. "Go get it, now."

"I can't." I could see the anger returning to his face. "You don't understand, I don't have access to the building outside office hours and only the manager has keys to open the safe."

Wilson glared at me, studying me carefully. "All right," he said reluctantly. He casually leaned back in his chair and said, "You can go, but I want that map tomorrow. Bring it here, do you understand?"

"Yes...yes, I understand, I will," I said as I got to my feet. "Come on, Emma." I reached out for her hand, but Hank wrapped his other arm around her and then Wilson spoke again.

"The girl stays here, just to make sure you don't get thinking any foolish thoughts."

Emma started to cry.

"Don't fret, pretty girl, I'll treat you real nice," Hank told her as he puckered up his lips threatening to kiss her. Tears streamed down her cheeks as she tried to push his face away.

"Anderson! I'll keep my men in line, just bring me what I want and then you can take your lady friend home."

I looked at Emma. I was lost for words and overwhelmed with a sense of total helplessness. Her face dropped into her hands as she tried to cope with her despair.

I heard the door being pulled open behind me. The Mexican stood beside it waiting for me to leave. He was grinning, relishing in my unfortunate situation. I walked out, receiving a rough shove to help me on my way. The door slammed shut behind me and as I stood outside, I was tortured by the pitiful whimpering of Emma, who was now left alone with these rough men.

THREE

Harper's Hotel

The road leading to the city seemed longer and lonelier than it ever had before, and my thoughts were a maelstrom of regret and self-criticism. I slowed Eclipse enough to allow me to fall out of the buggy without suffering serious injury and I was violently ill at the side of the road. I crouched on my hands and knees, retching like a drunk that had indulged beyond his capabilities. When I could vomit no more, I sat sobbing like a helpless child. I cursed my inability to do anything in the face of danger. My sense of shame was only witnessed by my horse, my creator, and the star littered sky above.

But what could I have done? They were armed and I was not. They were three of them and I had Emma's welfare to consider. Regardless of what argument I presented to myself, the fact remained that I should have done something.

For one of the few times in my life, I thought about my father. What would he have done? I recalled Larsen's telling of how he had given Craig Wilson a thrashing for harassing my mother. But my only knowledge of his demeanour was vague childhood recollections and a snippet of information supplied from a stranger. For the first time I began to regret never having received the guiding words and advice that a father divulges to a growing child.

I stood and fixed my crumpled clothes, before taking some slow breaths in an effort to bestow a feeling of calmness upon myself. It had always been my practise to adopt a clinical and logical approach to problems that arose in my council position so I decided to approach this dilemma in the same fashion.

In return for either a map or instructions leading to my father's gold, Wilson promised to release Emma. But I knew nothing about the whereabouts of any such gold. However, I suspected Bill Larsen had information concerning its location. It was the reason he came to visit me that night, but I'd declined to meet him at his hotel. But what hotel was it? I closed my eyes and sank my head into my hands in an effort to concentrate. I struggled to recall, it was near the harbour. The name came to me slowly, Harper... Harper's Hotel.

I climbed into the buggy and continued on my way, urging Eclipse to run faster than he ever had before. But would Larsen be still there, after all those weeks? I had no way of knowing, but I was determined to find him.

The buggy bounced wildly over the rough surfaces as Eclipse galloped along the dark and narrow country roads. As we got closer to the city, the tree lined roads widened and fashionable houses began to appear on both sides of us. They were partially illuminated by the moonlight and the dim glow of oil-filled lamps hanging in porches. The housing became denser as we reached the city's inner limits and the roads became surfaced, easing our ride.

Reaching the city's centre, it was quiet and void of the normal crowds that thronged the streets during the day. Only solidarity figures could be seen walking and the occasional carriage conveying people home. The impressive modern commercial buildings that fill Boston City lay in darkness, waiting for the morning's return of their employees.

I made my way through the city and continued towards the harbour. A fresh sea breeze chilled my cheeks and the acidy taste of salt found its way onto my lips. The evenly paved road surfaces gave way to older cobblestone. The streets grew darker as the city's gas lamps did not extend to the port. Office buildings petered out as they were replaced with warehouses and storage depots.

It was my intention to ask directions, as I was unfamiliar with Harper's Hotel; a fact I found strange because my office dealt with the granting of commercial licences to businesses within Boston. We slowed to a walking pace, but the narrow streets were desolate of people. As I passed dimly lit taverns, the rowdy shouts from drunken sailors and port workers spilled out. Boisterous laughing, singing, and music were resounding from within.

I could see no sign of the hotel, but then I noticed a man walking along the pavement in my direction. The collars of his coat were turned up, protecting him from the cold ocean breeze, and his cap was pulled low over his eyes. He walked purposely and kept his hands thrust deep into his pockets, his head down as if concentrating on his boots.

"You there!" I attempted to attract his attention, but he paid no heed to my call. I shouted out a second time. He glanced up for a brief moment but then returned his stare downwards and quickened his step.

I kept going, scanning the buildings left and right for a sign above a doorway that would display my destination. We turned a corner and two women stood loitering outside a doorway. One of them said something to me, but I failed to comprehend her words. I continued my pace without answering.

"Looking for company, sir?" she said in a louder voice and this time I understood.

"No, thank you," I replied politely.

They cursed me with a barrage of foul obscenities, most of which I had never heard uttered from the lips of a woman before. As I continued further along the narrow cobblestoned street, I could still hear them laughing, their course shrieks echoing between the buildings that lined both sides of the narrow road.

I saw another man ahead of me. He had just come out of a doorway and paused while he attempted to light a cigarette. I pulled on the reins and Eclipse came to a halt. I got out of the buggy and walked over to him. The stench of stale beer filled my nostrils as I got close, but he seemed to be steady on his feet, and I assumed he would not be too drunk.

"Excuse me, sir." My voice caused him to look around, but he did not answer and waited for me to speak again. "I'm looking for a friend."

"Good evenin' to ye, can I be of assistance?" He had a strong Irish accent and tipped his hat in a friendly manner.

"I'm looking for someone. He's staying at Harper's Hotel."

"Harpers, is it?" He rubbed his chin as he thought about it. "Can't say the name Harper's Hotel means anythin', but down the end there—" He looked to indicate the direction— "there's a small tavern run by a fella named Harper. Sure now maybe that's the place you're lookin' for."

I thanked the man and offered him a dollar for his trouble, but he waved his hand in the air, refusing any reward for his help. I returned to my buggy and continued the short distance to the end of the street.

The last dwelling on the left was a narrow three-story building. There was faint light coming through the ground floor window and the entrance door was slightly ajar. Above the door was a small length of wood crookedly nailed to the doorframe and written upon it in crude and faded lettering was the name, Harpers Inn and Hotel.

I tied Eclipse outside and entered the premises. There were five round wooden tables, each with an odd assortment of stools and chairs. The room was quiet with a few solitary figures sitting at different tables. At the back of the room was a makeshift counter consisting of two long planks laid across several upturned wooden barrels. The floor had a coating of sawdust that gave a twirling effect whenever anyone's feet moved. The room was dim, lit by two oil lamps suspended from blackened ceiling beams.

I approached the counter. The innkeeper was slouched forward with his elbows resting on the crude bar. He watched me as I crossed the room, but showed no reaction to me approaching him.

"I'm looking for a friend. He may be staying here. Bill Larsen. Do you know him?"

The barkeeper seemed uninterested in my question and shook his head slowly.

"Do you want a drink?" he asked.

"No. Please, I must find my friend. It's vital that I find him." My distress must have appeared obvious and I got the feeling that he was trying to decide if he should tell me anything. He leaned forward and looked me up and down. Perhaps he perceived that I was unlikely to be a threat to Larsen as he nodded in the direction of a small alcove. It was off the side of the main room and I had not noticed when I came in.

I walked over to the alcove. I could feel the piercing stares from the tavern's patrons following my every move. The small recess had just enough room for one table and a man and a woman occupied it. The woman was scantily dressed in dance hall clothes, which seemed to reveal more of her body than they covered. She was slumped forward across the table's surface, her outstretched hand gripping a half-empty glass of whiskey. The man sat facing me. He was in his mid-forties, clean-shaven, and wore a western style hat. His eyes appeared to be studying me in great detail. I turned to re-question the innkeeper, but a familiar voice stopped me.

"Kid," the man at the table called out.

I turned around to find him smiling. I looked at him closely, squinting my eyes in the dim light. "Bill...Bill Larsen?"

"Who'd you expect?" he said.

It was him, but he bore little resemblance to the stranger that called to my house some weeks ago.

"Sit down." He nodded towards a chair.

I sat facing him with the unconscious woman to my right. I looked at her and wondered if she was alright, but before I could mention her condition, he pre-empted my question. "She's alright, kid, just a bit too fond of the whiskey. Don't worry about her."

She moaned a little and rolled slightly to one side so that I could see her face. I felt sorry for her. I found it hard to estimate her age as her face appeared crunched-up from years of alcohol abuse. But to be dressed as she was and having drunk to such excess, I could only wonder with sadness as to the kind of life she led.

"I thought you weren't comin'?" Larson's words disturbed me from my thoughts concerning the woman.

"I wasn't, but something has happened and I need your help."

His expression did not alter and he waited for me to continue.

"Wilson. He's here." There was alarm in my voice and the name startled him.

His posture straightened as he leaned forward. "You've seen him?"

"Yes," I said and proceeded to tell him the whole story. He listened intently without interruption. When I finished, I asked him a direct question. "Do you have the information that Wilson wants?"

Larson pondered on my question for a moment and then he looked over my shoulder to make sure nobody could hear us. He looked down at the woman slumped across the table and used one finger to prod her shoulder. She grunted and mumbled something incoherent before lapsing back into her unconscious state.

"Not here...upstairs, I got a room."

We stood, and I followed him to a door next to the counter. As we went through the doorway, I could still feel the curious eyes from both the innkeeper and his customers watching our movements. The door led to a small lobby. There was a spiral iron staircase with wooden steps leading upstairs. We walked up in darkness. Every third of fourth step was loose, and I could feel them shifting beneath my feet. Those that were not loose creaked as we put our weight on them.

On the second floor, we walked along a dark corridor. In the half-light from two wall lanterns, I could see the grimy wallpaper ripped and peeling from the damp walls in numerous places. Larsen stopped at a door and fumbled in his pocket for a moment before producing a key, which he used to unlock the door. We entered the room and once inside, he turned and locked the door behind us, leaving the key in the lock.

The room was dark and Larsen struck a match, using it to light a lantern that hung from the ceiling. The shadows receded to reveal a grubby room in which even the dim light failed to conceal the dirt. A round table with two chairs sat in the middle of the room. Next to the window was a locker and upon it, a washbasin and water jug. Besides an untidy bed, the only other furniture was a tattered leather chair.

"I thought it would take him longer to find you," Larsen said as he pushed out one of the chairs for me.

"Can you help me?"

"Sit down." He did not answer my question. Instead, he opened the locker and produced a bottle of whiskey and two glasses.

"Look Tom." It was the first time he had addressed me by my Christian name. "If you have any noble ideas about exchangin' your gold for Emma, you better forget them."

"So the gold does exist?"

"It sure does and if you can survive another day or two I'll tell you about it. But first, we have to sort out this problem of yours. Like I was sayin', you got no idea about the kind of men you're dealin' with. If you go back, Wilson will kill you. Sure as there are wolves in the Rockies. The girl, too."

"What are you suggesting?" I said.

"I'm not suggesting nothin'. I'm just tellin' you how it is."

"Well, regardless of what you think, I have to go back. With or without a map."

Bill sniggered to himself and shook his head while looking at the floor. "Yep, stubborn just like your old man."

"What would he have done?" I asked.

Larson bit his lip. It was obvious he did not want to answer, but felt obliged to tell me the truth.

"Hell, he'd of gone back, stubborn fool that he was."

I could tell that he was speaking affectionately about my father.

He continued with similar reluctance. "And I'd of gone right along with him."

"Will you come back with me?" I had a good feeling about Larsen. His loyalty to my father told me a lot about his nature.

"Darn it all to hell, don't reckon I've got much choice."

He tried to display anger, but I could see right through it. I held out my hand across the table. He looked at it for a moment and then lifted his own hand to grasp mine. Nothing was said, nothing needed to be. Bill Larsen had a new partner, Johnny Anderson's son.

He poured two glasses of whiskey and slid one of them across the table. I did not drink, but I felt it was not the time to say such a thing. This was his way of sealing our friendship. We lifted our glasses and drank their contents. The burning sensation of whiskey hit the back of my throat and scalded my windpipe before settling in my stomach. Its searing heat gave me the feeling that somebody had lit a fire in my belly. It was too much to bear. I leapt to my feet and grabbed the water jug from the locker. I poured the liquid down my throat in an effort to quench the flame. Bill broke out in a fit of laughter, his chair rocking from side to side, and I thought the legs were going to snap from his shifting weight. It lightened the atmosphere for a brief moment.

I stood and said, "Well, what are we waiting for?"

"Sit down, Kid. If we do this, we do it my way." He spoke as he refilled his glass and I watched a serious expression spread across his face.

"First of all, we wait till mornin'."

"The morning?" I was horrified at the thought of leaving Emma there all night.

"Yep, waste of time tonight, because they won't be there."

"I don't understand?"

"You see, Kid, you don't know these men... I do." He settled back in the chair. "Wilson ain't stupid. He knows you might return with help. So he'll be camped out on high ground watchin' the cabin. When nothin' happens, him, the Mex and the ugly fella whose name is Kelly will come back down in the mornin' to wait for you. He'll think things are workin' out, so that's when he might get careless. You go blunderin' in there tonight and you'll never see that girl again, alive anyways."

The thought of leaving Emma alone was a hard reality to face and a painful one, but I had to trust Larsen. I had no other choice.

"What do you know about this man named Kelly? And the Mexican?" I asked.

"I know them. They work for Wilson. The Mex is a gunman, and a real fast one. Rarely speaks, lets his gun do his talkin'. Kelly's a despicable character with no morals. He does all the dirty work, and he don't care who he does it to, man, woman, or child."

Bill stood up and stretched his arms back while yawning. "We got a lot to do tomorrow, best turn in."

He walked over to the bed and started to fix his pillows before sitting down to pull off his boots.

"Take the other end if you want." He picked up one of the pillows and tossed it to the end of the bed."

"No, I don't think I could sleep. Besides, I better tend to Eclipse."

"There's a livery stable out back. Ask Harper about it," he said.

I left the room, leaving Larsen to get his rest and retraced my steps back downstairs to see Harper. Little had altered. The same lonely figures were still sitting at their tables nursing their drinks. Harper was still leaning forward on the counter, watching.

"Bill told me I'd be able to put my horse in the stable for the night," I said to him.

"Two dollars." He continued to look forward, not bothering to turn his head while answering me.

I pulled some coins from my pocket and placed two dollars on the counter.

"Around the back, make sure you close the gate after you." Still without looking at me, he used one hand to slide the coins off the counter where they dropped into his other waiting hand.

I walked to the entrance door and glanced across at the alcove to see the woman was still there. She was sitting up and giggling while another man, now at the table was refilling her glass.

My faithful horse Eclipse was waiting outside for me. I patted him tenderly on the head as I untied his lead rope from the post. He was exhausted, his coat damp and glistening with sweat. He needed food and rest. I walked him and the buggy around the corner to the back of the hotel. A hastily constructed wooden gate made from strips of rough planking nailed together led to a small yard. The livery stable had four horses in it. I unbridled Eclipse and released him from the buggy. He was pleased to be free and wandered around the yard while I sought out grain, which I found in a barrel. There was an empty stall and when I opened the gate, he trotted in without any coaxing. He looked better after I wiped him down. I placed food and water in the stall before I left.

FOUR

Man in the Mirror

I woke with a jolt and without any memory of dozing off. I remembered sitting in the chair next to the bed and that was my last recollection from the previous night. There was no sign of Larsen. His bed was empty and the blankets were thrown back in an untidy jumble. I lifted myself out of the chair and walked across to the window. I pulled the curtain open to find the glass caked with dirt, and it was with difficulty that I peered through its filth at the misty cobblestone street below.

It was not long after dawn judging by the hazy daylight. Despite the earliness of the hour, the street was a hive of activity. Goods-wagons weighed down with barrels and wooden crates trudged along the street as they made their way to and from the port. Men walked alongside the wagons, whipping the horses in an effort to urge them forward, and their loud shouts broke the early morning silence. A steady stream of women pushed handcarts, making their way to the early morning markets. Some carts were stacked high with boxes of vegetables, while others were packed with fish and ice.

I was exhausted and felt as if I had never slept. My body ached from the confinement of the chair. I used water from the jug to wash my face in an attempt to freshen myself. There was only one towel and it was filthy. Instead, I opted for my jacket sleeves, which I used to dab my hands and face until they were dry.

I began to wonder were Larson was, but as I did, the door swung open and he marched in carrying a rolled up blanket across his two outstretched arms.

"Sleep well?" he said.

I could tell by his smile that he was being sarcastic.

"Yes, fine thank you." I lied, and his smile broadened in acknowledgement of my lie.

He dropped the blanket onto the bed and the centre of the mattress sunk under the weight of the blanket's contents.

"What have you got there?" I asked.

He did not reply. Instead, he answered my question by unrolling the contents onto the bed. I stood in silence, my body locked in a vice-like paralysis fuelled by fear. Larson read my panic as easily as one would read a headline in a newspaper.

"They won't give her back. We gotta take her from them," he said as his jovial smile gave way to a solemn glare.

I did not answer and my body remained frozen in a state of shock. The array of weaponry and ammunition laid out before me was something that I was not used to.

He picked up a rifle and held it out towards me. "It won't bite."

He laughed at my reluctance to take it from him. With hesitation, I held out my hand and gripped the rifle. As I did, my arm dropped with the weight of it and I had to reach out and grasp it with my other hand.

"It's a Winchester seventy-six repeater, fires six rounds just as fast as you can count them."

"I've never fired a gun before."

"Hell, Kid, I know that. Knew it by the look on your face as soon as you laid eyes on it."

He took the rifle back and swung it around with a sense of ease and familiarity as he showed me how to use it. "Bullets go in here, squeeze the trigger and they come out here." He reached down and grabbed a handful of shells from a box. He loaded the gun, pushing six bullets into it, one after another. He handed the rifle back to me with one more instruction. "Safety," he said, pointing to a small lever on the side and just above the trigger.

I inspected the Winchester, trying to familiarise myself with each individual part. I did not tell him, but guns frightened me and the thought of shooting someone sickened me. I tried to imagine what a gunshot wound might look like. The vision of a gaping hole, spurting with blood and surrounded by torn flesh made me feel weak.

Larson lifted a gun-belt from the bed. It was the type that could be worn at one's side. While the leather belt was worn and frayed, the gun appeared to be in good condition. He pulled the weapon from its holster and used his right hand to roll the chamber along his outstretched left arm. Each click was clearly audible as the chamber spun around. He opened a box of cartridges and upturned the box, emptying its contents onto the bed. I watched as he filled the empty cylinders with bullets. He slid the gun back into its holster and held out the belt to me. "It's yours. Try it on."

I put my arm through the belt and fixed it over my shoulder. I was instantly aware of the peculiar feeling of six pounds of weight strapped to my side. I turned to face the window, which was so dirty that it acted more like a mirror and reflected my image back at me. A strange feeling overcame me as I studied the reflection. A man with a gun, but the image did not reflect my inner fears or the crippling terror that gripped every muscle of my body. If it was not for Emma, I think I would have been sick. But the thought of her waiting for me to return was the only thing that kept me going.

I pulled the gun out of its holster. It slid out with ease. I used the palm of my hand to spin the cylinder around and listened to the whirling noise it made as it spun. I moved it around and passed it from one hand to the other as I tried to get used to its weight. I aimed at the gunman in the window and wrapped my finger around the trigger. I stared into the eyes of the man facing me and I wondered if he would have the courage to pull the trigger..., to kill another man. I could not answer my own question, but I prayed that if the need arose, the man in the mirror would have the courage to do whatever it took to save Emma.

"You'll do just fine, Kid."

Larsen's voice disturbed me from my thoughts.

"I...I don't know if I can do it, Bill."

He walked over and put his hand on my shoulder.

"Kid, there are two kinds of people in this world. Those who know what's right but fail to follow the path, whether through fear or lack of will. And then there are those that can be relied on to do the right thing. Why? Because they know there just ain't no other way."

He stared me straight in the eyes. It reminded me of Wilson's glare but with a different meaning to it.

"You're one that a man can rely on...can trust. I can see it in your face. I saw the same in your father. You're just like him, except you don't know it."

I nodded, pretending to understand his meaning. I did not know how to answer him. He was comparing me to a man I did not know. From the little I did know, I doubted very much if I was like my father. But I was determined to go through with this. Emma's pitiful face was etched vividly into my mind, and her heart wrenching cries tore at my very soul. I could still hear them, and I knew if I failed her, they would destroy me.

I sat at the table and watched Larsen prepare. He seemed to know what he was doing, as if he had prepared like this a hundred times before. He loaded and checked two handguns. One, he placed into his side holster before gripping it by the handle and sliding it in and out several times. Each time the gun came out, it gave an impression that hand and gun were one. I saw a strap from the holster going up towards his shoulder were it disappeared under his coat. He held one side of his jacket open and pushed the second gun into his belt. Both pistols would be concealed when he fastened his coat. He picked up two boxes of cartridges and shoved them into his coat pockets, one each side.

A second rifle lay on the bed; it was unlike mine, its barrel noticeably longer. He picked it up and pushed his arm through a strap fixed to the rifle before slinging it around his shoulder. Then picked up his western style hat, and using both hands, fixed it securely on his head. He turned to me and said, "Let's do this."

FIVE

The Cabin

Bill took the lead as we made our way through the city streets He trotted at a steady pace and I followed, my buggy pulled along by Eclipse. The city had burst into life. Storekeepers were opening their shops and many of them were placing stock outside to attract the buyer's eye. The pavements were thronged with people, all hurrying to their places of work. The roads were busy with buggies and carts jostling for right of way.

I glanced across the main city square. I saw the Town Hall, which was one of the oldest buildings in Boston. Its elegant façade ensured it stood out from the drab buildings adjoining it. Deep in the bowels of that building was my small paper-cluttered office. It would remain devoid of my presence that morning. Normally a diligent employee, my work paled into insignificance when compared to the task that lay before me.

We left the hectic city centre behind us and entered the more serene suburbs. The elegant houses that I had seen the previous night, silhouetted by the moonlight, were now standing proud, displaying their architectural finesse in the early morning sunshine. Most had maintained gardens, and the colourful array of flora filled me with a surreal feeling considering the darkness of our intended deed.

Bill eased the pace and dropped back to trot alongside me.

"How ye doin', Kid?"

"I'm alright." I lied. My body was numb with the sensation of fear and my mouth was so dry, I doubted if any quantity of liquid could dampen it.

"Here's how we'll play this, you listenin'?"

I nodded as I found it difficult to speak; such was the pain of my parched throat. Bill appeared not the slightest bit scared and I envied him his courage.

"We'll hold up about a mile from the cabin. You'll have to wait for a bit while I work my way around the back. You got a watch?"

"Yes." I reached into my jacket to confirm I still had my pocket-watch.

"Wait an hour then ride your buggy in, real slow."

"Alone?"

"Yep, let Wilson think things are workin' out for him. Like I said, ride in slow. Stop short of the cabin, maybe around two hundred feet. Try to hold up near a tree or somethin' that will give you cover when you need it."

"What will I do after I pull up?"

"Nothin'."

"Nothing?" I said, having no idea whatsoever as to his intended plan of action.

"Wilson will be watchin' from the cabin. He'll be feelin' pretty darn confident. When you stop, he'll reckon it's because you're scared."

"I am," I said.

"Sure, Kid, I know you are. No shame in it."

His comment made me feel a little better. I was still scared, but no longer felt embarrassed to show it.

"Anyways, if all goes to plan, he'll come out front if he ain't there already. The Mexican might come out with him. He may not feel the need to give cover from a window."

"What about Kelly?" The image of the second man's ugly features returned vividly to my mind.

"He'll stay inside with the girl."

"Why not the Mexican?" I asked, intrigued by his reading of these men.

"Because Mex is the gun-hand. I know Wilson; he'll leave Kelly watchin' the girl."

"What will I do when they come out?"

"Wait," he replied.

"For what?"

"For me. When Wilson and the Mex come out front, I'll go

in through the back. I'll try to get Kelly with my knife. Then I'll blast Wilson and the Mexican from behind."

"In the back?"

"Look, Kid, get those honourable notions out of your head. When you're goin' to shoot a snake, you don't wait for him to turn around and bite you first."

He dispelled any thoughts I had about a civilised gun-fight, if ever there was such a thing.

"When you hear gunfire, jump for cover and then let off a few shots from that rifle of yours. Don't worry about hittin' anythin', not from that range, because you won't. Just keep your head down and keep blastin' away."

Bill pulled up his horse and I did the same.

"With you out front and me behind, I reckon they'll run like rabbits. What do you think?"

"Good, it sounds good," I replied.

I was unlikely to think of an alternative plan. The only consolation was that there would be a couple of hundred feet between Wilson and me. A vision of Bill plunging his knife into Kelly flashed into my mind, but I forced it away.

"You clear? Want me to go over it again?"

"No, I'm clear."

There were a hundred questions screaming in my head. They all began with, what if. What if Wilson does not come out? What if he has more men that we do not know about? What if he is not there? I declined to mention them. I felt I was getting to know him and I could envisage the type of sarcastic answer he might give me.

We continued along the road until we came to the turn-off that led along the narrow and rough dirt trail. We made slow progress up the track and I wondered how I had been able to travel so fast before in the dark.

After a short while, I called Bill to hold up. I was not sure, but I estimated we were close to the cabin. Bill grabbed Eclipse's bit and pulled him off the track and into a cluster of trees where we concealed ourselves. He went over the plan again just to make sure I understood.

"Don't forget, when you hear me let loose, dive for cover."

"You don't have to tell me that."

He smiled and held out his hand. I reached forward to grasp it.

"Good luck, Bill."

"You'll do just fine, Kid."

Bill coaxed his horse around and started off. He twisted his body around and placed one hand on the back of his saddle. "One hour." He held up one finger to confirm what he had said. Without waiting for an answer, he turned forward again and urged his horse onward. I watched as he disappeared behind a mass of bushes.

I was alone and the silence was only broken by the gentle swish of tree branches as they rose and fell with the breeze. I checked my pocket-watch, the minutes ticked by with agonizing sluggishness. It occurred to me that I had not eaten in almost two days. It mattered little, as I doubted my body was capable of holding down food.

I checked my watch again. Barely three minutes had passed since I last looked. I decided to busy myself by checking my guns and making sure I knew how to use them. I emptied a box of shells onto the buggy's seat. Drawing the handgun, I pulled on the small lever that caused the cylinder to swing out. I tried to push one of the bullets into an empty chamber but my hand shook so much I was unable to line the tip of the bullet to its intended slot. I tried again, this time pushing the shell against the cylinder and sliding it across until it found its position. I loaded each bullet using this technique.

My mouth still ached from dryness. I took a canteen from beneath the seat and quenched my thirst. I checked my watch – thirty minutes left. The tension inside me had built up so much that I felt as if I might explode at any moment. I thought about running. Just turn the buggy around and take-off. I was close to doing it, but where would I be then? Cowering in my house waiting for Wilson and his killers to come for me? What would I tell Emma's father? How would Bill take it? He might even shoot me himself. No, I had to stay no matter what was going to happen.

I checked my watch again – ten minutes to go. I sat in quietness, a still silence that was only eased by the gentle rustling of leaves as the breeze filtered through the tree branches.

It was finally time to move. I climbed into the buggy and picked up the reins. Eclipse turned his head to look at me, his eyes wide open. He seemed to know there was dangerous work ahead of us. Although we had never been in mortal danger before, I somehow knew that whatever was going to occur, I could rely on him.

I snapped the reins and he started to move. His hooves struggled to get a grip on the loose soil leading back onto the dirt trail. We trotted towards the cabin. I hoped Bill was in position. I felt very alone without his guidance.

We passed through a small opening that was defined by two upright wooden posts. They were almost obscured by overgrown weeds and tall grass, and the gate that had once swung between them had long gone.

The cabin came into view and its dilapidated state was more prevalent in the daylight. Even from this distance, I could see numerous planks loose and lopsided. The roof sagged at one end and it gave me the impression that it might collapse at any moment. There was no sign of Wilson or his men. I assumed they were observing me from one of the two windows either side of the door.

I slowed Eclipse to a walking pace while I scanned my surroundings for a safe place to stop. Larsen had suggested a tree, but there were none close enough to the path between the gateposts and the cabin. But there was a ditch running adjacent to us. It was about three feet deep and of a similar width. It was dry and the bottom was cluttered with leaves and broken branches. There was a small bend in the path leading to the cabin and the ditch turned to run alongside it. I decided this would be the best place to stop. It was closer than I had wanted, but it was the only suitable place to provide cover that I could see.

We continued at the same pace until we reached the bend. I tugged on the reins and we came to a stop. It was eerily quiet. Eclipse dragged his hooves back and forth uneasily on the ground. He seemed to sense that something unexpected was about to occur.

I watched the cabin, but there was no sign of any movement. I wondered if Larsen was in position. Perhaps he was watching me? I did not want to look anywhere other than straight ahead in case I gave the plan away.

The agonising silence was finally broken by a slow creaking noise as the cabin door opened inwards. A tall figure dressed in dark clothing appeared at the doorway, but he did not step out any further. The man shouted something and I saw his arm rising to beckon me forward. I held my hand up to my ear to signal that I could not hear him. I had to hold my nerve until they came out.

"Come on in," he shouted.

I understood his words this time, but I stayed put, hoping they would come out. A shadow crossed the inside of the window. I was being watched and there were at least two men inside. The figure finally stepped forward from the shadows. It was Wilson and he took two steps out onto the porch. He stood and watched, obvious wondering why I was not advancing.

"Come on, Mex, come on," I whispered under my breath, trying to coax the other man out by sheer force of will.

He did not appear. Wilson studied the surrounding fields with a sharp eye and slowly began to step backwards into the safety of the cabin. Something was not right and he knew it.

It all happened with terrifying speed. A bright flash from within the cabin lit up the dark doorway. The loud sound of a gunshot startled both Wilson and me. Eclipse's body instantly tensed and his head rose up with alertness. Wilson spun around and crouched simultaneously to face back into the doorway. The inside of the cabin erupted with gunfire. The darkness of the door and windows lit up in a series of bright flashes that resembled a terrifying lightning storm. Eclipse bucked and broke into a frightened run. I dived from the moving buggy, throwing myself towards the ditch while clutching the rifle. I crashed to the ground several feet short of safety. I franticly rolled through the undergrowth until I fell down into the scrub that littered the bottom of the ditch.

The ferocious gun battle continued without abate. I clambered up to look over the edge of the ditch. Wilson was crouched outside a window and was loading his gun. Another figure emerged from the doorway with great haste. It was the Mexican. Without looking around, he was firing wildly back into the cabin. He stumbled and fell, but immediately regained his composure and jumped to his feet before seeking cover on the opposite side of the doorway to Wilson.

This was it and it was my time to act. I lifted up the rifle and rested its barrel on the rim of the ditch. I tried to aim, but a mixture of excitement and fear made it impossible. I wrapped my finger around the trigger and squeezed. My eardrums almost exploded from the sharp crack of the rifle discharging. The weapon jerked backwards slamming its butt into my shoulder. The searing pain made me cry out in agony. The instant I fired, the Mexican spun around and began to shoot at me. Clumps of dirt were exploded beside me and particles of grit were thrown up into my face. I fell backwards in a motion of part sliding and part rolling. The rifle was left sitting on the rim of the ditch. I reached down and pulled out the handgun from under my coat. I aimed up and held the handle firmly with two hands. I started to blast away, aiming directly up into the air. The noise was deafening and I hoped it would have the desired effect. I fired six shots from the gun before the clicking sound of the gun's hammer hitting empty chambers signalled it was out of bullets. I listened and could hear no sound. I scrambled up the side of the ditch, but I was too scared to raise my head over the edge for fear there would be a gun aimed at me. It remained silent for what felt like an eternity.

"Tom!" Larsen yelled.

"What's going on?" I shouted back to him.

"Come on out, it's all over."

I stood up, still gripped with the fear of being shot. Larsen was standing out front holding his rifle by his side. There was no sign of Wilson or the Mexican. I picked up my rifle and stumbled towards him. He turned and walked back into the cabin and I followed him.

Inside was a scene of carnage. The table was lying on its side and chairs were strewn around the room. Shreds of broken glass lay everywhere and crunched under my shoes as I walked. Sitting down with his back against the stove was Kelly. He was alive, but his face was contorted in pain and he was clutching his side. Blood was oozing out between his fingers as he tried to keep pressure against a wound. A crimson pool of blood was forming on the floor around him.

I turned to Larsen and said, "Emma?"

He nodded towards an open door that led to the back of the cabin. I went through. There was a door in front of me that was open and led out to the back. It must have been the way Larsen came in. There was another door to my right and it was closed. I opened it slowly, not knowing if I would find Emma alive or dead.

As I pushed the door open, a blue dress lay on the floor before me. It was covered in dried mud stains and was torn almost into two separate pieces. Across the room was a window with its curtain drawn. Below the window was a bed with Emma lying on it. She was on her side facing into the wall. She was naked and motionless.

"Emma, Emma!" I cried as I covered the distance of around six feet in one giant stride.

Her eyes were open and her body was trembling. I picked up a crumpled blanket from the floor and spread it over her. I placed my hand on her shoulder.

"It's over Emma...it's over," I said in little more than a whisper.

She did not reply and a tear rolled down her cheek to be absorbed by the mattress.

"I'm so sorry." I did not know what else to say.

"Tom." Bill's voice came from behind me.

I turned around to see him standing in the doorway. He was holding out a clean blanket and his long coat folded up in his outstretched arms. I took them from him and placed them on the bed beside Emma.

"We'll be outside. Take your time, we're going to bring you home."

I left the room and pulled the door closed behind me.

Larsen was standing over Kelly, looking down at him. "Watch him. I'm goin' to round up the horses."

I pulled my gun out and rummaged in my coat pockets for some loose shells. I started to reload the gun. I paused for a moment and looked at my hand. It was steady and not shaking like before. I pushed three bullets into the cylinder and clicked it shut.

Kelly was struggling to breathe. I righted a chair and sat down facing him. His eyes were open and staring forward. He moved and tried to push himself off the floor, but there was no strength in his arms.

I had never witnessed a man dying before, but now here one was, right in front of me. The life was ebbing out of his body and his face was starting to turn pale. I was calm and surprised at my indifference to his suffering. He moaned and moved his lips as if to speak, but no words came out. I heard the noise of hooves stomping and Eclipse neighing outside as Larsen returned with the horses. I started to turn towards the door, but a deafening bang threw me off my chair with fright.

Kelly's body pressed back hard against the stove before slumping forward again and falling to one side. I jumped to my feet. Emma was standing at the back door with a gun that she gripped tightly with her two hands. Smoke was seeping from its barrel and it was aimed at Kelly's lifeless body.

There were heavy footsteps as Larsen came rushing in with his gun drawn. He stopped and took in the scene before him.

Kelly's body was sprawled across the floor surrounded by a fresh pool of blood that was seeping down between the cracks where the floorboards joined. Emma was standing motionless like a statue with the gun she was holding still aimed at Kelly. She was wearing his long-coat, fastened at the front. A blanket was wrapped around her waist like a skirt, but only the bottom could be seen as the coat hung down below her knees. The blue bow she'd worn was gone, and her hair was wild and partially blocking one side of her face. I was struggling to get to my feet. My eyes were darting from Emma to Kelly's body and back again.

Larsen holstered his gun and walked over to Emma. He put one hand on her shoulder and squeezed gently. The other hand he placed over the gun she was holding. After a few seconds, Emma released her grip. She fell to her knees and began to sob. Bill put his hand under her arm and helped her to stand up. He picked up one of the upturned chairs and put it down properly. He guided her to it and did not remove his arm until she was sitting down. He gestured for me to follow him outside, which I did. I looked back at Emma, but I was lost for words. I had no idea what to say that might be of any comfort.

We stepped out into the sunshine. The horses were tied to one of the upright porch posts. Eclipse had calmed down and raised his head when he saw me.

"We gotta get her home. She's in a bad way." Larsen said, and his anxious look showed his concern for her.

"I know. I'll bring her out."

Before I turned to go in, I held out the rifle to Larsen.

"It's yours, Kid." He turned to tend to his horse.

"What about Wilson and the Mexican?" I asked. My concern for Emma had caused me to forget all about them.

"They high-tailed it out. With me in the cabin and you blastin' away out front, it was enough to convince them to take-off." He turned to face me. "You did alright, Kid." Without waiting to see my expression, he turned his attention back to his horse.

I felt proud of myself. It was true I did not hit anything as I was mostly shooting into the air. But I went through with it. I had stayed in the face of danger when I could so easily have run.

"I'll get Emma," I said.

I placed the rifle under the buggy's seat and returned into the cabin.

Emma was still sitting in the chair. She was no longer crying, but her face was red and her cheeks blotted from the tears she had shed. Her eyes were transfixed on Kelly's body.

"Emma, we're going to take you home now."

She did not reply, nor did she change her posture. I put my hand under her arm and coaxed her to stand-up. We walked out with me guiding her every step. Emma stared straight ahead and appeared to be in a trance-like state.

Even after I helped her into the buggy, she continued to stare into thin air. I untied Eclipse's rope and climbed in beside her.

"I'm sorry, Emma. I'm so truly sorry."

She did not respond. It was as if she could not hear me.

Larsen trotted away from the cabin and we followed. We travelled slowly along the dirt trail for Emma's comfort. When we reached the main road, we turned in the direction of the O'Brien house. How could I explain this to Mr O'Brien? Could he forgive me for the horrible fate forced upon his beloved daughter? I doubted it, for I was unable to forgive myself.

As we approached the house, Emma leaned forward and reached out to grab my hand. She did not look at me, but for the first time she spoke.

"I can't go home, not like this. Bring me to Aunt Mary's house." She released my hand and sat back to resume her trance-like state.

I called out to Larsen, and he turned around and began to trot back towards us. I nodded, indicating a turn farther up the road.

I had met Emma's aunt many times. She was a sister to Emma's father. She was a spinster and had played a large part in the upbringing of Emma, taking on a motherly role to a large extent. Her small cottage was not far, roughly one mile farther along the road. It did not take long to reach it. We came to a halt outside a small wooden swing gate that gave access to the path leading past colourful rose bushes and to the cottage. Emma climbed out of the buggy unaided. I stepped down, but she hurried through the gate, letting it swing shut behind her. She did not look back. It was obvious she did not want my company. I stood outside, holding Eclipse by his bridle as she hammered on the door with her fists. When the door opened, she stumbled in pushing it closed behind her. I did not even catch a glimpse of her aunt because it all happened so fast.

I turned to face Larsen. He was leaning forward, resting his elbows on the head of his saddle.

"She's in good hands now. Ain't nothin' else you can do for her."

I looked back at the cottage. He was right and I knew it. But deep down I desperately wanted to help, but what could I do? Her safety was my responsibility and I had failed. Perhaps she blamed me for her misfortune? If she did, I would not have blamed her as I held myself to account for what had happened. It was with a heavy heart that I climbed back into the buggy. We turned around and headed back to the main road.

"Where to now?" Larsen asked.

"My house. There are things we need to discuss."

SIX

Gold Fever

The country lane leading to my home had an almost tunnel-like appearance. Tall elm trees encroached in from both sides and gradually leaned in towards one another, joining overhead in a tangled mass of entwined branches. My unconscious easing of the reins caused Eclipse to slow and allowed Larsen to trot on ahead into the distance. I was in no particular hurry, and my mind was awash with mixed emotions.

I reflected on the morning's events. I had redeemed myself to some degree, in the sense that I had faced danger and risked my life in the confrontation with Wilson. Emma was safe, but what of the horrific ordeal that she had endured at the hands of Wilson's men? My heart sank at the thought of it. Her pitiful face, swollen from a dark night of continuous crying was painfully etched into my mind, and I could not dispel the image. She had changed. Of course, I realised that she was traumatised, but it was more than that. Something was gone, something deep within her. Emma would never be the same again, and I held myself largely responsible for her suffering.

Before this horrible mess, had someone told me that she could have killed a man, I would never have believed it possible. Yet, she did just that. I had wrestled with my own conscience as to whether I could kill another human being; it took a traumatic experience to cause Emma to pull the trigger. I wondered what would it take for me to do the same.

Larsen pulled up his horse and turned, waiting for me to

catch up. I was taking him to my home, but as I got closer, I could not help but wonder, where was he taking me?

The smell of smouldering wood filled the air long before we came upon the scene. My home, the house that my parents had purchased twenty-five years ago, was gone. In its place was a darkened pile of scorched wood with small plumes of whirling smoke still escaping from the crackling mound.

I climbed out of the buggy and walked around the devastation that once was my house. There was little left. Every possession of mine, from the smallest cufflink to the grand piano that my mother took such delight in playing was destroyed, burnt almost beyond recognition.

The small stable next to the house was the only thing that had survived, although not intentionally. For I could see scorch marks on the roof where a lighted torch had landed, only to roll off and burn out harmlessly on the ground.

"Why?" I asked myself as much as I did Larsen.

"Wilson's callin' card," he said. "Just pure meanness. He don't need no particular reason."

Eclipse neighed and raised his head. He sensed my feeling of loss. I patted his mane and he crooked his head to one side. It was a trait he had always displayed to show his affection.

I turned to Larsen and said, "What now?"

He tilted his hat back and leaned forward. He rested his elbow on the front of his saddle and used the same arm to support his head while rubbing his chin at the same time. "The way I see it, you got two choices. Stay here and put your life back together, course, you will always be lookin' over your shoulder, waitin' for Wilson. Or you can come with me."

"Where?"

"Canada."

"Canada!" I blurted out in disbelief.

He nodded. "That's where I'm goin'. I was only waitin' for the weather to break up north. I'm goin' to collect my gold. Half of it belongs to you. Expect I'll run into Wilson along the way."

For the first time since yesterday the mention of Wilson's name did not leave me with a sickening feeling in the pit of my stomach. Maybe it was because I had seen him flee back at the cabin and I realised that despite his evilness, he was just a man, no different from any other.

I felt a sensation of change within me. My job and peaceful existence no longer seemed as important as it once did. I had no great urge to travel north as my father had done, but something unseen was gnawing at my soul. A feeling there was something that I had to do, that I had unfinished business to attend to. What is was, I did not know and I was confused. Perhaps it was to find my father's gold or maybe I was destined to put an end to Wilson. The only thing that seemed certain was that I would not find the answer here, living in Boston.

"I'm coming with you," I said.

"Never thought it would be any other way." He smiled, satisfied that he knew my character better than I did myself.

We tended to the animals. There was hay in the stable and Larsen spread it out on the ground. I unhitched Eclipse from the buggy and he trotted straight over to feed alongside Larsen's stallion.

While the horses ate, I sought out an old saddle from the back of the stable. It belonged to my father, but had lain unused for a long time. It was filthy and had a coating of mildew covering it. I set about cleaning it with some dampened cloths. As the dust and grime gave way from a vigorous scrubbing, the brown leather began to shine, renewing it to its former glory. The metal stirrups had a light coating of rust and I was unable to do much about that. Despite its lack of use, it was in good condition.

After the horses finished eating, they trotted around, happy to roam free in the garden while we picked comfortable spots to lie down and rest. I dozed off – the past two days had taken a lot out of me. It was some hours later when Larsen prodded me with his boot. I clambered to my feet, still groggy, but the warm afternoon sun helped to revive me.

Eclipse was stomping the ground, nudging me with his head. He was eager to be on the road again. I saddled him, letting out the leather straps to fit around his broad frame. He was so used to pulling a buggy, that I wondered how he would react to a rider on his back. I need not have worried. I put one foot into a stirrup and pulled myself up while throwing my other leg over his back. I settled myself into the saddle and he stood patiently, waiting for my guidance as to direction.

We trotted side by side away from my home. Without slowing, I turned sideways in the saddle for a last look. The small plumes of smoke had died out and all that remained was a charred heap of burnt wood.

"Which way?" I asked.

"South, it's too risky to go back into the city. Wilson knows I'm here now and he's probably already found out where I'm stayin'. Him and the Mex might be waitin' for us at Harper's. When we don't show, he'll know what our plans are. They'll be makin' for Canada, just like us."

For the rest of the day, we travelled south. It was our intention to board a westbound train at Providence, a small town, one hundred miles southwest of Boston. We left the main roads and cut across country, skirting the large farms that dominated this part of the countryside.

As night approached, we stopped to camp by a fast flowing stream. I use the word camp in the widest of terms, for we possessed little that would normally be associated with the pursuit of camping outdoors. Without a canvas sheet or even bedrolls, I was not looking forward to bedding down for the night.

Larsen produced a length of coiled wire from his saddlebag and set about trying to catch fish in the stream. I looked after the horses. They needed tending to, after their day's labour. When I finished, I left them tied with long lengths of rope to allow them to graze with relative freedom. After seeing to their needs, I collected scraps of wood, which lay around in abundance. I built a large campfire, as the evening's cold was beginning to take hold.

It took two hours for Larsen to catch three modestly sized sliver carp fish. I watched as he prepared them. Using his knife, he skilfully set about gutting and scaling the fish before removing the bones. We used long thin sticks to pierce them and then lightly roasted them above the flames. It was a meagre meal, a few mouthfuls and they were gone. I was still hungry and the low growling noises from my stomach confirmed it.

The night grew dark and the clear sky displayed a vast array of dazzling stars above us. We settled down using an old fallen tree to sit on. The roaring fire emitted enough heat to ward off the cold night air.

"Hell, I'd give my share of the gold for some coffee now," Larsen said, before reaching into his coat pocket and producing a pipe and tobacco pouch. He began to pull out clumps of tobacco using two fingers and started to pack it into the pipe.

"Tell me about the gold, Bill."

"Well I reckon it's about time you knew the whole story."

He struck a match off a stone and held it over the pipe. The flame was pulled down into the tobacco as he sucked feverously in an effort to light it. Puffs of grey smoke indicated it was lit and he shook the match before tossing it aside. A look of contented pleasure spread across his face as he inhaled the smoke deep into his lungs. He paused for a moment, nurturing the feeling, and then exhaled a long stream of smoke. The greyish cloud was carried off with the wind to evaporate into the air.

"When the war ended," he continued. "I drifted up north. Thought I'd try my luck at prospectin'. Worked a few claims, made a livin', but never more than enough to start diggin' someplace else. I ran across your father in some small town, can't recall the name, but it sure did my heart good to see Johnny again. He told me about Jenny livin' in Boston with his son, that would be you, I reckon." He broke into a laugh, gripping his ribcage as if it might bust open.

"I guess he had gold fever, too?" I said, interrupting his bout of amusement.

"Gold fever? Why you stupid greenhorn! Your Pa was probably the only man north of the border that didn't have gold fever."

"I'm sorry...I don't understand?" I said, trying to calm

him down.

His attention went back to his pipe, which had gone out.

"Gold fever," he continued, "is the curse of desperate men. It takes over their lives, consumin' every thought and every dream until it becomes an obsession that often destroys them. I don't lie when I say many a good man has lost his way, driven by the pursuit of wealth."

"But, if my father did not have gold fever, then why spend all those years searching for it?"

"For you, Tom, and your mother. Hell, Johnny would have been happy livin' out on the range without a cent to his name. But him and Jenny wanted somethin' better for you. They wanted you to get a good education, a proper job. I guess they wanted you to live a decent life and not have to survive by your wits day after day as they had done."

When he finished speaking, there was a long silence. We were both lost in our separate thoughts. He was reflecting back to his friend, my father. I was doing the same. Although I had not really known him, I began to feel a sense of guilt. He had been devoted to me and my mother, and I had not appreciated his efforts.

"As for me," he spoke again. "I reckon I had a touch of the fever. There were other things I could have bein' doin' instead of spendin' my years prospectin' in the hills."

The fire was dwindling. I bent down and used some of the smaller logs to build it up again. I sat back and waited for him to continue at his own pace.

"Anyways, me and Johnny headed for the high country, the Canadian Rockies. Most others were headin' for the Yukon, but I'd spent time trappin' in those parts and I'd seen some promisin' signs. We stocked up in a small town below the treeline. But what we didn't know was that one of the Wilson clan ran the supply store and word got back to Blake."

"Blake Wilson." I don't know what prompted me to repeat his name, perhaps it was to remind myself of the hatred that was growing inside me.

"Yep, Wilson," Larsen continued his story. "Well, we got lucky, set up our mine at the right spot and hit it big. But don't you go thinkin' it was easy." He leaned forward, pointing his finger towards me. "Gold don't come jumpin' out of the ground. Nope." He leaned back, resuming his relaxed posture. "Two years we worked that mine, seven days a week for two long years. Backbreakin' work it was, froze in the winter and summers so hot, the sweat burnt our eyes. Every four weeks, one of us would make the trip into town for fresh supplies. We'd bring a small amount of gold dust and use it to buy food, coffee, and anythin' else we needed." Larsen buttoned up his coat; the cold of the night was starting to bite, despite the warmth of the fire.

"It turned out that Wilson was informed every time one of us went into town. He knew about every pound of coffee, how much meat we bought. He knew everythin'. That bastard was just sittin' back and lettin' us do all the hard work before he made his move."

"What happened to my father?"

"Well, I guess that's where we made our mistake. When it came time to leave, we decided we needed two extra mules to carry the gold. I made the trip into town, bought supplies and the mules. While I was gone, Johnny stayed to close-up the mine. 'Repairin' the mountain,' he called it. I reckon it was only fair. That mountain was good to us, seemed only right to put her back to the way she was before we arrived."

Larsen paused again to attend to his pipe. I had come to the conclusion that his two greatest pleasures in life were coffee and his pipe. I threw some extra wood on the fire, which was beginning to dwindle again.

While he occupied himself, tapping his pipe against the tree trunk in an effort to clean it out, I stared out into the surrounding darkness. I thought about my position. I was heading to Canada and my only possessions were Eclipse, my father's saddle, two guns, and the clothes I was wearing. Only two days previous, my circumstances were so different. I owned my own home, had an occupation, and I was beginning to think about the future, maybe even marriage. I wondered what the future held in store for me now.

"When the mine was closed up," Larsen continued. "We packed our belongin's, the gold too, onto the mules.

"How much was there?" My curiosity had finally gotten the better of me.

"We reckoned about a hundred thousand dollars' worth."

He smiled at the look of astonishment on my face. "A lot of money, Tom. Enough to rebuild your house and set you up real nice for the rest of your days."

"And half is mine?"

"Sure is, Kid."

"What happened then?" I urged him to continue.

"We were makin' our way down out of the mountain, headin' for town. That's when Wilson struck. Him and maybe half a dozen more ambushed us. They picked their spot well. We were passin' through a narrow gorge when they let loose. To this day, I'll never understand how we got out alive. The mules bolted, Johnny rode at full gallop, standin' up in the stirrups and blastin' away at them. I followed, couldn't get a shot off though. I was hanging onto my horse for dear life."

I sat in silence listening to Larsen's account of my father's actions. It occurred to me that he was a man of great courage; it was something that did not come quite so easily to his son.

"We caught up with the mules soon after. It was gettin' dark and we were able to slip off the trail and cut through the woodland. It was the next day before they picked up our tracks. It gave us some time."

"Is that when my father was shot?"

"Yep. Turned out he took a bullet through the side." He placed the palm of his hand on his lower right side to show me where he meant. "It went straight through without hittin' any major organs; even the bleedin' wasn't too bad. I done some doctorin' on him, plugged the wound and stitched it up. I thought he would be alright, but the next day he felt real bad and only got worse after that." Larsen went quiet for a moment before continuing. "Tough old sod he was, and the best friend I ever had."

Once again, he went silent while attending to his pipe. I could see the emotion in his face, even though he was trying hard to conceal it. I remained quiet and waited for him to continue whenever he felt ready.

"Anyways, with Wilson searchin' the mountains and Johnny sick, we reckoned it best to hide the gold and get to a proper doctor. So that's what we done. We buried it. The next day we let the mules loose and travelled fast after that. Our plan was to go back when he was well enough. We left Wilson searchin' and we made our way down to a minin' camp. By then, Johnny was in a real bad way."

"Was there a doctor there?" I asked.

"Sure was, fresh out from the east. He was a greenhorn

in that part of the country, but he seemed to know his doctorin' pretty good. Turned out Johnny had a real bad infection that had spread through his body. Doc done his best,
gave him all sorts of tablets and injections. He seemed to
improve for a few days, but then he had a relapse. He died
soon after, peaceful like, while he slept. Damn shame."

I felt a welling up of sadness. It was the first time I had
ever had such feelings towards my father.

Larsen composed himself before continuing. "The day before he died, he called for me. He knew what was comin'.
Told me to get a message to Jen and to give his half to the
both of you."

"That's why you came to Boston?"

"Sure. I cabled Jen with the news, but I weren't about to
mention gold in no telegram. That's somethin' that's better
passed personal like." Larsen leaned back and stretched out
his arms, "I'm done in, Lad. Not as young as I used to be.
We'll talk more tomorrow."

We used the saddles to rest our heads on. We had no
blankets, so I built up the fire with the remaining wood piled
beside us. Larsen fell asleep immediately. I lay awake for a
while listening to the flowing water, which had a therapeutic
effect on my weary mind. Despite the cold, I drifted off into a
deep sleep, peppered with dreams of gold, the high country,
and my father.

SEVEN

Olaf's Farm

The hill below us descended steeply before levelling out to a gentler slope where it met the wooden perimeter fence of a small farm. The greenness of the grass incline changed shades as the silhouettes cast from clouds drifted across its surface.

"We need food," I said, and Larsen nodded in agreement.

From our vantage point, we could make out two figures walking to and from a farmhouse and various outbuildings. The farm was not large. Its boundaries were visible by the picket fence that surrounded it. Sheep and cattle grazed in separate fields while others were used for crops, mainly wheat. The long rows of wheat appeared to be dancing in unison as the shoulder high sheaves swayed back and forth before the wind.

We started down the hill, leaning back in our saddles as the horses thread awkwardly on the steep slope, feeling out each step as they went. It took a while to reach the bottom and when we did, we sat upright again as the going became easier.

Having closed the distance, we could see the two figures were a man and a woman. They looked up and saw us approaching, but kept about their business. We rode along the outside of the fence until we reached the entrance gate. I leaned down to push it open and we went through, making sure to close it behind us. The man and woman, whom I presumed to be man and wife stopped their work and stood waiting for us to reach them.

"Howdy," Larsen addressed the man.

"Good afternoon," he replied, welcoming us with a strong Swedish accent, but there was a look of apprehension in his face.

His wife stood to the side of us. She was holding two pails, one in each hand. She remained silent but shared the same uneasy look. At that moment it occurred to me; we were strangers and our appearance must have been rather shabby, as we had slept rough. Added to this, we were armed, which was not a common sight in this part of the country.

Larsen did the talking. "I'm sorry, we did not mean to alarm you. We are travellin' to Providence. If you could spare some food we'd be happy to pay for it." He put his hand to his coat pocket, indicating that he had money.

His tone seemed to put them at ease and the man's expression changed to one of friendliness. He smiled as he stepped forward to shake hands with Larsen. Then he walked around to me. I reached down to grip his hand. He had a firm handshake and I had to control my expression as he squeezed my hand.

"Welcome, welcome, we have food and you are welcome to share. My name is Olaf and this is my wife, Ingrid."

Ingrid smiled politely and somewhat shyly, her cheeks taking on a redness, which contrasted against her natural white complexion. Olaf spoke to her in Swedish. She put down the pails and hurried into the house.

"My wife does not speak English. She will prepare a meal for us." He reached up to pat Eclipse's head before continuing. "Your horses are worn out. Come, we will look after them."

We dismounted and followed Olaf, pulling the horses behind us. He led us into the barn. There were six stalls, two of them occupied by large workhorses. I led Eclipse into an empty stall while Larsen did the same with his horse. While we unsaddled the horses, Olaf brought grain and water. There was hay stacked at the back of the barn and we used it to cover the floor of the two stalls. We left them to feed and rest as Olaf ushered us across the yard and into his home.

Larsen and I exchanged glances. The aroma of fresh food filled the farmhouse and hit us the moment we stepped through the door. I felt weak with anticipation of what was to come and I suspected he had the same sensation.

The kitchen table was a sight to behold. A freshly baked

loaf, two dishes of apples and a large plate of homemade biscuits converted an ordinary table into a hungry traveller's delight. As we sat down, Ingrid placed bowls of thick turnip soup in front of us. She hurried back to the range and then returned with plates, which were full of fried corn fritters. We thanked her, but her only reply was a shy smile that highlighted her beauty.

A petite girl, she had a natural innocent look about her. I guessed she was no older than I was, while Olaf, I estimated to be in his late thirties. I was curious as to why she spoke no English, because Olaf, despite having a strong accent, spoke both languages. I put the question to him as we ate.

"Ingrid," he told us, "only arrived from Sweden three months ago. I have lived in America for many years. Our families arranged it. They thought it would be a good match." He reached out to hold her hand. The looks that they exchanged showed their love for each other and Ingrid's smile confirmed it. "But," he added, turning back to face us, "soon she will speak English good. I will teach her to speak it, myself."

We finished our soup and corn fritters. Ingrid cleared the used bowls and placed clean plates before us. In the middle of the table she placed a roasted chicken and beside it, a bowl of boiled potatoes. Having eaten nothing for the past few days except for some carp fish, I was exceptionally hungry, and it had been a long time since I enjoyed a meal prepared by a woman.

We ate until we could eat no more, and afterwards coffee was poured, much to Larsen's delight. Olaf was a pipe smoker and the two men relaxed with coffee and tobacco while discussing a wide variety of topics, ranging from American farming techniques to traditional Swedish customs.

I needed to move around after such a big meal. I went to check on the horses and then helped Ingrid to feed the fowl. After that, we spent the next two hours gathering hay from an adjoining field and moving it to the barn. There was little conversation – Ingrid only knew a few basic words in English. I envied them their simple life, their farm, their love for each another. They had much to look forward to.

Larsen emerged from the farmhouse. He was carrying two croaker sacks and he made straight for the barn. I followed him in. Olaf had supplied us with food, coffee, blankets and even two tin cups.

"We best be movin'," he said as he pulled his saddle off the stall fence.

"Couldn't we stay the night?"

I was enjoying the comfort afforded to us and relished the thought of sleeping in a proper bed.

"Better not. I've got a bad feelin'."

Olaf's farm was idyllic and I failed to understand how anyone could not help but feel the benefits of the peaceful atmosphere here. But I was learning to trust Larsen's instincts and after our encounter with Wilson, I realised he was a man with vast experience of dangerous situations.

I set about saddling Eclipse. We packed the saddlebags with food and tied the rolled blankets across the back of our saddles. Anything that we could not cram into the bags, we had wrapped in the blankets.

We were discussing the next stage of our journey when the peaceful ambience was shattered by the high-pitched screaming of Ingrid, which was immediately followed by Olaf shouting in Swedish. A shot rang out. There was a moments silence before Ingrid wailed in despair.

Larsen pulled his rifle out from under the blanket and ran to the barn door. I grabbed my handgun and rushed to his side. He held out his arm ensuring I would not run out through the open barn doors. We stood just inside the door, obscured by the shadows. Olaf was lying on the ground with Ingrid kneeling and hunched over his body, cradling his head in her hands. Blood was flowing from his skull. He was dead – there could be little doubt about that. Beside him lay a stranger, he was facing up and his arms were outstretched. There was a handgun next to his body. A pitchfork had been thrust deep into his stomach and remained lodged firmly in position, its handle pointing skywards.

"What's happening?" I asked, looking to Larsen for an explanation.

"Wilson's men, they must have tracked us here from your house."

He pointed to the hill, the same one that we had descended earlier that afternoon. Half a dozen men on horseback were trying to negotiate the steep slope. Larsen bolted from the barn, hunched low as he ran across the yard and took up position behind a three-rung fence that ran parallel to the house. He swung his rifle over the top and rested it on the top rung. He took a moment to aim before blasting off a shot. The riders, unable to move fast on the slope, either jumped or fell from their horses. They scrambled in various directions attempting to find cover behind small bushes that peppered the hill.

Keeping low, I crawled on my hands and knees to Olaf's body. It was a horrific sight. He had been shot in the forehead and the bullet had exploded out through the rear of his skull. I grasped hold of Ingrid's arm and tried to pull her towards the safety of the farmhouse. The atmosphere was alive with the crack of gunfire. The sound of each blast seemed to last for a few moments before waning as the wind carried away its thunderous echo. The men on the hill had taken cover and were returning Larsen's fire. But the range was great and while I could hear the whizz of bullets passing through the air, they seemed to be a long way off their mark.

Ingrid clung to her husband's body and refused to let go. She was screaming and her face was glistening with tears. I pried her fingers loose, one by one, and only then could I drag her along the ground towards the open door. Small clumps of dirt were jumping into the air close to us – the men's aims were improving. I fell in through the doorway and pulled Ingrid in after me. She was distraught, trying to push me away so she could return to Olaf. I managed to pin her arms down and stretched out my foot to kick the door closed. I couldn't let her up. If I did, she would be shot.

The gun battle raged outside. I knew Larsen would need help, but I was struggling with Ingrid.

"Tom!" Larsen shouted.

I could think of no other way and it was sheer desperation on my part. I punched Ingrid on the side of her head. Her body went limp and her arms fell to the floor. She was unconscious. It was the first time I had ever hit someone and of all people it had to be a young woman. My hand ached and I feared I might have broken a finger.

"Tom!" Larsen's yelling broke my thoughts and I forgot about any injury I might have incurred.

I pulled the door open, but stood to the side so as not to offer myself as a target. Larsen was crouched low and using the fence for cover. Wilson's men were scurrying from one hedge to another making their way down the hill, while firing the odd sporadic shot at him.

"I'm out of ammunition!" Larsen shouted and held up his rifle to signify its uselessness without bullets.

I knew the cartridges were packed into the saddlebags. My rifle was there, too. I had to get to the barn, a distance of about fifty feet across the yard. I stepped back a few feet, took a deep breath, and then charged as fast as I could out the door. I reached the halfway point before they had time to react. And then, they got me in their sights. Bullets cut through the air creating a whizzing sound as they passed. Despite running at full speed, I was sure I could feel the movement of air as they passed within inches of me. I dived forward to cover the last ten feet and landed roughly between the barn doors. There was no time to spare. I rolled forward into the safety of the shadows and jumped to my feet.

The horses were agitated by the gunfire. They were twisting and turning in their stalls and Larsen's horse crushed me up against the stall door as I tried to root out a box of cartridges from his saddlebag. Pushing the horse back, I managed to grip two boxes and pull them out. I clambered back over the wooden partition into Eclipse's stall. Eclipse was also upset and thrashed around his stall. On hearing my voice, he calmed down, allowing me to pull out my rifle before running back to the barn's entrance.

"Bill!" I threw one of the boxes to him and it landed at his feet.

We loaded our rifles at the same time, but reflecting back later, I did not recall pushing the bullets into the chamber. Larsen's lessons on guns must have had some effect on me, that I was able to do it without thought.

Wilson's men were approaching the outer fence. Larsen's lack of shooting had encouraged them to come out into the open. I took aim through a gap in the door between the frame and the door itself, resting the barrel of the Winchester on the door hinge. I had one of them in clear sight. I lined up the gun's pointer to his body and squeezed the trigger. The rifle discharged and jerked upwards. I was holding it firmly against my shoulder as I remembered how it had kicked back violently at the cabin. As a puff of smoke drifted away with the breeze, I scanned the hill expecting to see a body sprawled on the grass. Instead, I saw the man that I had just shot at, running on unhindered.

Larsen was kneeling and aiming his rifle through the horizontal rungs of the fence. I watched as with incredible speed he fired off six shots. Their advance was halted and they scrambled for cover.

"Tom!" Larsen called out. "Cover me, I'm comin' back to the barn."

I nodded and pushed an extra bullet into the rifle to replace the one I had fired. Larsen waited for me to give a signal. I took a deep breath and readied myself. I realised that the chances of me hitting any of them was remote. They were too far away and while I knew how to shoot, I did not know how to shoot well. I nodded to Larsen and began to fire in the direction of the hillside. I fired three shots, enough time for him to run back to the barn. Wilson's men kept their cover – they had no idea as to the extent of my marksmanship. I remained at the door, firing off a shot every time one of them stuck their head out from behind a bush. Larsen, breathed heavily while reloading as he tried to regain his composure.

"I've scattered their horses," he said, and took a few deep breaths before continuing. "We can ride out and around the back. It will take them hours to round up their animals."

"What about Ingrid?" I said to him.

Larsen did not answer, he just stared at me.

"We can't leave her!" I read his thoughts, but I was thinking back to Emma's ordeal at the hands of such men.

"Jesus, Kid. We'll be lucky to get away as it stands."

"I can't leave her. You go if you want."

"Damn you Andersons!" There was no venom in his tone, despite his best efforts to display it. He lifted up his rifle and fired a shot; one of Wilson's men had stepped out from the protection of a thick clump of shrub. A puff of dirt rose into the air, inches from his foot and he jumped backwards to his previous position.

Larsen stepped forward to get a good view of the hill. He trained his rifle on the slope and every time one of the men dared to show themselves, he would blast off a shot, convincing them it would be more prudent to remain concealed. They did manage to return fire, but under pressure from Larsen's aim, their bullets were badly aimed.

"We got to work this out." He spoke without turning around. "One of us will have to cross the yard and get her.

"It will have to be me." I was the obvious choice. I was half his age and would be able to run faster. Also, I would not have the ability to keep them pinned down as his accurate shooting was doing.

"Leave me your rifle." He agreed without discussing the matter. I put my rifle down, leaning it against the doorframe, but before we could discuss the plan further, our attention was overtaken by screaming from the farmhouse. Through the kitchen window, we could see the silhouette of two figures struggling with each other.

"One of them must have worked his way around the back...quick, the open window!" Larsen's raised voice stressed the urgency; he nodded up, towards an open window at the side of the farmhouse.

It was all happening too fast and I did not have time to dwell on the danger I faced. Had I time to think about my intended actions, I doubt I would have done anything.

Larsen leaned out of the barn's entrance and began to fire one shot after another at the men on the hill.

"Go, go!" he yelled at me.

Keeping my head drooped low, I ran towards the open window. As I got close to the house, I saw the window frame split in half as a bullet tore through the wood. Splinters exploded outwards in all directions. I dived through the gap, not thinking of where I might land – my only concern was to get out of sight from Wilson's men.

It was luck and for no other reason that I found myself crashing down onto a soft mattress. It was the bedroom that I had entered so unconventionally. My forward motion caused me to roll across the bed and fall uninjured onto the floor. I got to my feet. The gunfire outside had ceased and the only noise I could hear was Ingrid, pleading in her native language to the intruder.

I pulled out my handgun and checked it. It was fully loaded and I pushed the small safety lever up. I made my way out of the bedroom and into a narrow passageway that lead to the kitchen. They had not heard me enter the house and were unaware of me approaching. My heart was thumping wildly – it felt as if my chest would explode at any second. My hands were wet, saturated with sweat, unlike my throat, which ached with dryness.

I took one step at a time, placing each foot down on the

wooden planked floor as lightly as I could. The kitchen door was open and I stepped through, holding the gun in my outstretched arm. The man had his back to me. He was holding Ingrid in a chokehold, his left arm wrapped around her neck and he was walking her towards the front door. I saw a gun in his right hand, which was down by his side. I realised his intention was to use her as a shield as he went out the door.

I aimed the gun directly at his back and my whole body tensed. I wrapped my finger around the trigger, but I could not do it, I could not shoot. Larsen's words were screaming in my head, *"When you're going to shoot a snake...don't wait for him to turn around and bite you."*

I tried, but was unable to apply that tiny bit of extra pressure that would fire my gun.

They were at the doorway. Two more steps and they would be outside. I could see Ingrid's legs kicking wildly, his grip around her neck had lifted her off the ground.

"You there, stop or I'll shoot!"

He released his grip on Ingrid and spun around to face me. There was surprise on his face, but it was his eyes that I noticed more than anything. They were black, black as the darkest night, and they were wild with fury. I was unexpected and we stood looking at each other for what seemed like an eternity. Ingrid fell to her knees, coughing and rasping from the chocking. I saw the man's arm rise slowly.

"Don't...please don't," I pleaded to him.

He appeared calm, unlike the scared and terrified image that I must have presented to him. He continued to raise his arm and it all seemed to be happening in slow motion. I knew I should shoot, but I was frozen in a state of fear. He could see it. He could read my reluctance to kill and he was willing to test my fear with his life.

I don't know how I did it – I don't remember making a conscious decision to shoot. The gun jerked in my hand. There was a blinding flash and a loud explosion as the gun discharged. The man's face twisted in pain, his body was pushed backwards and his arms were thrown both up and forward. His gun went spinning to the floor. He stumbled back against the wall and his hands came down to his chest in a natural reflex to cover a wound. His wild eyes stared at me in disbelief.

I watched his eyes roll upwards as he turned sideways,

his weight pressing hard against the wall. He stayed that way for a moment, his face continuing to contort with the pain. After a few moments, his weight began to shift as he went crashing down to the floor without the normal reaction of reaching out to break one's fall. When his body hit the ground his head and legs bounced off the stone flagged floor before falling back down. He lay still and a red stream of blood began to flow outwards from beneath his body.

I had killed a man, but there was no time to think about or dwell on my actions. Ingrid had gotten to her feet and was stepping out the door. Her arms were waving in confusion and she was wailing with despair, or maybe it was shock.

"Ingrid, no!" I yelled as I ran to stop her.

I reached out to grab her arm, but she was too fast. She ran out into the open and made straight for the body of her husband. As I showed myself in the doorway a volley of gun-fire rang out. I fell back and rolled to the side and out of view. Bullets came tearing through the open door, speeding across the room in search of human flesh. The gunfire from the hill ceased as Larsen's covering fire forced them to crouch down again.

I got to my feet and looked out the window. Ingrid's body was slumped across Olaf. She was not moving and I could see two red blotches on her back, the blood standing out sharply against the pale yellow of her dress.

"Tom, come on, Tom, while I have them pinned down!" Larsen was yelling from the barn.

I stumbled out the door and ran in a confused daze back to the barn.

"You alright? You ain't shot, are you?" he said as he looked me up and down.

"No...no, I don't think..." I couldn't get a proper sentence out, I was in shock.

Larsen hurried to the stalls and led our horses out.

"Let's get goin'," he said.

I didn't answer, I couldn't move.

"Come on, Kid."

He lifted my leg, pushing my foot into a stirrup and then heaved me up onto Eclipse. Larsen grabbed his saddle and swung himself up onto his horse in one swift movement. He reached out and held Eclipse by his reins.

"Yehah!" He let out a roar and prodded his horse with the

heel of his boot. Eclipse followed, being pulled for the first few feet.

Leaving the barn, we turned and rode around the side, putting the building between us and the hill. We galloped out of the yard and into a wheat field. The horses cut through the sea of sheaves leaving a trampled trail leading away from the house. We emerged from the golden wheat forest into the open, about fifteen strides from the outer fence. Larsen led – he leaned forward, urging his horse on. They rose into the air before me. Every muscle in the black stallion was taut and working in unison as it lifted its giant frame off the ground. Its front legs found purchase on the other side as its back legs curled to clear the top rung of the fence.

I closed my eyes and hunched down, putting my trust in Eclipse. I felt my stomach heave as we went up, seemingly pausing for a moment before the motion of coming down was felt. We landed hard and I was almost thrown off, but I clung on, throwing my arms around his neck. Eclipse instantly regained his balance and quickened his stride to a gallop as he chased Larsen's horse.

We fled across a green valley and away from the farm, leaving Wilson's men to search for their scattered horses.

EIGHT

Life on the trail

"Here, Kid, get this into you."

The heat from the mug radiated through my cupped hands. Larsen began to break up the fire with his boot. He stomped and ground the glowing embers into the dirt until they were all extinguished.

"We can't risk a fire tonight...there'll be no more coffee till mornin'."

The scalding black liquid made me wince, from the taste as much as the burning sensation of it hitting the back of my throat.

"You'll get used to it. Milk is a luxury you won't have on the trail."

He was probably smiling, but I could not tell for sure, as we sat in total darkness, shivering in the cold night air.

"You alright, Kid?"

"I...I don't know." It was the first time I had spoken since this afternoon. I had spent most of the latter part of the day clinging to Eclipse as he followed Larsen south and away from the carnage at Olaf's farm. "What have we done?" I said.

"What do you mean?"

"Ingrid...Olaf, my God, what have we done?" I cradled my face in my hands as I shook my head from side-to-side.

"Look, Tom, I'm real sorry about what happened back there, but it weren't our doin'."

"Not our doing? They'd still be alive if it wasn't for us," I said, angrily, annoyed at his attempt to distance us from blame.

"I know you feel bad, even that we are responsible, but we're not. Tom, you got to get things straight in your head. We didn't know those men were doggin' us. Wilson has left a trail of dead both sides of the Canadian border. Don't blame yourself for the crimes of another man."

Deep down, I knew he was right, but it did not ease the pain. I felt a share of the responsibility, just as I did with Emma.

"I killed a man, Bill."

Shooting Wilson's man was another action that I was finding hard to come to terms with.

"The man in the farmhouse?"

"Yes, I shot him. I aimed and I shot him."

"Well hell, Kid, it was him or you."

"Maybe, but it was ghastly, his face, the blood...I feel sick."

I leaned forward, feeling that I was going to vomit.

Larsen griped my shoulder. "Killin' is always ghastly, but you get used to it."

"No..." I struggled to speak while retching, "I could never get used to that."

"Get some sleep, Tom. We got to start early tomorrow."

He placed a blanket on my lap. I wrapped it around myself and then turned up the collars of my coat before lying down – curling up in an effort to get warm.

And there we spent our second night on the trail. Lost in the darkness, huddled among the boulders of a rocky outcrop and surrounded by low grassy hills – like a dried up oasis encircled by wave after wave of rolling sand dunes.

Dawn came slowly and I had hardly slept, continuously waking during the night, haunted by visions of death. My body was numb with the intense cold. I sat upright, keeping the blanket wrapped tight around me.

Larsen woke. He sat up with an annoying enthusiasm as he stretched his arms back to work the stiffness out of his body. He got to his feet and scanned the surrounding hills. To look at him, one would think he just emerged from a cosy hotel bed, while I on the other hand was useless. I sat pathetically and huddled in my blanket, shivering while he did everything.

I watched as he set about gathering loose wood for a fire. He used small twigs and clumps of dried grass first. He struck a match and held the small flame against the driest of the grass. The flame took hold, the brown strands of grass quickly shrivelling up in a wisp of grey smoke, but not before lending their flame to the thin twigs stacked above them. He patiently fed the fire strips of bark and thicker twigs until the flames danced higher, calling out for broken-up branches and any small logs that were to hand. I moved closer to the dancing flames, and the crackle of dry wood burning was like music to my ears. The emitting heat was a glorious sensation and never had I enjoyed the pleasure of a fire so much.

I was still too cold to talk, so I continued to watch as he emptied the last of our water into the coffee pot. He nestled the pot into the fire and the flames licked the sides of the already blackened vessel. From his saddlebag, he pulled out some bread and a few strips of salted meat.

Olaf had been generous in supplying us, and as I thought about him and Ingrid, a vision of their crumpled and bloodied bodies came flooding back into my mind. For the first time in my life, I wanted for another man's death. Whether on the gallows or by the hand of Larsen, it did not matter.

"Coffee," he said, thrusting the mug into my hands and disturbing me from my line of thought.

"Food." He handed me a plate of bread, meat, and corn fritters.

We ate without conversation. The food was good. I was hungry and the hot coffee was welcome, even without milk. Its heat travelled down my windpipe and slowly radiated around my body. It felt good and I was beginning to understand why Larsen was obsessed with coffee.

After finishing our breakfast, we sat – content to watch the rising sun gain strength in the clear western sky. Larsen produced his pipe while I rejoiced with the feeling of returning warmth. I felt able to engage in conversation again.

"We might make Providence by tonight?" I asked, eager to hear his reply.

"We better talk about that," he replied.

A serious expression spread across his face.

I wanted to ask what the problem was, but he became momentarily absorbed with the action of filling his pipe. I was learning to expect him to explain things at his own pace and sure enough, after a few minutes he continued.

"Think about it, they tracked us south from Boston. I reckon they'll have put two and two together and realise that we are makin' for the rail line. There are only a few stations that we could be headin' for and they'll have split-up to cover them."

"So, what do we do now?" I asked, my tone echoing both my frustration and my disappointment.

"Well, I've been puttin' some thought into that. Here's what we'll do..."

He crouched down onto one knee and used the back of his hand to smooth out a patch of dirt on the ground. Using his index finger, he scratched a small circle. "Boston...and we're about here, about twenty miles south."

Another mark, this time an X. Larsen pulled a smouldering stick from the fire and scratched a long wavy line above the other markings.

"This is the Canadian border, about one hundred miles to the north-west."

He straightened up and held his chin in his hand, pondering on his plan. He nodded as if agreeing with himself. The smouldering stick came into use once more and an oval shape appeared within the rough map.

"We can head north-west to Lake Ontario."

Larsen dragged the now extinguished stick along the dirt to show the route.

"We should be able to get someone to take us across to Toronto, on the other side. From there, we can travel north and pick up the train that connects Montreal in the east to Winnipeg in the west."

Larsen dug the stick into the ground, one foot away from his map to mark Winnipeg and the distance that lay ahead of us.

I had sat and listened patiently. Now I sat in silence, overwhelmed by the distances laid out before me. I had only left Boston once before and that was a short holiday to see the sights in New York. Now I was facing a journey on horseback of over a hundred miles, and that was just to reach Lake Ontario. After that, I found it hard to comprehend the vast distances involved to reach the western regions of Canada.

"Well, let's get movin'," he said as he stood.

He wasn't waiting for my thoughts on the plan.

We made good progress over the next two days, covering more than thirty miles on each day. We were well stocked with provisions and avoided small towns that lay along the route and went around any farms that we happened across. We ate twice a day, once in the morning and again in the evening. While our stock of food lasted, our diet consisted of salted beef and biscuits that had been dipped in bacon grease. At night we would sit and talk while a roaring campfire would keep us warm. When we'd tire of talking, Larsen would suck on his pipe and drink coffee. Eventually tiredness would overcome us and we would turn in, snug and comfortable under our waterproof blankets. The rain held off and I had to admit to myself that I was enjoying the journey. The sense of freedom that came with living on the trail was in stark contrast to my life back in Boston.

Larsen was confident that we had lost our pursuers and as a result, the journey was easy going. When our food supplies ran out, he showed his expertise in hunting. Small game such as rabbits, squirrels and birds became our daily diet. Should we happen to come upon a stream, we would stop to fish.

I was used to preparing food, but while I bought my food in the markets and stores of Boston, here we were self-sufficient. I learned how to make and set traps using wire and sticks. We would set our traps in the evening and check them the following morning. For every half dozen set, we might be rewarded with one and sometimes two successes. The only drawback to finding our own food was that it slowed down our journey. However, Larsen did not seem to be in a hurry and I was enjoying the new learning experience so much that I welcomed the easy pace.

I looked forward to our nightly conversations. Larsen was a man who liked to talk, and I learned much about things that I was ignorant of, such as the war. His recollections of the sheer slaughter and wanton waste of human life made me sick to the stomach.

I learned much about my father, realising I was more like him than I thought. Not in courage or daring, but in the way he approached problems and situations. His thought processes were much like my own in the way we logically came to a conclusion concerning a line of action that must be followed.

Larsen had begun to interest me greatly. I was intrigued by his ways and his peculiar quirks. He seemed to live by a code, a code that was only understood by him alone. He liked the small pleasures in life, coffee, female company, his pipe, and friendship. The order of preference was something that I had not yet worked out. His word was his bond and he expected the same from others. He detested evil men and for this reason, I had spent some time considering something that happened back at the barn. It was when I asked about Ingrid, as we stood by our horses, ready to flee. He gave me the impression that perhaps we should leave her – as we would be lucky to escape with our own lives and that should be enough. I realise now that he would not have left her. He was letting me make the decision. Whether it was a test to see what I was made of, or it was his way of allowing me find my inner courage, I did not know.

Each afternoon we would stop to rest. It was during these stops that he took the opportunity to show me how to use my gun. I was taught that there was more to using a gun than simply being able to aim and shoot. I learned all aspects of weaponry. He dismantled our weapons and explained how they worked, how different models differed in their design and purpose. I spent many hours taking apart my rifle and handgun to reassemble them again, cleaning and oiling all the fine parts as I went. There were shooting lessons as well, although we had to act sparingly as we could not afford to waste cartridges.

I realised an immense satisfaction growing within me. Learning the basic skills of survival and self-reliance filled me with a sense of pride and achievement. It is something that did not show on the outside, but within my being, a new-found confidence began to develop. It was true my proficiency with guns was basic and the ability to hunt food successfully was still beyond my grasp, but I knew what to do and that was the important thing. As with all skills, success would come with time and practice.

I wondered if I would be able to resume my old job when this was all over, assuming they would take me back, that is. Could I cope with the confines of a small office after tasting the freedom of the outdoors? I wasn't sure and for the first time in my life, I didn't particularly care. In the short space of one week, I had learned to take each day as it came and not to burden myself with thoughts about what tomorrow might bring.

NINE

Lake Ontario

It was late afternoon when we reached the shores of Lake Ontario. I knew we were getting close as I had been noticing signs for the previous two days. It reminded me of approaching the Atlantic coastline. There was a cool dampness carried along with the breeze. There was no salt in the air, but I could imagine it. With the breaking of dawn, flocks of birds, mostly gulls, flew high and all in the same direction to fulfil their daily ritual of fishing in the vast lake. In the late afternoon, the same birds would be seen returning, flying low and stopping to perch in trees – their bellies swollen after a day's feasting.

The lake revealed itself as we emerged from the dense woodland that followed the lake's contours. It was a magnificent sight. The pale blue waters stretched out as far as the eye could see, only to disappear over the hazy horizon. A pillar of grey smoke rose into the air, far out in the distance – a steamship making its way across the fresh water lake.

"Heading for Canada?" I asked.

"Probably there already, the border cuts across the middle of the lake," Larsen said as he lifted himself up in the saddle to peer across the open water. He was impressed with the scene before him, just as I was.

"Will we cross on the next one?"

"No." He sat back down before continuing. "I reckon Wilson is headin' home. He knows we'll turn up sooner or later. Better not take any chances though. We'll head south along the shoreline where there'll be some fishin' villages. We should be able to get someone to bring us across."

We turned west and made our way along the shore until darkness began to set in. We were setting up night camp when dim lights further along the shore caught our attention. It was a fishing village or a settlement and as the distance did not seem to be great, we decided to push on.

We followed the water's edge, threading our way carefully in the dark. The weak lights became brighter as we got closer. It was late when we arrived at the source of the light. There was a motley collection of cabins and hastily constructed shacks. They were spread out on a low sloping hill that ran down to the water's edge. There was no apparent thought or planning put into their placement and there was no road or path linking them. The only common feature shared among them was that they all faced towards the lake. There were several boats anchored out in the water. It was difficult to judge their size or type, as only glimpses of their silhouettes were visible when the moonlight shone down between parting clouds.

One cabin was noticeably larger than the others. It had three windows to the right of its door and each window was lit with oil lamps sitting inside on their corresponding sills. Voices and occasional bursts of laughter echoed from within. There was no sign indicating its purpose, but we assumed it was an inn. We decided to go in with the intention of acquiring passage to the Canadian side.

I was not in the habit of frequenting taverns, but the few I visited bore no resemblance to this one. The ceiling was low, but the room was well lit with a mixture of lanterns and large wax candles that sat upon every table. A cloud of acrid tobacco smoke hung motionless in the air and my eyes began to sting as they became watery. The tavern's patrons paid us no heed and continued their individual conversations. Larsen led the way to an empty table. As we walked across the room, I heard both English and French been used at various tables. We sat down and Larsen nodded at the innkeeper to get his attention.

I found the situation intimidating. Although our presence was not acknowledged, other than by the occasional glance, there was an unusual atmosphere. There were over a dozen men present and I guessed they were a mixture of trappers and fishermen. The fishermen were easily identified by their waterproof clothing; oilskin trousers and knee-high seal skin boots. I assumed the other men were trappers, judging by their warm clothing which mostly consisted of fur-lined coats and boots. Several of them wore beaver hats and had long hunting type rifles, which were propped up against the wall near the entrance door. The vast array of long bladed knifes was frightening and it appeared that every man was armed with a sheathed blade strapped to their waist.

"Good evenin', Gentlemen," the innkeeper said and what an unpleasant fellow he was. He was short, standing no taller than five foot. A sickly gaunt face exaggerated his thinness with his cheekbones sharply outlined against his skin. He rubbed his sweaty hands together in anticipation of new money that may be about to cross them. His grubby clothes matched his character.

Larsen uttered just one word. "Beer."

"Not many strangers come here...passin' through?" he asked.

Larsen did not answer and I decided to do the same.

"We have a room out back if you want to stay the night or...if you gentlemen would like some company..." He looked back over his shoulder to a half open door at the end of the counter.

I looked at the door he was drawing our attention to, but the room beyond it was too dimly lit to see inside.

"Just beer." Larsen's tone was abrupt.

"Certainly sir, certainly." He turned, returning to the bar with an unusual walk that made me think of a snake slithering through the undergrowth.

I leaned forward and whispered to Larsen, "Why didn't you ask about a boat?"

"All in good time, Lad, best not to rush things."

His vision was taking in the room and its occupants. The vile innkeeper returned and put two tankards on the table.

"Our finest ale, Sir." He addressed Larsen and did not bother to look at me. Without waiting for a reply, he returned to his bar, but I noticed that he continued to observe us with a devious eye.

The ale was strong and after two gulps, I felt the disorienting affect it had on my head.

The innkeeper shouting caused me turn in my chair to see what the fuss was about. He was coming out of the back room and pulling a reluctant Indian girl who was clad in tanned buckskins. He thrust a broom into her hand and began to point at various points on the planked floor. The girl, who could not have been older than eighteen, threw the broom down in an act of defiance. She folded her arms and turned her back to him. The innkeeper flew into a fit of rage. He pulled a long bamboo stick from a shelf behind the bar and proceeded to beat her across the back. The whip of the stick created a sharp whooshing sound as it cut through the air. The girl fell to the floor and curled up, tucking her knees under her chin and using her hands to shield her head. He continued with the thrashing, his face glowing red from exertion and all the time cursing the girl with a torrent of foul obscenities. The men in the tavern seemed indifferent to the scene. Some looked out of curiosity while others paid no attention to the girl's misfortune.

I had not noticed Larsen standing up or crossing the fifteen feet between us and the counter. He just seemed to appear behind the innkeeper as he was stretching his arm upwards, higher than before with the intention of delivering an extra hard blow. Larsen gripped the man's wrist. The innkeeper turned, hunching down at the same time to reach for the handle of a knife that was protruding up from his boot. Larsen twisted his wrist and the man grimaced in pain as he contorted his body to lessen the effect of the twist.

"Enough," Larsen told him.

At first, the innkeeper seemed to be complying, but his free hand continued to work its way down to the knife. Larsen twisted the wrist again and I expected to hear the crack of a bone breaking. The man cried out in agony.

"Enough, I said!" Larsen yelled.

"All right, Sir, all right."

The innkeeper's hand moved away from his boot. He had obviously thought better of the situation. Larsen let go and the innkeeper stood up, massaging his twisted wrist while holding it against his stomach.

The girl clambered to her feet and turned towards the

room that she had been dragged from in such an undignified manner. Her face showed the bruises from previous beatings. Both her eyes were blackened and her bottom lip was swollen to twice the size of the upper one. She ran back into to room, slamming the door shut behind her.

"No harm done, no harm Sir." The innkeeper stared at the floor as he addressed Larsen.

The few customers that had shown the mildest interest in the episode had resumed their conversations.

"Please, Sir... You sit down and I'll bring more ale, on the house, to show there are no hard feelins'."

Larsen returned to our table without answering him.

When the innkeeper returned with two fresh tankards, he was still grovelling.

"Sit down, Innkeeper, I want to talk." Larsen stretched out his leg to push out a chair.

"What is your name, Innkeeper?"

"Campbell, Sir, John Campbell."

"Well, Campbell, we wish to get passage across the lake. Who should we talk to?" Larsen pulled a dollar coin from his pocket and slid it across the table.

Campbell took the coin most willingly and sat up straight as he pocketed the money.

"Captain Vennard, Sir. He's the man to help. He's here now," Campbell said, looked across the room. "He's that big fella over there."

"Tell him we have business for him."

"Yes, Sir, you leave it to me. Captain Vennard will look after you alright."

We watched as he crossed the room to whisper in the ear of the man he told us about.

The captain was sitting at a table with three other men. The table was littered with discarded tankards and empty bottles. Even from this distance, his huge size was apparent. Although sitting down, he towered above the short innkeeper who stood beside him. His chair, which was practically hidden under him, seemed like something a child might sit on. The stature of the men around him made it obvious that he was the dominant man at the table. Campbell continued to whisper into the man's ear, his eyes pointing down to the floor in a similar fashion to the way he addressed Larsen. Campbell returned to his bar, nodding his head as he past us to indicate that he had done what he said he would.

Vennard looked us up and down from a distance. The other three men leaned in towards him to discuss the matter in whispers. After a few minutes, the big man stood up, his legs pushing back his chair like it was a pile of useless wood in his path. He walked to our table and stood towering over us and casting a wide shadow across our table.

"You want go Canada, yes?" His broken English was dominated by a heavy French accent.

"Yes," Larsen replied, adding, "and our horses."

"You not take steamboat, it leave close to here every day, no?"

"No, we don't want to travel on the steamboat. Campbell said you might be able to take us?"

"Why you not go by ferry, you run from law, maybe?"

"We got our reasons. Are you going to take us or not?"

"You can pay, yes?" His eyes scanned Larsen as if wondering where he kept his money.

"We can pay," Larsen answered without moving his hands and left the captain's eyes still wondering.

"Twenty dollars each."

"Ten dollars," Larsen replied.

The captain rubbed his chin before replying. His hand was bigger than both of mine put together. "Fifteen."

Larsen nodded – it was agreed.

A smile broke across the Vennard's face. "Good, we make deal." But then his smile gave way to an apprehensive look. "I not sail in night. Be at wharf come dawn, we sail then."

Larsen nodded again.

Vennard returned to his table. He was in a cheerful mood, jesting with other men as he passed them. When he sat down, the three men leaned in towards him once again to converse in whispers.

"Can we trust him?" I asked.

"Nope, nor that innkeeper neither. Best be on our guard tonight."

"Where are we going to spend the night? We need rest," I said.

He thought for a moment and then looked over my shoulder. "Innkeeper!" He called out.

Campbell scurried over in his usual snaky manner.

"You have a room? We wish to spend the night."

"Of course, gentlemen." His greedy hands began to rub one another. "Four dollars for the room and you can use the stable around the back."

Larsen produced four dollar coins from his coat pocket and placed them on the table, but Campbell seemed more interested in the pocket that they had come from. Larsen read the innkeeper's thoughts and leaned back in his chair, resting his left hand on his thigh, but purposely using his arm to brush his coat open to display the handle of his gun. It was his way of giving Campbell a message and the innkeeper's expression confirmed that he got it.

The room was basic, the only furnishings consisting of two beds and a washbasin that sat upon a small table. Moss grew in the joints between the wall's wooden planking and the ceiling bore numerous damp patches where the first signs of mould were beginning to form. I peered out the window, but darkness concealed any view that I might have had. I pulled the moth-eaten curtain across to give us some sense of privacy.

"No key," Larsen said as he was fiddled with the door handle.

"Can we wedge it shut?"

"With what?" There was a mild tone of sarcasm in his voice as he looked around the bare room.

"I don't trust that innkeeper, Bill."

"You're right not to, a thief if ever there was one."

I sat on one of the beds – I was tired and struggling to keep my eyes open. The ale had not helped matters.

He could see my exhaustion, and said, "You get some sleep. I'll keep watch and wake you in a few hours."

I was too tired to argue. I lay back on the bed and drifted into a deep sleep.

No doubt, it was only a couple of hours, but it felt like minutes later when I felt my body rocking from side-to-side. Larsen was pushing my shoulder in an effort to wake me. I swung my legs out and got to my feet. I made use of the washbasin to splash cold water onto my face.

"Wake me at dawn," Larsen said as he lay down and

rolled over to face the wall.

Within the space of two minutes, he was snoring.

The wax candle beside the washbasin was the only source of light in the room and it flickered intermittently as it neared the end of its life. Its melted wax was congealed with thick lumps welding it to the table's surface. There was a second unused candle beside it, but I decided to let the flickering flame run its course and burn out naturally.

The candle eventually burnt out and I sat on the bed in the darkness. My gun lay beside me and I felt ready for anything that might happen. The wind howled ghostlike calls outside and the constant tapping of tree branches tipping against one another added to the surreal atmosphere. My mind drifted from one thing to another as I stared into the wall of blackness that surrounded me. I lost track of time as minutes and hours merged together.

It was as if a ghostly apparition had surrounded me. I felt the distinctive fine point of a blade pressed against my throat. I reached out to find my gun, but my hand was pressed into the mattress under the weight of a foot. There was no sound. I remained still, frozen with terror and expecting to feel the warm trickle of blood running down my neck. It did not happen. A match was struck and a thin arm clad in buckskin reached out to light the second candle. It was the Indian girl and she was kneeling on the bed behind me with her left arm reaching around to hold the knife against my throat. She removed her arm and as I turned around, she held a finger to my mouth and whispered something in a language that I did not understand. While her words meant nothing to me, it was obvious she wanted me to keep my voice down. I nodded, thankful to be still alive.

"What do you want?" I asked quietly.

She pointed at Larsen and made a hand motion of pushing. I reached across to grab his leg, shaking it until he came to. He sat up, rubbing the back of his neck.

"What in tarnation..."

The girl interrupted him by repeating the words that she had said to me and once again, put her finger to her lips.

"She wants to talk to us," I told him.

"Hell, Tom. How'd she get in, were you asleep?"

"No, she just came in." I did not go into detail of how I had failed in my guard duty so miserably.

The girl got off the bed and walked to the window. She pointed out towards the lake and began to speak excitedly in her own language.

"Hold on, girl," Larsen said, reaching out to grab her arm. "We don't speak no Indian talk, you speak English?"

She looked at him with a blank expression.

"Eng...lish?" he said slowly.

She shook her head and began to speak again, but this time in French. Larsen put his hand up to stop her and then turned to me. "You know any French talk?"

"I took French during my first year in college, but I changed courses. I know some, but not much."

"Well, see if you can get any sense out of her." He stood and routed in his coat pockets for his pipe. "I'm goin' out to get some air. Good luck, Kid." He opened the door and stepped out into the hall, closing the door gently behind him.

I sat on the bed facing the girl. I found it hard to judge her age as I had a feeling her face was aged beyond her years. The fact that her face was swollen and discoloured with bruising did not make it any easier. She spoke low and in her native tongue again and seemed to be getting frustrated that I could not understand her.

"I don't understand." I shrugged my shoulders to display my confusion. "Parlez-vous français?"

"Oui, oui," she replied with a smile, relieved that we were making some progress and launched into a torrent of French, which bewildered me.

I had to put my hand across her mouth to stop her.

"Lent. Très lent s'il vous plait," I asked in my best schoolboy French, hoping she would understand.

She did understand and at last began to speak slowly, carefully pronouncing each word before moving onto the next one.

We talked for almost an hour. Although I studied French for a year in school, I had never actually had a conversation with anybody before in the language. To make matters more challenging, Canadian French had a dialect all of its own and differed greatly to the language I knew. Nevertheless, we managed. Between French, the odd English word and many hand gestures, she conveyed her story to me.

I was handing a cup of water to the girl as Larsen re-entered the room. I felt quite proud of myself that I was able to pass on the whole story to him.

"Her name is Taipa and her family lives on the Canadian side of the lake. Two months ago, Captain Vennard kidnapped her and sold her to Campbell. I don't have to tell you how she is treated here. She told me that after we left, she overheard Vennard and Campbell talking. They've come up with a plan to kill us. Vennard intends to cut our throats before we reach the Canadian shore and throw our bodies overboard. Him and Campbell plan to split any money that we might have and to sell our horses, and belongings. If anyone ever asks about us, Campbell will tell them that we stayed the night and rode out early the next morning. That's why Vennard wants to sail at dawn. There'll be no witnesses to see us getting on his boat."

I patted Taipa's arm and thanked her. "Merci...merci beaucoup." I turned back to Larsen, "what are we going to do?"

I was thinking that we could get our horses and simply ride away, but he had other ideas.

"Blasted French, never trusted them, never," he said, almost spitting as he spoke.

The girl stood up. She was anxious to get back to her room in case she was discovered. I tried to stop her; I grasped her arm and tried to explain that we would help her. She shunned my offer, shrugging off my hand and left us alone once more.

With the girl gone, I turned back to Larsen and repeated my question as to what we were going to do. He had a confident look on his face, a look I had seen before.

"We cross the lake, just like we planned."

"But, there're going to kill us!"

"No, Kid, they ain't."

I knew him well enough now to know that he had it all worked out.

TEN

Vent du Nord

The Vent du Nord lay tied to the wharf that reached out from the pebbled beach into the blue-green waters of the lake. A moderate westerly breeze drove a gentle swell against the shore and the wooden sailing ship bobbed up and down as it met each incoming wave.

She was a thirty-foot sailing schooner and was ten foot across at her widest point. The deck was void of any structure that would occupy space such as a cabin or wheelhouse. The open deck was designed for the storage of whatever cargo Captain Vennard happened to be transporting. Today, we were his cargo and for once Captain Vennard had no intention of delivering it.

"Bonjour!" Vennard waved to us from the stern of his boat. His broad smile displayed a row of pearly white teeth that hid his treacherous intentions well.

We nodded in reply, too cold and too tired to muster anything more enthusiastic. We stood on the beach with the pretence of checking our horses and supplies. In reality, we were going over our plan. My part was to kill Vennard. As distasteful as it was, the alterative of having my throat cut and being dumped overboard ensured no encouragement was needed from Larsen. His job was to take care of the crew. We needed them alive to work the sails, although, just one would do, he had told me earlier.

"Got your gun, Lad?"

I patted the side of my coat. I had shoved my handgun into my trouser belt and concealed it by fastening my coat.

"All right, Tom, let's go."

We walked the horses along the wharf. Vennard called out to his men and one of them slid a wide board consisting of five half planks lashed together out from the boat, its far edge resting on the wharf. We led the horses across and on-to the deck. A wooden cross-pole had been fixed across the handrails near the bow for us to tie them to. They shifted uneasily as they adjusted their balance to the moving ground beneath them.

The deck was empty, save a pile of canvas sails folded and stacked near the stern.

Vennard came forward, still smiling. "You pay now, yes?"

Larsen handed him thirty dollars, which the captain counted and recounted.

"We sail now. You sit here, keep out way of crew, all right?" His smile had disappeared. Now that he had our money, he felt no need to be overly pleasant anymore.

We sat on the side-rail and watched the crew at work. Vennard stood at the tiller and shouted orders to his two crewmen.

"The two men," I whispered to Larsen, "were at Ven-nard's table last night." He did not answer and I added, "Maybe what the Indian girl told us was not true?"

"Could be," he replied. "But why would she lie? Just keep your wits about you, and remember, watch Vennard. Ain't nothin' gonna happen unless he starts it."

One of the sailors began to haul a rope, feeding it through his hands. A triangular jib sail began to rise from the deck and it fluttered noisily in the stiffening breeze. The other man re-leased a rope at the bow that was tied to the wharf. The boat began to swing out, eager to be under way. He ran the length of the deck to release a second line tied aft.

Vennard pushed the tiller all the way over and the wind caught the jib sail, filling it so it became taut and lost its creases as it strained at its lines to pull us away from the wharf. Both sailors helped to haul the mainsail up. It rose foot by foot until it pulled the boom so hard that it creaked under the strain. The boat heeled over to such an acute angle that myself and Larsen almost fell backwards into the water. We decided it would be safer to sit on the deck with our backs against the rail. Captain Vennard roared with laughter at the two landlubbers aboard his vessel. I looked to see how our horses were faring, but they seemed unfazed by the sloping deck and shifted their weight to compensate accordingly.

The land faded into the distance as the Vent du Nord cut her way through the water. The wind was beginning to change direction and blow from the north, and it meant Captain Vennard had to beat a zigzag course across the lake.

The Canadian shore was nothing more than a dark line on the horizon and the Vent du Nord continuously changed direction as Vennard worked his way into the wind. The breeze began to strengthen and the boat's motion reflected the growing choppiness of the lake. Water began to splash over the rail as the bow rose and fell with each wave. We got wet as water found its way into every piece of our clothing. Vennard and his crew were better prepared with sea-boots and oilskins.

Each time Vennard changed direction he would let out a roar in French, just before he would push the tiller away from him. As the bow cut across the wind the boom came swinging across the deck with tremendous force as the wind filled the opposing side of the mainsail. We sat with a comfortable two feet between our heads and the heavy boom, but even still, we would duck as it passed violently above us.

The shoreline became more visible and vast forests of green spruce filled the horizon from east to west. I was unable to enjoy the view as my attention was focused on Vennard. The captain paid little heed to us. The big man stood at the helm holding the tiller and concentrating on the sails. He continuously made slight adjustments to our course, keeping the sails full and working at their most efficient.

It was a nod from the captain that first alerted me. It had been so quick and so slight that had I not been watching intently, it would have gone unnoticed. I turned, pretending to take in the view and I noticed the two sailors casually stand-up and move from their positions on the other side of the horses. One of them walked to our side and stood, gripping the rail as he looked out across the lake. The second man moved closer to the centre of the boat. He acted under the pretence of checking ropes that were coiled around the mast.

I used my elbow to nudge Larsen.

"This is it," he mumbled under his breath.

I opened my coat to allow my hand easy access to the gun concealed under it. My heart was pounding and my mouth was dry.

We sat and waited, trying to give the appearance that we were ignorant of what was coming. The sailor gripping the rail made the first move. He turned and walked straight at us with a long blade in his right hand. Larsen jumped to his feet just as the man reached him. The sailor lurched forward, his knife held firmly in his outstretched hand and directed at Larsen's stomach. Larsen stepped backwards as the knife passed within an inch of him. The sailor lost control of his balance momentarily as he stabbed into thin air. Larsen seized the opportunity by stepping forward again and grabbing the knifeman's arm. He twisted it while using his other hand to push down on the back of the twisted arm's elbow. I heard the sharp crack of bone snapping, even above the howling wind. The man cried out in excruciating pain and his knife fell to the deck.

Still holding the crippled arm, Larsen grabbed the sailor by the back of his oilskin leggings and bundled him towards the rail. When just three steps away, he broke into a run and lifted the man off his feet and threw him at the rail. The sailor landed on the side rail, the upper half of his body draped over the other side. Larsen reached down and grabbed the man's foot, lifting it into the air, higher and higher. The murderous sailor's good arm wrapped around the rail as he tried desperately to prevent himself from going over – but his own weight proved too much for him and he went sliding headfirst into the water below.

The second crewmember stood watching, and like his friend, had a knife in his hand. He had hesitated when the attack begun, probably put off by Larsen's speed and aggressiveness.

I turned to look at Vennard. He had lashed the tiller and stood facing me. There was disappointment across his face. His crew had failed and now he had to do his own dirty work. He walked towards me with a purpose, his immense size appearing all the bigger as he got closer. I pulled the gun out of my belt and began to take aim, but as I did, a small lead pipe slid from Vennard's coat sleeve and he threw it at me. It came spinning through the air and hit my wrist. The sharp pain from the impact caused me to cry out and the gun fell from my hand. In an instant, Vennard took two giant steps towards me and reached out to grab my throat. His massive hand wrapped itself around my neck and with apparent effortlessness. I was lifted off the deck. My dangling feet kicked out, looking for something solid to stand on, but the deck was several inches below them. His fingers began to squeeze and I felt as if my throat was gripped in a vice. I was looking straight into his face. He was grinning, a grin dominated by two perfect rows of perfectly polished teeth.

I used my hands to try to pry his fingers loose, but it was useless. I had never known such strength. My eyes started to bulge and my lungs, deprived of oxygen, felt as if they were about to explode. My arms fell to my side as my strength waned. A strange calmness began to overcome me as the daylight faded before my eyes. Vennard was still grinning, taking pleasure in watching the life drain out of my body.

I must have been within seconds of death when for some reason his grip loosened. My feet felt the firm wooden deck again and Vennard's expression began to change. His callous grin faded as his face altered to a strange blank expression. I summoned up enough strength to try again at prising his fingers loose. This time they gave way easily. I stepped back, gasping for air. Vennard stood motionless for a few seconds before his arm fell to his side. He continued to stand there, staring but not focused. It was as if he was looking straight through me.

The big man took one step forward and came crashing down onto the deck in the manner of a tree falling. The impact of his huge mass colliding with the wooden surface sent a thundering vibration throughout the vessel.

The handle of a knife, its blade unseen, was protruding from his back. Behind him stood Taipa, the young Indian girl who had warned us of the captain's treachery. The pile of canvas sails that were stacked aft lay scattered around the deck. I realised then, that she had concealed herself under them before anyone had boarded this morning.

She stepped forward and placed one foot on the dead man's back. Reaching down, she took hold of the knife's handle and pulled it from Vennard's body. Its blade was red and she wiped it clean on the captain's coat, first one side and then the other until it its metal surface showed. I watched her face the whole time. Her expression never changed, showing as much indifference that one would might display while cleaning a kitchen utensil.

I turned around to see Larsen standing with his back against the mast. His face was white and a knife was stuck in his shoulder. He slid his back down the mast until he was in a sitting position. There was no sign of the second sailor.

I ran towards him, but after only a few steps, the deck started to pitch violently to one side. The boat heeled over and I fell, sliding until my body crumpled up against the side rail.

"Drop the sails!" Larsen shouted to me.

He was clinging to the mast after wrapping his good arm around it, but he was unable to get up.

The boat had turned side-on to the wind and was on the verge of broaching. The water was level with the port rail and beginning to wash across the deck. The horses had fallen over and their legs were kicking wildly as they thrashed about, trying to get to their feet.

I could not move, the deck was at an acute angle and my own weight pinned me against the rail. We were a tangled mess of men and horses and the cold water was rising around us. There was nothing for me to grasp that I might pull myself towards the mast. It seemed hopeless – we were about to capsize.

Just when all appeared lost, the Vend du Nord began to lurch violently. Her bow kept rising several feet out of the water before crashing back down again. As the bow rose again, this time higher than before, I braced myself – waiting for the inevitable thump as it came crashing down again. But, it did not happen. Inch by inch, the sturdy boat began to come level, draining out the water that had swamped the portside.

Still clinging on, I turned to look back. Taipa was sitting on the side-rail with one leg over the side. She held the tiller with both hands and with all her might was pulling it towards her.

The sails were battling the gale, trying to force the bow to starboard. Gusts of wind began to fill the reverse side of the sails and the boat slowly swung across as hoped. The force of the wind filling the mainsail sent the boom careering across the deck with such ferocity that I thought it might rip the mainmast out of the boat. Taipa eased off the tiller as she climbed in over the rail. Once again, I owed my life to this young Indian girl.

The Vend du Nord steered towards the Canadian shore-line. Taipa did not hold the bow so close to the wind as Captain Vennard had done and as a result, we cut through the water at a more relaxed pace. Eclipse and the stallion managed to clamber to their feet and appeared to be unruffled by their experience. Vennard's body had been washed over-board along with the spare sails.

Larsen had managed to hang on with one arm. He sat leaning against the mast and clenched his teeth as he coped with the pain of the shoulder wound.

"Bill..." I did not know what else to say as I knelt down next to him.

"I'm all right, done worse shavin'." He tried to smile, but his teeth clenched again with the pain. After a brief moment, he continued. "That damn sailor...threw his knife and then jumped over the side. I hope he can swim." He looked past me and out across the water. He turned to face me again. "You got Vennard?"

"Well, not quite," I looked over my shoulder. "She did."

Taipa was not looking at us. Just as Vennard had done, she devoted her attention to steering the Vend du Nord.

Larsen tried to speak again, but his face twisted in agony.

"What should I do?" I asked.

He took a deep breath and exhaled slowly as he summoned up the energy to talk. "You got to pull it out."

I nodded, and taking a firm hold of the handle, I readied myself.

He raised his hand to get my attention. "Do it quick, one fast movement. Don't go diggin' for no gold in there."

I smiled at his humour. I took a few short but slow breaths and counted to three in my head. As the four-inch blade came out, he tilted his head back and closed his eyes – he did not make a sound. I could only try to imagine the pain he endured. I threw the bloody knife overboard. Larsen flat-tened the palm of his hand on the deck and pushed himself upright.

"That's better." His clenched face relaxed. "Get me some-thing to stop the bleedin'."

From Eclipse's saddlebag, I pulled some cloth that had

been used to wrap food. I folded it several times and Larsen took it from me. He shoved it inside his shirt and pressed it hard against the wound.

"It will need stitchin'," he said, trying to look at his shoulder.

"We'll be ashore soon." I looked out at the approaching land. "Can it wait?"

"Yea, it can wait." He looked back at Taipa. She was standing at the stern, steering the boat with one hand. "Damn useful girl, that."

I nodded, "She saved my life more than once today."

I got to my feet and walked back to her. She appeared indifferent to my approach and kept her eyes trained on the shoreline.

"Merci," I said.

Without turning her head, she gave a brief nod in recognition of my gratitude.

Taipa was the first Indian I ever met. She was someone I found hard to understand and I wondered if all Indians were like her. I had yet to see her display emotion of any kind. While she did warn us about Vennard, I could not help but suspect that she harbours a hatred of all white men and warning us was simply to suit her own plans for escape. Perhaps she cared nothing of our fate and we were just a means to an end for her. Whatever her motivations, we were indebted to her.

The Vent Du Nord's wooden frame groaned as its hull strained under the pressure of running aground. The horses shifted their weight to compensate for the deck leaning hard to one side as the boat ground to a halt. I climbed over the rail and jumped down into two feet of clear lake water. I walked forward until I stood on the grassy shore. Ahead of me was a solid green barrier of spruce trees that stretched as far as I could see in both directions. The cool damp smell of the forest replaced the fresh water smell from the lake and I inhaled deeply, filling my lungs. I had arrived in Canada and the first stage of my journey was over.

ELEVEN

Canada

We rode deep into the woodlands, following remote trails that were scarcely visible. Overhanging branches reached across as if purposely attempting to hinder our path. Taipa sat back of me with her arms wrapped around my waist. Larsen followed behind, clinging to his horse and grimacing in pain with every movement of the black stallion. He did not look well and I was worried. I wanted to stop and tend to him, but Taipa kept waving me forward and insisting we go deeper into the forest, and further away from the lake.

We rode all day and waited for the sun to dip below the treeline before we stopped. I helped Larsen down from his horse. I had to take his full weight and Taipa, seeing me struggling, helped me to carry him. We put him down on a soft bed of moss and I rolled up my coat, using it as a pillow to prop under his head.

His clothes were saturated with sweat. He was exhausted and wanted nothing more than to sleep. I pulled his shirt open and removed the blood-soaked cloth that covered his wound. A two-inch gash confronted me. The bleeding had stopped and dry blood congealed the cut. The sight of torn flesh made me feel nauseous and I leaned back, feeling that I might faint. Taipa knelt on the other side and studied the injury. She started to probe the wound with her fingers. Larsen groaned, feeling the pain from even the most delicate touch.

"Le sang...mauvais sang."

I shook my head – I did not understand her words.

She made a circular motion over his shoulder with her hands. "Mauvais."

She frowned with frustration at my lack of understanding. She stood and pointed into the forest, before throwing out a deluge of words in her native language. I shrugged my shoulders. Taipa waved her hand in a dismissive manner and walked away mumbling to herself. I watched her disappear in among the trees. She did not look back. I did not know where she was going or if she had any intention of returning.

The night wore on. I built a fire and put two blankets over Larsen. He had become delirious and shivered uncontrollably. I realised it was infection that had taken hold of his body, similar to the one that killed my father. Other than cleaning the wound, I did not know what else to do. The gash needed stitching, but I had neither needle nor thread. I decided to wait until morning. I would tie him to his horse and seek help. But I feared he would die before I found a doctor.

I could not sleep so I sat beside him, wiping the sweat from his face and trying to keep his temperature down with a damp cloth. The night was quiet except for the crackling fire and the distant howling of a lonely wolf.

A noise disturbed me. I listened, wondering if I had imagined it. A few moments later, I heard the distinctive crack of a twig breaking. I continued to listen and then I heard the rustle of leaves as branches were pushed aside. Somebody or something was out there in the darkness, and coming straight towards us.

I picked up my rifle and waited. The sounds continued and as they got closer, I was able to determine the direction they were coming from. I aimed my gun into the wall of darkness and readied myself. I began to wonder if it might be a bear.

From between two narrow tree trunks that stood side-by-side, Taipa emerged from the dark and into the flickering light. I eased my finger from the trigger and exhaled a breath of relief, thanking my own luck for not shooting out of fear or panic.

She was carrying a bundle of what looked like dried mud and leaves. She made straight for Larsen without even acknowledging my presence and knelt beside him. He was asleep and his body, gripped by the infection that was killing him, shook in an uncontrollable spasm every five or six seconds. She pulled the blankets back and shook her head in dismay at his state.

She turned to me and said, "Eau."

I understood the word water and filled one of our tin cups from my canteen. I was handing it to her when she stopped me. Pointing at the cup and then the fire, she said, "Chauds...chauds," repeating it slowly the second time so I would understand.

I sat the cup into the fire and while I waited for the water to heat, I watched Taipa. She had opened the bundle onto the ground and was dividing its contents into separate piles. There were plant roots, berries, herbs, and what looked like small strips of tree bark. She proceeded to crush and break-up each ingredient between her hands and then used a rounded stone to produce a rough powder of what remained.

I checked the water – bubbles were beginning to break on the surface. The tin cup had become so hot that I had to use my shirtsleeve to protect my fingers as I pulled it from the flames.

Taipa took the cup and poured some of the water out, leaving the vessel half-empty. She emptied a portion from each crushed pile into the cup and used a stick to mix the concoction until a thick sludge developed. I knew nothing of Indian medicine, but Larsen was in a bad way and I feared he was close to death. I decided that whatever Taipa did was unlikely to make his condition worse. Using two fingers, she scooped blobs of the gooey substance and began to smear it around the wound. She moulded it into a small mound above the gash and when finished, covered him with the blankets.

I slept, but my last vision before my eyes closed was of Taipa kneeling over Larsen's shivering body, rocking back and forth, and chanting in an Indian dialect.

The gentle whoosh of treetops swaying back and forth in the morning breeze woke me. I sat up to find Taipa still sitting beside Larsen. He was sweating profusely and his head rocked from side-to-side as he murmured nonsensically.

"How is he?" I asked.

"Malade. Larsen très malade. Il faut du temps pour guérir."

I understood the word, time. We had no choice but to stay and wait until his fever broke.

We had no food and only a little water so it was left to me to provide for all of us. I spent the morning constructing traps. I broke off suitable branches that were both thin and strong enough for their intended purpose. I cut notches to hold lengths of wire, of which there was a coil in the saddlebags. Having made six snares, I walked from the camp and placed them at strategic locations. I found an entrance to a rabbit hole and put the others between narrow gaps of fallen trees where small animals might run. I had nothing to use as scent, so I was relying on pure luck and nothing else. I returned to camp. Nothing had changed. Larsen was still ill and Taipa was keeping vigil over him. I did not think she slept during the night as she refused to leave his side.

I saddled Eclipse and packed the empty canteens along with my rifle and the last of the steel wire. I intended to travel further afield in search of game. I told Taipa that I would return before dark and while she seemed to understand, she seemed indifferent as to whether I returned or not. At least, that was the impression I was left with.

Riding out, I travelled north along the trail. I leaned forward to pat Eclipse's head. "We're a long way from Boston!"

Eclipse had spent his life pulling a buggy, but I had never seen him happier than he was now. He trotted along with his head held high, anticipating every little turn I wanted to make even before I could tug on the reins. I stopped at regular intervals to take note of landmarks; a hilltop or a break in the trees, anything that would help me find my way back.

The afternoon sun shone down from a clear sky and the scenery was magnificent. I had been travelling uphill, and far below the lake from which we crossed came into view. The sun reflected off its surface and glinted back as if the calm blue water was a mirror.

The forestry became sparser and soon we were crossing open ground that was only broken by small clusters of trees and rocky outcrops. In the distance, I saw two mountain goats feeding on grass that protruded from crevasses on one such rock pile. We turned and made towards them. Before coming within rifle range, their heads rose up, alerted by the sound of Eclipse's hooves stomping the dirt. Without any apparent sense of urgency, they moved around the boulders and out of sight. When I reached the rocks, I saw that they had moved further away. We followed, but the same scene was played out time and time again. There was no air of panic about them, they simply kept their distance and frustrated my efforts to get within shooting range.

I decided to continue on foot, believing that I could travel quieter if not on horseback. Eclipse was content to graze while I set off in a wide circle to surprise my prey. However, I was continuously outwitted. Every time, I reached the goat's position only to find that they had already moved on. I watched from a distance. The two goats appeared oblivious to my presence, but a sixth sense seemed to tell them when to go. For two hours the game of cat and mouse continued. Had it not been for my hunger, I would have given up, but a hungry belly was a powerful motivator.

At last my luck seemed to be changing when a steep slope of small boulders and loose stones leading back down to the woods hindered their progress. They walked along the hill's rim as they looked for a way to descend. I saw my chance and rushed forward as fast as my legs would carry me. I closed the distance to within a hundred feet, but as I knelt and took aim, they disappeared over the edge and down onto the rocks. I ran on and watched from the edge as they worked their way down the hill in a zigzag fashion. I set about descending the slope, confident that I could cut them off before they reached the bottom and vanished into the woods.

But I misjudged the steepness of the hill. I found myself jumping from one rock to another with such momentum that I was unable to stop. My feet landed awkwardly on one boulder and I leapt forward hoping to recover my balance on the next one, but the forward motion of my body was beyond my control. I fell forward and crashed to the ground, landing on my side. I continued down the slope, sliding and rolling as I collided from one boulder to another. I let out yells of pain as my body was battered against hard rock. I had no recollection of reaching the bottom. At one point my head bashed against hard stone and I was knocked unconscious. When I came to, I was lying in a crumpled heap at the bottom of the hill. Every bone in my body ached and a large lump protruded from the back of my head.

It took time to come to my senses. I limped around in circles as I felt for broken bones. Other than cuts and bruises along with the mother of all headaches, I had escaped without serious injury. I searched the hill for my rifle and by the time I found it, the light was fading. I did not feel up to the long journey back and I doubted if I would be able to retrace my route in the dark. I decided to camp in the woods and wait for dawn before making my way back to Eclipse.

TWELVE

A Wanted Man

I did not know what had disturbed me from my sleep. Maybe it was the noise of a gun's hammer being drawn back or perhaps they had prodded me with their boots. Maybe it was my subconscious becoming aware of their presence. Whatever it was, I sat up to find myself staring into a forty-five calibre cylindrical tunnel that hid a bullet deep within its dark shaft. A handgun, barely three inches from my face and a nervous look on the man behind it.

"Get up...nice and easy like," the man said.

I obeyed, too scared to speak.

"Where's your partner?" Another man, much older and wearing a heavy coat, and not dressed in a dark uniform like the others, spoke to me.

"I don't know." I spoke slow, terrified that any sudden movement could cause the man facing me to shoot.

"All right, Constable, ease off there," the older man said with the sound of authority in his voice.

The man took a step back, using his thumb to return the gun's hammer to its normal position and lowering the weapon at the same time. Another Constable had picked up my rifle and with his other hand patted me around the waist to make sure I had nothing concealed. I noticed the writing on his shirt collar – Royal Toronto Constabulary.

"Where's your partner?" The older man spoke again.

"I don't know."

"What's your name?"

"My name?"

"You've got a name, haven't you?"

"I'm Tom Anderson. What's this about?"

"We're taking you in."

"Taking me in...why? I've done nothing."

"I wouldn't call murder nothing." The man's face grew more serious.

"Murder?" I gasped.

"That's right, for the murder of John H. Campbell and Captain Jules Vennard."

"But...I didn't—" I was not sure what to say. In any case, I was interrupted.

"Save it for the judge, son."

They shackled my wrists and helped me onto a horse. After satisfying themselves that I was alone, we set off back down the trail. I did not bother to protest my innocence, as I realised it would do no good. I was confident I would be able to sort out the misunderstanding when we got to wherever it was we were going.

Our line of horses travelled slowly down the narrow trail. After some hours we came to a clearing at the bottom of the hill. There was a wagon there waiting for us. It was specially constructed for the transport of prisoners. A large steel cage was fixed onto the wagon's flat surface. A single wooden bench was all that was inside. A lone policeman stood tightening the straps and ropes that joined the wagon to the two horses that pulled this moving cage.

I was pulled down from the horse and suffered the further humiliation of having my ankles shackled. The policeman that had been waiting put down a crate for me to step on and into the cage. It was not easy. My hands and ankles manacled left me with little balance. The chain joining my feet was no more than a few inches in length. I could only shuffle along and lacked the ability to reach out my arms to steady myself. Aided by two policemen, each holding one of my elbows, I managed to stand on the box and rather indignantly fell forward through the small opening.

The wagon trudged along at a slow pace as it made its way towards Toronto. At first I had sat on the fixed bench, resting my back against the metal bars, but every time one of the wheels hit a rock or dropped into a small hole, I was thrown off the seat. Without the full use of my hands to reach out for protection, it was not long before I became badly bruised. I decided it was safer to sit on the floor for the remainder of the journey. Seven men escorted the wagon – the driver and six riders. Although surrounded by men, I had never felt so alone in all my life. I looked back at the tall spruce trees that were fading into the distance and I remembered back to only yesterday when I felt like the freest man alive.

My thoughts turned to Larsen and I wondered if I would ever see him again. I feared he might die if indeed he was not already dead. And even if he did recover, what would he think about my absence? He might find Eclipse and with no sign of me, presume I had fallen off and broken my neck. After a day or two, he would continue his journey without me.

It was late when the wagon rolled noisily through the streets of Toronto, and I welcomed the dark and empty roads. It was humiliating enough to be caged like a wild animal, but had I been paraded down busy thoroughfares, the shame would have been unbearable, even before the eyes of strangers.

Heavy iron gates that needed the strength of two men to pull open marked the entrance to a small-enclosed courtyard at the rear of the city's police station. I was helped down from the wagon and led through a narrow arched doorway. I had to stoop my head when entering. A spiral stone stairwell led down into the basement of the building. I had to negotiate each step with caution as my chains only allowed the toes of one foot to touch the step below before I would have to hop to bring down my second foot. At the bottom of the stairwell was a narrow corridor, dimly lit by two gas lamps that were fixed to the wall. Steel doors lined both sides of the passageway, each one an individual cell. The second to last one on the left was for me.

I was pushed in and found myself standing in the centre of a small room, roughly eight feet long and five feet wide. The cell was dark and the only light was that which came in from the gas lamps in the passageway.

"I need to speak to someone," I said, hoping to make some progress on sorting out my situation.

"Tomorrow," one of the guards answered as he knelt to remove my shackles.

A second guard stood behind me in case I had notions of

starting trouble. The heavy shackles came off and I massaged my wrists in relief. My skin was chaffed and I felt wet streaks of blood on the palms of my hands as I rubbed them.

The guard stood up and I questioned him again. "When tomorrow?

I thought he was ignoring me as he turned to leave, but he spun around and drove his fist hard into my stomach. I fell to my knees, coughing as I struggled to breathe. His second punch caught me on the side of my head and I crumpled up in a heap on the cold stone floor.

When I came to, I was alone and in darkness. I reached out and held the side of the bed as I pulled myself up off the floor. The mattress was thin and the wooden bed-boards felt as if they were protruding through. I stumbled around the room and waved my arms out in front of me as I tried to become familiar with my surroundings. The room contained little in the way of luxuries. Other than the bed, the only other furniture was a small stool and a round table, the surface of which was no bigger than the top of the stool. A metal pail sat in the corner. I only discovered it when I accidently kicked it over. I could feel a draught of fresh air on my face. I ran my hands along the cool surface of the cell walls looking for the vent or window that was the draught's source. I found nothing so I used the stool to stand on to investigate higher up. On the back wall I found it. It was high up and close to the ceiling – a small opening guarded by thick metal bars. Even standing on my toes, I could only reach the sill's surface and touch the bars with the tips of my fingers.

I sat on the edge of the bed and prepared to wait until morning. Hours passed, or at least it felt like hours, as in the total darkness I was becoming disoriented. It was a surreal feeling. The passing of time was impossible to keep track of and even the space around me seemed dreamlike. I stood up, but when I did I felt dizzy, unsure of which way was up and which way was down. It was as if I was floating in a chamber where gravity itself was confused. I sat down again and lay back on the bed. I reached out to touch the wall as I tried to keep a sense of position.

I did sleep, but I suspect it was not for long. When I awoke, the first shafts of daylight were beginning to come in through the tiny window. The dusty rays of light did little to vanquish the depressive ambience of the cold cell. I heard a voice and then footsteps passing the opening. The window was just above ground level with the rear courtyard where I was brought in the night before.

I was not the only one to wake. From other cells, voices began to echo and resound throughout the basement. There was a mixture of laughter and despair from the unseen voices. Their echoes mingled together so as it became impossible to hear any particular one with any degree of clarity.

I waited as there was not much else I could do. After the beating I received from the guard, I realised it would be pointless to call out for attention. I checked my pocket-watch, but its hands were stuck at three o'clock as it had been several days since I last wound it. The cell brightened as the morning took hold. At last, I heard something besides the confused bellows of caged men – a steel bolt noisily drawn back and a door opening. Voices sounded outside my cell. Near the bottom of my door, a flap fell outwards and a tin tray was pushed in. I jumped off the bed and grabbed it before it fell to the floor, spilling its contents. The flap was promptly pushed shut as the guards moved on to the next door.

Breakfast was a bowl of foul smelling fish chowder, one slice of stale bread, and a mug of water. I sat at the table to eat, but the taste of the fish stew was even worse than its nauseating aroma. I ate the hard bread and emptied the bowl's contents into the pail.

The morning passed and it was late afternoon before my cell door finally opened. A guard stood just outside and the man who questioned me yesterday entered. I stayed sitting on the bed, not sure what to expect.

"My name is John Thornton. I'm the Chief Constable with the Toronto Constabulary."

He still had the air of authority about him, but his manner was polite and I felt that I had nothing to fear from him in the way of rough treatment.

"Mr Thornton, I need to speak to someone about why I am here."

"You'll get your chance."

"I need a lawyer."

"Have you someone in mind?"

"No, I don't know anyone in Canada. I'm from Boston."

"Well, the city will appoint you one."

"When?"

"In a few days. I've just come from the courthouse. Your trial is scheduled for the week after next."

"Trial?" I was shocked at the mention of the word. This was going further than I had expected.

"That's right. In the meantime, keep your nose clean and don't cause us no trouble."

He turned and left the cell, leaving me speechless. Trial? I felt a sickening panic spreading throughout my body.

The guard did not close the door.

"Grab your pail and let's go," he said.

I stepped out into the passageway and he pointed me forward towards the stairwell that led up to the courtyard. I walked up and out into the sunshine. The bright light hurt my eyes and I held my hand up to shield them. The guard prodded me in the back with a cudgel. "Empty your pail over there. You get one hours exercise every day, so make the most of it."

The courtyard had six other prisoners in it. Three were keeping their own company while the others sat in a corner talking. Not counting the guard behind me, there were two guards wandering around the courtyard. Both carried shotguns and although holding them casually, appeared ready to use them at a seconds notice.

The police station enclosed the yard on three sides and countless windows looked down on us from the three-story building. The fourth side was the rear wall. It must have been twenty feet high at least. The only exit was through the large gates which were fixed shut with a heavy timber post laid across them, both ends fitting snugly into recesses in the wall. There was a small gap between the bottom of the gates and the ground. I could see the shadows cast from people's feet as they passed by in both directions.

I spent the next hour pacing the courtyard. The other prisoners were the roughest men I had ever seen and I thought it wise to keep to myself. I spoke to no one and I was not bothered. The hour passed quickly and having collected our empty pails, we were escorted one at a time back to our cells.

The next three days followed the same routine. I sat in my cell day and night except for one hour when I was permitted to exercise in the yard. I did befriend some of the other prisoners during this time. Their curiosity as to my reasons for being there spurred them to confront me. I tried not to become too involved with them. They were a rough bunch of characters and were a mixture of Irish and Canadian French. It did not take me long to realise that the two groups had a deep hatred of each other. It was a hatred that was fuelled by land wars that had flared up on the outside. I was an American and as such seemed to be accepted by both sides. I also learned why there were so few of us in this part of the jail. We were separated from other prisoners who would have committed lesser crimes such as theft or public drunkenness. Every man here had been charged with murder and was apparently destined to hang or be sentenced to a life of hard labour. It was for this reason we were considered to be desperate, men that had nothing to lose.

It was on the fourth day that I received some unexpected but wonderful news, news that informed me I was not forgotten by the outside world. It was late morning when I received a visit from the Chief Constable. He entered my cell while one of the guards stood at the open door. He held a piece of paper and took a moment to glance over it before speaking.

"You must have friends in high places, Anderson," he said in an unfriendly voice.

"What do you mean?"

He did not answer, but handed the piece of paper to me. It was a telegram and it was addressed to the courts.

To: Court Registrar, Royal Canadian Courts Department **STOP**

Boston Law firm, Wallberg and Branbery have been instructed to represent Mr. Thomas Charles Anderson in all legal proceedings Pertaining to charges regarding warrant issued 10th February 1888 **STOP**

A representative from said company is on route to hold council with their client and is expected to arrive in Toronto in two days **STOP**

I trust all counsel/client privileges will be afforded Mr. Anderson's legal counsel **STOP**

Mr. Thomas O'Brien,
President,
O'Brien Land Corporation.

I sat reading and taking in every word with a sense of renewed hope. As I read, Thornton stood, waiting for me to finish. He did not ask for the telegram back, but his presence and his posture made it clear that I was to return it to him. He folded the telegram before sliding it into his jacket pocket.

"It came this morning, so you can expect a visit the day after tomorrow."

"Yes, I understand, thank you."

He gave me a strange look before turning to leave. It was a sneer of disapproval and I was left in no doubt that my having friends in high places, as he had put it, was not to his liking.

Alone again, I stretched out on the bed. I constantly moved, shifting my weight as I attempted the impossible task of finding comfort on the thin mattress. I couldn't believe my luck. Emma's father had solicited the most prestigious law firm in Boston to handle my defence. I could only but wonder at the expense involved. And why would he do such a thing? My only explanation was that Emma had exerted influence on him to come to my aid.

I thought about Emma. I was still racked with guilt and her pathetic image still haunted me. She must be coping, I thought to myself. How else could she organise such a thing?

Darkness came again as the day grew late. But my gloom and mental suffering was eased by the thought that help was coming.

THIRTEEN

Miss Arabella Woodhall

The rain did not fall in as much as it seemed to linger in a mist-like form as it gradually penetrated everything it came into contact with. Every minute or so, a loud thud reverberated around the courtyard as another sash window was pulled down. The building's office workers were afforded the luxury of being able to shut out the damp miserable weather with the simple action of closing a window.

Below the long rows of wooden window frames surrounded by dreary walls, the half dozen wretched men that trod the gravel-covered courtyard each afternoon knew no such luxury. Whatever the weather, be it wet, freezing, or scorching beneath a blistering sun, the routine never altered. One hours exercise to break the monotony of been locked in a small cell for twenty-three hours at a time.

I was one of these men, shivering pathetically and wallowing in self-pity at my miserable predicament. My feet dragged along the ground as if weighed down by invisible weights. Although treated reasonably well, the loneliness of my cell coupled with a diet of bland food and the realisation that my freedom had been taken away was having an adverse effect on my mental state. The thought of a trial no longer terrified me. Anything, even a legal argument where my very life itself would be at stake would be a welcome relief to the monotonous existence I was presently enduring.

"Get your pails!" One of the guards called out from a sheltered doorway. It was time to return to our cells, but as I crossed the yard, the calling of my name stopped me. I turned to see a guard standing in an open doorway. He waved, indicating that I was to come over to him.

"This way, Anderson. You got a visitor," he said.

I stepped in through the open door where a second guard was holding the now familiar shackles in his hands.

"We don't want you getting no stupid notions, now do we?" the guard said before clapping them around my wrists, tightening them until I felt the pain of their restriction. He knelt and put on the leg irons next, looking up as he did, and grinning when he saw me winch as he turned the securing bolts.

I was brought up a rear staircase. Its wooden steps had space for three men abreast. A window at every turning provided ample light than shone off the finely carved and varnished spindles. I had left the dismal surroundings of my basement prison and was entering the world of normality again.

On the second floor, we stopped at a door halfway along the corridor. One of the guards grabbed my arm and pushed me against the opposite wall. The door had an obscure glass panel and through it, I could see the blurry outline of two people silhouetted by the light from a window. They were talking and I was able to hear the conversation coming from within.

"I don't like it. It's not the normal procedure we follow here." I recognised the voice of John Thornton.

"Chief Constable—" the second voice surprised me, as it was that of a woman— "Our client is to stand trial in four days' time. He has a legal right and an entitlement to adequate council. Given the time frame and Mr Branbery's unavoidable delay, it is of the upmost importance that I interview Mr Anderson. If you refuse me access, I will have no choice but to get a court order. And I can assure you, the delay will be brought to the attention of the trial judge."

There was a pause before Thornton spoke again. "All right, but one of my men stays in the room."

"That is not acceptable, Chief Constable." Her voice had risen to a higher tone and at that moment, I would have given anything to see the look on his face.

"Well...well the door remains open and my man waits outside." The frustration in his voice was obvious. "I don't like the idea of a murderer alone with a woman, even if he is your client."

"Alleged murderer, Chief Constable, there has been no conviction yet," she said, rebuking his last comment.

The door burst open and Thornton stormed out. His face was glowing red and he was seething with anger. When he saw me, he stopped and stared straight into my face.

"Don't you cause trouble or you won't live long enough to stand trial." He turned to the guard. "You stand here and don't take your eyes off him, understand?" Without waiting for a reply, he turned and marched down the corridor. A clerk carrying papers had to sidestep out of his way, as the Chief Constable had no intention of yielding.

The guard pushed me and said, "Inside, and remember, I'll be right here."

The room was magnificently bright, the walls white-washed to reflect the incoming light from a large sash window. Filing cupboards lined the far wall and a table with two chairs was centred in the room.

The woman was no more than a girl in her early twenties and she stood displaying a look of shock at my ragged appearance. She regained her composure and stepped forward to shake my hand. Her white gloved fingers were greeted by my shackled hands and she showed a momentary glint of embarrassment.

"Please sit down, Mr Anderson." She pushed out one of the chairs for me and walked around the table to sit facing me.

I watched as she struggled to sit. The large bushel at the back of her skirt forced her to sit forward on the edge of the seat. She removed her bonnet. Her hair was auburn, reminding me of autumn leaves. It was tied up to fit beneath the hat. She exhaled a sigh of relief as she placed it on the table next to a folder filled with loose sheets of paper.

"Mr Anderson, my name is Miss Arabella Woodhall and I work for Mr Branbery who will be representing you during the forthcoming trial."

I cleared my throat – I was taken aback as it had been some weeks since I last spoke to a white woman. "Please, call me Tom, Miss Woodhall. I am sorry, but I'm a bit surprised as I've never met a female lawyer before."

"Oh no, Mr...I mean, Tom. I'm not a lawyer. Please let me explain." Her face showed genuine concern at my misinterpretation of her, and her eagerness to clear up any confusion was obvious.

"I am a second year law student and I work part-time for Mr Branbery to help fund my tuition."

"I did not realise there were any practicing women lawyers, forgive me," I said, hoping she had not thought me patronising."

"Not in Boston, not yet," she said, apparently not having taken offence at my remark. "I hope to be one of the first to qualify and practice law there."

"Well, I wish you good luck with that. Judging from the way you handled Thornton, I'd say you will make a formidable legal practitioner."

"Thank you," she said, looking down modestly for a brief moment. "Now, Tom, there is much to do." She looked back up at me, her twinge of embarrassment gone and a more serious business-like look on her face. "First of all, Mr Branbery sends his apologies. A family bereavement has delayed him and he will meet you in Ottawa the day after tomorrow."

"Ottawa?"

"Yes." She leaned a little forward. "Has nobody told you?"

"No, told me what?"

"Apparently this captain..." She opened the folder and flicked through the pages searching for the name. "Vennard...was a brother-in-law to the Governor General and he has taken a personal interest in the case. He has arranged for the trial to take place in the newly built state courthouse in Ottawa. You are to be transferred there tomorrow. I will be travelling also, and Mr Branbery will meet us there on Thursday, the day before the trial. That is my reason for being here now. He instructed me to get a statement from you regarding the facts of the case so as to save time when you do meet."

"I see," I answered, a bit bewildered by all the information that was been thrust upon me.

I raised my shackled hands and used my sleeve to wipe my forehead. Water was trickling down from my wet hair. Her eyes displayed pity and I could see she was sympathetic with my chained and beguiled situation. She leaned back as much as the bushel would allow her, shifting her shoulders, apparently uncomfortable with the tightly laced corset she wore.

"Well, Miss Woodhall, what do you want to know?"

She searched the folder for blank paper on which to make notes. It seemed we both felt a momentary distraction had occurred.

"This, Mr Campbell, what can you tell me about the events leading to his death?"

"Nothing, I did not even know he was dead. The last time I saw him was the night before we sailed across the lake."

Miss Woodhall paused as she stared at the open door. The guard was standing at the doorway and feeling the intense glare directed at him, he took a step back into the corridor.

She turned back to me. "I'm sorry, you were saying?"

"Like I said, he was in good health when I last saw him, other than that, I don't know anything."

I watched as she noted down everything I said.

She searched through the folder again, pulling various sheets of typed paper out and placing them in different positions on the table. She spoke as she sorted out her paperwork.

"John Campbell...proprietor of Campbell's Tavern. Shortly after you left, his body was discovered. He had been stabbed in the back. Also, there are eight affidavits describing how your travelling companion, Bill Larsen, attacked him, and later, threatened him." She looked up at me, waiting for my reply.

I shrugged my shoulders. "It wasn't like that, not like that at all." I was thinking as I spoke. An image of Taipa pulling her knife from Vennard's back came into my mind. It was beginning to make sense, but I thought it better not to mention Taipa's name. I owed my life to her and I could not repay that debt by implicating her in a murder.

"Are you saying these men were lying?"

"They were friends and customers of his and we were strangers. No doubt their accounts of what actually happened, favoured Campbell."

"Alright, and what about Captain Vennard? His body was found washed ashore, also with a stab wound in the back. And there are two eyewitnesses who will swear that you and Bill Larsen attacked them while crossing the lake."

"What two witnesses?"

"Two crew, employed by Captain Vennard."

"I thought they drowned."

She looked a little shocked. "Well, I would not say that in court if I were you."

"Look, Miss Woodhall, Vennard was killed in self-defence."

"A wound in the back is difficult to pass off as self-defence, Tom."

"I know, I can't explain it, but it's true, I swear it. If Bill Larsen was here he would be able to confirm everything I'm saying."

"Ah...Bill Larsen. Now there, we have a problem," she said.

Miss Woodhall picked up different sheets of paper, casting her eye across them before putting them down and selecting others. "Here we are." She found what she was looking for and her eyes moved from left to right as she worked her way down the page. "This man called Larsen, is he a good friend of yours?"

"Yes, I would say that, a good friend."

She shook her head in disapproval, "I think it might be a good idea to play down your friendship with this man."

"But why?"

Using her pencil, she pointed at different paragraphs on the typed page as she spoke, "Bill Larsen. Warrants issued in Wyoming, Utah, and Arizona for a catalogue of offences including murder, robbery, and fraud." She ran her pencil further down the page, "Here in Canada he was arrested for unlawful prospecting and...vagrancy."

Miss Woodhall put down her pencil, straightened her glasses, and looked me straight in the eye. "I have to be honest, Tom. You are going to stand trial for two murders. One of the victims was a relation to the Governor General and there are eyewitness accounts that go against you. And the only defence you have, would be a statement from a notorious outlaw, whose location is not known to us."

I did not answer as I did not know what else to say.

"We can blame the killings on Larsen. As you have never been in trouble with the law before I think it's your only option."

I shook my head. "No, no. Bill did not kill those men. I can't lie. I just can't."

There was silence for a few moments and then Miss Woodhall did something quite unexpected and very personal.

Removing her glasses, she reached out and placed her hand on mine, "Tom, is there something you are not telling me?"

I looked into her eyes. They were beautiful eyes. Had the situation been different.... However, I had to face reality. She was a talented law student with a brilliant future ahead of her while my future looked rather short. And even if it wasn't, what would I have to offer? Without a home or a job I was hardly in a position to present myself to any young lady.

Her voice disturbed my thoughts. "You do realise, Tom, you will be on trial for your life?"

I nodded. There was so much I was not saying, but to do so could mean Taipa having to face a trial for murder. I wondered what kind of justice an Indian girl could expect for killing two white men. I decided there and then that I would never reveal her part in this no matter what the consequences might be for me. She had saved my life and I owed her a debt. And if even if repaying that debt meant walking to the gallows, then so be it.

"Well, that's about it," she said.

Her hand withdrew and she started to place the papers back into the folder. "I'll type up a report for Mr Branbery and we shall see you in Ottawa two days from now. Is there anything I can get you? I'm sure I can get permission to send in some food or some reading material if you like."

I shook my head. "No...no thank you, I'll be fine." My mood had lapsed into that of depression and I seemed to have little enthusiasm for anything.

Miss Arabella Woodhall left me alone while I waited to go back to my cell. I stared at the window, looking forward and not concentrating on anything in particular. The light faded as dark clouds passed overhead, and as the light darkened outside, my reflection became visible in the glass. A scruffy unshaved man was facing me with a blank expression upon his face. I cast my mind back to Vennard and the similar look he expressed just before he fell. Was I falling? Was this the end of a brief but exciting adventure? I thought about these questions, both there and later in the dark confines of my cell. Seeing no way out of my predicament, I decided that, yes, it was the end for me.

FOURTEEN

Second Class

Breakfast came and it was no different from what I had become used to; a meagre helping of cornmeal and bread that had the first signs of mould beginning to show. I was sitting on the bed and lost in my own thoughts when the heavy clunking of the lock turning disturbed me, its sound amplified by the solid walls of the cell. The door swung out, its weight straining the three steel hinges that were buried deep into the wall. The guard that had so brutally welcomed me on my first night and the Chief Constable were standing there. The guard entered with a bundle of clean clothes, which he placed on the bed.

Thornton spoke as the guard returned to the passageway to pick up another bundle off the floor. "Clean yourself up, you're going on a train ride."

"Ottawa?" I asked.

"That's right, and we can't have you looking like a vagrant in front of the other passengers, now can we?"

The guard re-entered the cell and the second bundle he put down contained a towel, soap, razor, and a small yellow stained mirror.

"Two of my men will be going along. You will be shackled and they have orders to shoot if you try anything stupid."

The third time the guard came in was to place a ceramic bowl of hot water on the table. Steam billowed upwards as the water came into contact with the cold air of the room. Thornton stood back as the guard pushed the heavy door shut.

"You leave in thirty minutes." The noise of the door shutting drowned out his voice and I was alone again.

Warm water is one of those simple pleasures I never appreciated until it was taken away from me. I put my hands together and dipped them into the bowl. I lifted up a scoop of warm water and sank my face into my cupped hands. The pleasurable feeling of tepid liquid running down my face was a delight I promised myself never to take for granted again.

I only realised the true extent of the stench my clothes emitted when I inspected the clothes that had been left for me. They were not new. The trousers were threadbare at the knees, and the cotton shirt had a frayed collar and cuffs. But they were clean and compared with my present attire, could only be an improvement.

I stripped off my clothes and left them wrapped in a bundle near the door. Wetting the block of soap, I cleaned myself and used the same water to rinse off the soapy mixture as best I could. The water had cooled quickly and I began to shiver with the cold. I dressed and felt like a new man again. I pushed the table up to the wall and stood the mirror upright. I inspected my bearded face. I was twenty-four years old, but the man looking back at me could have passed for forty. My mind drifted back to the night that Larsen knocked at my door. I had thought he was an old-timer in his sixties, but the next time I saw him in Harper's Hotel he had lost between ten and fifteen years with the loss of his beard. Ten days of confinement had added nearly twenty years to my appearance, and it was with much satisfaction that I shaved and a familiar face was revealed to me.

Union station was three blocks away from the police station and it had been decided that we walk the short distance. Thankfully the leg irons were not used and only my wrists were shackled. Four guards accompanied me, but only two were detailed to board the train for the six hour journey.

The glances from people walking past was something I

would never forget. They were unable to make eye contact with me and looked down as if hypnotised by my chains. There would be a quick glance to see my face and then they would turn away before my eyes could meet theirs. I became oblivious to them, too weary to care anymore about the thoughts of others.

We walked along Union Street and the morning bustle heralding a busy shopping day was beginning to build. As we passed the open door of a bakery, the sweet aroma of freshly baked bread filled my nostrils. I tried to look in, to catch a glimpse of the ovens, but by the time my head turned, we had past. I glanced in the window of a teashop. An elegant lady and a distinguished looking gentleman were sitting at a table close to the window. The woman's nose rose as her head turned with disgust at seeing a shackled man pass so close to her. The gentleman gave me a disapproving glare, his bushy moustache flinching as the corner of his lip curled up. We had passed in an instant and I was angry with myself that I had not the wit or the gumption to return his glare with a sneer.

The barrel of a rifle prodded into my back prompting me to step out onto the muddy road. The mud squelched under our feet as we crossed. Carriages slowed as we made our way across to the opposite paved walkway. It occurred to me that it would have been a good idea for policemen escorting prisoners to the station to walk along the roads for the entire journey. The slippery mud would have made any thoughts of making a break for freedom pointless. It took all of one's attention and balance just to remain upright while walking, let alone running. Wet slippery roads or dry sidewalks, I had no intention of any such foolish heroics. I doubt I would have got ten paces before receiving a shotgun blast in the back.

We reached the stationhouse, a large timber building that was painted a dark shade of yellow. Above the entrance doors, a clock was fitted to the wall. It read ten minutes to eleven. The train was almost ready to depart. Huge plumes of hot steam were pumped out from the engine and drifted along the platform towards the rear of the train. Through the windows, I saw passengers making their way along the carriages as they sought out seating. Some were stretching upwards as they stored their baggage overhead. I stood on the platform with three guards while the fourth went to the cashier's counter.

"You got to go second class, Anderson. State doesn't rate you good enough for first class," one of the guards said and began laughing at his own humour.

The other guard returned and handed three tickets to one of the men that would be travelling on the train. A shotgun and rifle were handed to the guards that were going back to the station. They joked among themselves and I heard something about a whore in Ottawa that one of them was fond of – at least that is what the other three were trying to imply.

Although standing in the middle of them, their voices drifted into the background as my attention focused on a young woman that was buying a ticket. It was Miss Woodhall, and I watched as she struggled to carry a heavy carpetbag towards one of the front carriages. Her bonnet began to slip sideways and as she reached up to straighten it, the bag fell to the ground. A porter hurried over to lend assistance. She smiled with relief as he took charge of the bag. She pointed to the front carriage and he nodded as he picked up the bag with apparent effortlessness. She turned around, taking in the hustle and bustle of the station as she fixed her bonnet. She was pretty and without her glasses, she lost the formal look that goes with the seriousness of her profession.

She saw me, and a smile spread across her face. Her white gloved hand rose into the air as she waved. I nodded in reply as my shackled hands made it difficult to do anything else. She made her way towards us, her long skirt flowing sideways in the sturdy wind that blew down along the platform.

Of course, I realised she was part of my legal representation, but her complete lack of embarrassment or horror at the presence of a shackled prisoner was something I admired, and it helped me to remember that I was a man and not a wild animal.

"Tom, how are you?" She was still smiling as she approached.

Two of the constables had walked away, leaving two men armed with side-arms beneath their jackets standing on either side of me. They waited, allowing Miss Woodhall to exchange a few words with me.

"I'm alright, glad to be out of that cell."

"Well, at least they let you clean-up for the journey." She was still smiling as she talked and it was a beautiful quality to possess.

I suspect had it been a man I was talking to, the guards would have waved him away, but faced with a pretty female, they were somewhat embarrassed and did not want to appear rude.

"Mr Branbery will be waiting to meet you in Ottawa."

"Good, I look forward to meeting him."

"Have you food for the journey?"

"No."

Miss Woodhall looked at the guards, first one and then the other. "Will he get something to eat on the train?"

The guards shifted uneasily on their feet. One of them finally spoke. "No, the dining carriage is reserved for the first class passengers."

A look of concern spread across her face and she bit her bottom lip while she was thinking. "There will be a short stop at Smiths Falls. Can I bring some food back for Tom?"

The two men exchanged glances before one of them replied with a tone of uncertainty. "Well...I don't know—"

"Just something small," she said, before he could finish. "Surely you won't mind? Tom hasn't eaten very well over the last few weeks."

The other guard, feeling likewise embarrassed at the prospect of turning her down, answered. "I suppose it would be all right." He looked at his friend for conformation.

"All right, Ma'am," he replied with a hint of defeat in his voice.

"Oh, thank you. Thank you so much." Her smile confirmed her gratitude.

A high-pitched whistle broke the moment and the engine began to chug as thick plumes of smoke billowed into the air. Miss Woodhall turned and started to run to the front carriage. "Bye, Tom, I'll see you when we stop at the falls."

FIFTEEN

The Escape

The Canadian landscape rolled past my window and along with the constant clacking of the rail sleepers, it had a hypnotising effect. I drifted in and out of sleep with my head pressed against the vibrating glass.

The two constables, whose names I had learned were Murphy and Dillon, got up every now and again to stretch their legs. They would walk up and down the passageway between the seating, stretching their cramped muscles as they went. At one point, I asked if I could do likewise, but a firm no was the reply.

Murphy, I came to realise, enjoyed his position in the Constabulary because of the power it afforded him, power that he would never have attained in civilian life. He was the guard who had welcomed me with a beating on my first night in jail. I had learned from other prisoners that he took a sadistic pleasure in giving the Saturday night drunks a good thrashing. There was no doubt in my mind that beneath the tough image, he was a coward that took delight in preying on the weak and helpless.

Dillon was different. He was older, in his mid-fifties. A family man with a wife and children, but I gathered from listening to him that they were grown-up now and he and his wife lived alone. He was a tall man of thin stature. He seemed to lack enthusiasm for the job, content to put in the hours, collect his pay, and go home to where he could forget about work. He was reasonably pleasant and I felt that without Murphy's presence, he would have had no objection to me getting up to relieve the stiffness that comes with sitting in the same position for several hours.

A change in the rhythmic movement of the train made me sit up straight in the seat. My hands rose together as I rubbed my tired eyes. We were slowing down and I pressed my cheek against the window in an effort to look forward. We passed a small shed followed by two old freight boxcars. One of them was lying on its side and the other was stripped of most of its wood.

The carriage chugged as we rolled into the small town of Smiths Falls. There was a final jolt along with the sharp sound of the brakes pressing against the metal wheels as we came to a halt. A loud bellow of hot steam was released from the engine and filled the air both sides of the carriage. I pushed my face against the glass and tried to look forward again. I could see two men, partially obscured by whirling steam. They were standing at the base of a large water tank that was supported by stout wooden posts. One of the men was feeding a rope through his hands to lower a long pipe onto the engine's roof. His companion was waving his arms and shouting instructions to someone unseen by me on the engine's roof.

Murphy stood up and stretched his arms back, twisting them as he did so to relieve the stiffness. "We'll be here for fifteen minutes or so. I'm going for a stroll, don't take your eyes off him."

"I know how to do my job," Dillon replied, seeming annoyed at Murphy's dominant tone rather than by what he had said.

Murphy grunted as he turned to leave the carriage. Both men were getting irritable. Most of the passengers were also getting off, taking the opportunity to get some fresh air or perhaps buy a cup of coffee. I was going nowhere. Dillon sat on the outside of the seat facing me. I knew he lacked enthusiasm for the job, but his experience was evident. He stayed sitting upright and alert to everything that happened around him. Any movement, no matter how slight, and his eyes would dart sideways as his head turned, but never so much that his attention might be taken away from his prisoner.

I looked up along the carriage and out of the windows. Miss Woodhall had said she would come back with food and I waited eagerly. I was hungry and my stomach made embarrassing grumbling noises. Besides the prospect of eating, I was also looking forward to her company. I felt dreadfully alone, and her pleasant companionship was the only positive thing in my life. It might even be the last pleasant experience I ever had as my future was looking bleak.

Passengers began to return and they jostled past one another to take their seats. There was still no sign of Miss Woodhall and the thought that she may have forgotten saddened me. The carriage shuddered as the engine worked to build up power. Puffs of released steam drifted past the windows and Dillon moved his head from side-to-side as he struggled to peer through the moving grey mist. Murphy had not returned. Dillon got to his feet, seemingly unsure of what to do. He shifted his weight from one foot to the other as he anxiously looked out the window. I looked too, but it suited me if he did not return. His presence was something I would not miss.

A woman ran along the opposite side of the carriage. Appearing and disappearing as she passed each window. Her arm was stretched up and holding her bonnet in place as she slowed to glance in every window. It was Miss Woodhall. I felt my heart miss a beat as her face lit up, illuminated by a wide smile when she caught sight of me. She pointed to the end of the carriage to show me where she was going to come in. I smiled while nodding to her, but she never noticed in her haste to get aboard.

A loud, shrill toot echoed as the engine's whistle blew. Dillon paced up and down in mild panic at Murphy's absence.

"Tom!" Miss Woodhall said as she sat down facing me, struggling to regain her breath. "Oh my!" She patted her chest as she puffed.

Dillon showed little interest in her presence. He banged on the opposite window to get the attention of the stationmaster who was walking the length of the train. Both Miss Woodhall and I watched as Dillon frantically waved the stationmaster aboard.

She turned and gave me a warm smile, her cheeks glowing red from exertion. On the seat beside her, she placed a wicker basket that she had brought with her. It was covered with a red and black folded blanket. One could be excused for assuming that we were on a day's outing.

The stationmaster stepped aboard as another two loud whistles sounded. He was an old man in his sixties. Small and thin, his glasses were pushed forward, resting on the tip of his nose.

"We can't go yet, there's another constable and he's not back." In his panic, Dillon stuttered a little as he spoke.

The old timer's head drooped down as he squinted out between the rim of his glasses and the peak of his cap. "I can't hold the train on account of one man. Do you want to get off?"

"We're transporting a prisoner." Dillon looked towards me.

The stationmaster pulled out a pocket watch from his top pocket. Its gold chain swung as he tried to focus on the time-piece. He tapped it three times, each tap slow and deliberate. He was too old to get flustered. "I'll give you two minutes, that's the best I can do." He turned to leave, not waiting for a reply.

Dillon kept turning his head to gaze out across the empty platform and back to me again. He was under pressure as he tried to make a decision as to whether to stay put or get off. Beads of sweat rolled down his face and he pulled a handker-chief from his pocket to wipe them away. The two minutes passed quickly and the stationmaster, who was now standing on the platform, blew a whistle and waved forward to the engine's driver. A jolt that pushed me back into my seat and caused Miss Woodhall to lurch forward signalled our depar-ture. As the train chugged out of the station, Dillon sat on the other side of the carriage and continued to watch out for Murphy, but he never appeared.

"What happened to the other constable?" Miss Woodhall asked him.

"Damn fool went for a whiskey. He'll lose his job over this."

"Oh dear," she replied, but as she turned back to me, I thought I detected a slight smirk.

There was a notable difference in the atmosphere during the second part of the journey. The train gradually built up momentum to reach its maximum speed and once again, the countryside rolled past the windows.

Dillon had forgotten about Murphy and settled down for the remainder of the journey, still sitting on the opposite side of the railcar. It left me plenty of room to stretch out on the seat. Miss Woodhall sat facing me and was the most pleasant travelling companion that one could have wished for. Her cheerful and affable manner was a tonic to me and I relished her company. She shunned all notion of legal discussion as she proceeded to empty some of the basket's contents onto the seat beside her.

Fresh bread, salted strips of beef, and corn heads were arranged neatly on a plate for me. The taste of fresh food was most welcome and I enjoyed my feast, savouring every mouthful. I washed it down with a bottle of Jamaican Ginger, which was a drink I had never tasted before.

Miss Woodhall stood up and held out a plate of food similar to mine to Constable Dillon. His eyes widened with pleasure at the plate's contents. His face displayed a tinge of embarrassment at the kindness that was shown to him.

Miss Woodhall and I talked. She asked about my life in Boston and seemed genuinely interested in what I told her. I questioned her about Harvard, where I assumed she was studying law. I noticed, although I did not make an issue of it, that she had a habit of being vague about details or else she changed the subject whenever I asked something specific about her studies or about the college. I assumed she simply did not wish to divulge any information she deemed personal, and I was careful not to repeat questions or to pursue answers.

Dillon finished off his plate of food and leaned back as he rubbed his stomach in satisfaction.

"Would you like something to drink, Constable? The pork was a tad salty." As she spoke, she held out a bottle of Jamaican Ginger.

Dillon reached out, a grateful look upon his face.

The train continued its journey towards Ottawa. Conversation between us waned as the rocking motion of the carriage had a tiring effect on both of us. I dozed off with my head resting against the vibrating window.

I only dozed for a few minutes at most. As my eyes struggled to open, I was faced with an empty seat in front of me. I turned to see Miss Woodhall sitting beside Dillon and rifling through his pockets.

"What's going on?" I said.

She turned to me and held her finger to her lips. "Shush!"

In an instant, my whole body tensed. Adeline surged through my veins and it felt as if my heart was about to burst with the pressure. She showed a look of calm determination as she systematically checked each of Dillon's pockets in turn. I looked forward; the other passengers were oblivious to what was occurring. Most of them sat facing forward and those that did face us were asleep or lost in their own world of thoughts. I looked back at Dillon. I had thought he was sleeping, but looking more closely, I started to wonder if he had been drugged. His body was slouched over and his head flopped sideways against the rattling glass. His face was twisted in a strange fashion and his eyelids flickered occasionally.

She smiled with success as she pulled a set of keys from his inside pocket. Standing up, she brushed down along her skirt, straightening out any creases as if she had not a care in the world. She calmly walked back to take her seat opposite me.

"What's going on?" I leaned forward as I whispered.

"We're getting off." Her voice sounded different, her eastern accent seemed less pronounced.

"Are you mad?"

"Do you want to swing at the end of a rope?" She held out the keys, jangling them in front of me.

"But...you'll be in trouble." I could not help but wonder why she would destroy her career and throw away a promising future just to help me.

She giggled and it was out of keeping with her manner up to now. It was a reaction I could not easily associate with the business-like law student I knew.

"It's alright, Tom. Haven't you realised yet? There is no Miss Woodhall. This has all been a setup to get you out."

"But...who?"

She glanced out the window. "There's no time now, we have to get moving. I'll explain later."

I took hold of the dangling keys and set about unlocking the shackles from my wrists. I placed them gently on the seat beside me, terrified that any rattling noise would gain unwanted attention from the other passengers. I looked at Dillon.

"Don't worry about him," she said, adding, "He'll sleep for hours yet."

"Drugged?" I asked.

"His bottle was laced with horse painkillers. He'll be alright, maybe a headache when he wakes."

"And Murphy?"

"I took care of him in town. He wasn't as easy, almost made me miss the train."

Before I could speak again, she stood up. "Let's go, now!"

I followed her to the back of the carriage. As she reached the door, she stretched up to pull the emergency cord that ran the length of the carriage. We held on as the train's engineer applied the brakes. Passengers, startled at the braking motion, began to look around as they wondered what the problem was. A few that had been sitting on the edge of their seats fell off and landed in the space between the seating. Some luggage that had been stored carelessly overhead fell down, landing on the heads of their owners.

As the train slowed to a crawl, we opened the door and slipped out. We jumped from the slow moving locomotive and landed on loose gravel that lay on both sides of the track. We wasted no time and disappeared into the tall grass, which was scorched yellow by the hot summer sun.

Miss Woodhall, although I now knew that was not her real name, took to running through the long flowing grass and away from the train. I followed and had I not been gripped by the terror of being recaptured or even shot, I might have appreciated the ludicrous scene that we presented.

She was running as fast as her legs could carry her. Her arms were down by her side as she hitched up her skirt to just below her knees. Hampered by the heavy garment, she could only manage short strides. Her bonnet flew off her head, caught by a gust of wind. She paid no heed to the missing hat. The thick bustle behind her bounced up and down as well as from side-to-side in a wild fashion.

I followed in her tracks, running slow in keeping with her pace. I glanced back over my shoulder. The grass obscured the train, but I could still hear the steam engine chugging, and puffs of black smoke rose into the air to be carried off in the direction of the wind. I looked up at the blue cloudless sky and then down at my wrists, which were free of the heavy shackles. A warm breeze fanned my cheeks and I knew I was free.

SIXTEEN

Friends Reunited

"Hold on!" I cried ahead to the girl.

She stopped and turned back to face me. Her face was red and sweat dampened her cheeks and forehead. She took a moment, puffing heavily and holding her sides as she tried to regain her breath before speaking.

"We're almost there." She pointed ahead.

I had to stand on my toes to see over the grass, which was now the height of a man. I could see the tops of trees swaying in the breeze. It was a pine forest, no more than half a mile away and in the direction we were running.

"Almost where?"

She shook her head in apparent frustration at my question. "Just keep going, the sooner we get into cover, the better."

"Alright." I took the lead, using my outstretched arm to part the grass as we went. My other arm, I used to hold her hand and pull her along behind me. I had no idea what the plan was, or if there even was a plan, but I was free now and I had no intention of being recaptured.

As we got closer to the forest, the height of grass began to get shorter until it was no higher than our knees – its growth hampered by the shade cast from a solid green line of pine trees. The bright sunshine gave way to a cool dimness as we entered the woods. We stopped running and sat down on the soft ground, which consisted of a thick covering of matted grass and weed. We did not speak for a while. Both of us sat in silence as we tried to recover from the exertion expended in running from the train.

After a short rest, I stood and walked to the edge of the treeline where I looked back in the direction we had come from. The only noise was the gentle whooshing of the long grass in the wind. Far off, specks of black smoke appeared for a brief moment before they dispersed into the air. The train was gone, continuing its journey to Ottawa. I wondered if Dillon had come around, although, I cared neither one way nor the other.

I turned back to my companion. "Who are you?"

She got to her feet, but at the instant her mouth opened, the noise of a horse neighing startled us. I panicked and my stomach churned at the prospect of being caught. I sought shelter behind the stoutest tree trunk I could find. The girl did the same, but her movements seemed to lack urgency. We waited and I could feel my heart beating rapidly in anticipation.

It wasn't long before we heard the same noise again. As the intermittent sound of neighing and the occasional horse's snort got closer, I could make out at least two horses and maybe more. I began to hear hooves stomping the soft ground. They were making their way along the edge of the trees and getting closer all the time.

"Come on," I whispered. I wanted to move back deeper into the woods.

"No, wait!" She refused to move, straining her head out from behind a tree to see who was coming.

"We have to move back, now!" I pleaded to her.

She shook her head and used her hand to motion that I should stay put.

The noise of riders was almost upon us now and it was too late to run. I remained silent while holding my breath.

"Katherine!" A voice called out, not very loud, but just loud enough to penetrate the first barrier of trees between the rider and us. "Katherine!" he called again, but his voice was closer this time.

There was a certain familiarity about the voice, but before my mind could grasp the situation, the girl stepped out into the open and called out. "Bill?"

A man on a black horse turned into the trees. He was pulling two horses behind him. It was only as his face moved into the shade that I recognised him. It was my friend and partner, Bill Larsen.

He swung his leg over the rear of his horse to dismount. His feet had barely touched the soft bed of tangled moss when the girl flung herself forward, wrapping her arms around his neck. He laughed, stumbling backwards as he did so and almost fell over.

"Steady on." He struggled to speak while laughing.

The girl said nothing and her arms were wrapped so tight around his neck that she was able to lift her feet off the ground.

He walked towards me. She was still hanging on to him and had her face pressed hard into his chest.

"Hello, Tom." He held out his hand, which I grasped.

The girl let go, but not before smothering his cheek in kisses.

"It's good to see you. I thought—" I spoke, but did get to finish my sentence as he interrupted me.

"Thought what? That maybe I was dead?"

"I don't know. I thought perhaps you had gone on alone."

"Without my partner?" A broad smile spread across his face.

"I wouldn't have held it against you," I said.

He looked into the girl's eyes, but continued to talk to me.

"I'd never leave a friend behind. Katherine could have told you that."

"Katherine?" I asked.

"Yep, Katherine, my daughter."

"Your daughter?" I did not think I could be any more surprised than I already was. I never for a moment thought of him having a daughter, or any family for that matter. I just assumed he was alone in the world.

"Pleased to meet you, Tom." She grinned, and I got the impression she was trying to control herself for fear she would break into a fit of laughter. No doubt, she thought the whole affair, including my misconceptions about her, amusing. If there was any doubt in my mind about her being related to Larsen, her sense of humour put paid to that notion.

Eclipse was returned to me. He whinnied and stomped his front hooves into the ground when he saw me approaching. I patted his mane and pressed my cheek against his neck. He continued his display of stomping and whinnying.

I knew Larsen and Katherine were watching me, no doubt exchanging glances while raising their eyes to the heavens. I did not care. While most men look upon their horses as a tool, a convenience, I did not. While it is true that a horse is an invaluable means of transport, Eclipse was more than that. I witnessed his birth and helped my mother care for him when his own mother died giving birth. He became my best friend...and I, his.

I turned back to my companions, but the girl was nowhere to be seen.

"Bill, I have so many questions, I hardly know where to start."

"Not now," he said. "Best we get movin' and put some distance behind us. We can talk later."

Katherine appeared from behind some trees. She had sought privacy while she changed into clothes more suited for riding. She looked different, not just a little different, but like another person. Her hair which had been tied up was now let down. It reached halfway down her back and fine strands of auburn hair were lifted by a gentle breeze to flutter free in the wind. The long heavy skirt with its awkward bushel was replaced for trousers and the frilly white blouse swapped for a chequered shirt, which was tucked into her trousers. It was impossible not to notice her slender figure, as the tight fitting clothes displayed every womanly curve. I could not help but look and when she turned her face towards me and followed up with a grin, I replied with an awkward smile, before my embarrassment caused me to look away.

Larsen climbed onto his large stallion. Katherine gripped the front of her saddle and put one foot in a stirrup before hoisting herself up to swing her other leg over the horse's back. She mounted the horse with a motion of incredible ease and smoothness that I have never seen from a woman.

We rode along the edge of the treeline and followed its

contours before turning northwest. We crossed several miles of open ground before entering another forest. This time we went straight in and lost ourselves in the vast woodland where the ground never saw the overhead sun. Travelling through this ancient timber jungle was not easy. The ground was not smooth. Tree roots protruded at every step and of-ten concealed under thick moss, nettles or tangled clumps of weed. The horses walked, feeling the ground beneath their feet before committing their full weight onto their front legs. We continuously ducked under low and thick hanging branches or else pushed the smaller ones aside. Larsen led the way and Eclipse followed without any encouragement from me. Katherine was behind and whenever I turned to check on her, she grinned, and when she did, her whole face lit up with happiness.

As darkness set in, movement through the forest became both difficult and dangerous. We came upon a small hollow and decided to stop for the night. We worked well together. I tended to the horses while Larsen prepared a fire. Although it had been a warm day, the woods were permanently cool as the sun's full heat was unable to penetrate the thick canopy of leaves. However, the night brought a new level of cold – a freezing chill that bore right through a man's soul. Our blaz-ing fire warded off some of the cold that comes hand in hand with the dark. We hunched close to its dancing flames and listened to the crackling of burning wood, while we watched a bubbling soup pot Katherine had prepared. We ate. Hot leek soup and salted rabbit meat, washed down by black coffee. After our food we sat, surrounded by a wall of darkness. The glow from our fire lit the hollow and extended no further, and the air hung heavy with the smell of burning wood and dried moss.

Katherine did not talk much. Tiredness had overcome her and she settled down to sleep, covered with two blankets while lying close to the fire. We watched her drift into a peaceful slumber, her eyes flickering between open and closed until finally they remained shut.

Larsen settled back and filled his pipe. He picked up a long twig, which he held just above the fire's flame and used the smouldering stick to light his pipe. I pulled the coffee pot from the flames and filled two mugs, handing one of them to him. I took another look at Katherine who was in a deep sleep and lost in her dreams, before I turned to Larsen.

"I never knew you had a daughter. To be honest and I'm not sure why, but I just assumed you had no family."

He took a long intake of smoke from the pipe while looking at Katherine. I could see the proud look on his face.

"Well, Tom, I'll tell you, and I've never spoken of this before to any man except your father..." He leaned forward and took a good look to make sure she was asleep. "Katherine ain't really my daughter. I came across her when she was ten years old. Her mother was no good and abandoned her so she could run off to Frisco with some tin horn gambler. Katherine was workin' in a minin' camp saloon, moppin' up and emptyin' spittoons. Hell... that weren't no life for a kid. Anyways, I own a small spread in Montana, ain't nothin' special. I'm rarely there so a couple run it for me. Nice people and good friends. I brought Katherine home with me. I thought maybe they could raise her as their own, seeing as how they had no kids. Well, she grew up all right, but insisted on callin' me her Pa. She knew I wasn't, but I guess she needed to belong, so I just let it ride."

I refilled our mugs as Larsen tended to his pipe. The fire was dwindling so I poked at it with a branch. Glowing sparks rose into the air and floated above our heads. The lack of wind ensured they burnt out their short lives without leaving the hollow. His pipe filled, he continued.

"Well, we made sure she got schoolin' and grew up proper, but I gotta tell you. It weren't easy. Before she was fifteen, she could ride and shoot better than most men I knew. Kept gettin' in trouble at school for fightin' with boys." He laughed quietly, careful not to wake her. "When she was eighteen, we sent her to finishin' school in Ottawa. I tell you..." Larsen shook his head and smiled while thinking back. "Three times I put her on a train. The first two times she arrived back at the ranch, the third time I swore to her that I'd shoot her on sight if she came back."

I stoked up the fire again. I was starting to crave hot coffee. It was the best cure in the world for a night's chill.

"How long ago was that?" I talked as I worked the fire.

"Six months, but it turned out that instead of attendin' school, she got an office job in a law firm."

"That explains her convincing act back in Toronto," I said. I was starting to realise just how cunning she was. "But how did it all come about? How did you even know where I was?"

Larsen stretched out his arm, waving his coffee mug in front of me. "Fill her up, Lad. I reckon it's going to be a long night." His mug refilled, he continued talking. "I don't remember landin' in Canada. I guess I was out of it with the fever."

I nodded as I remembered how we struggled to lift him from his horse.

"All I know is, I woke up to Taipa chantin' and wavin' some damn string of beads over me. She told me... and it weren't easy in that blasted French of hers, about how she'd seen you taken down the trail by men in dark uniforms. I guessed it was the Toronto Police, considerin' the direction they were headin'."

"What about Taipa? What happened to her?"

"I'm not sure. After she told me about you, she vanished into the woods. I turned around and she was gone, never even said goodbye. I reckon she believed herself beholden to me. When I recovered, her debt to me was repaid and as such, she was free to leave."

I reached down for the last few logs and placed them on the fire. As I leaned down, I saw Katherine's face. She looked so innocent that I found it hard to believe what Larsen had said about her. I thought back to how she had fooled Thornton and I smiled to myself.

I could not but wonder what lay in store for me. Ever since meeting Larsen, I had been thrown from one escapade to another. I could not help but think that Katherine, despite her virtuous look, also possessed his uncanny knack of inviting adventure.

"Time we turned in." Larsen stretched back his arms as he spoke.

I unrolled my blanket, but I turned towards him; there was something I just had to say before I slept. "Bill, thanks for getting me out, I owe you my life."

"Me? Ain't nothin' to do with me, Kid." He looked at Katherine and nodded his head in her direction. "It was her doin'. As soon as I told her about you, she started plannin' the whole thing. Anytime I offered a suggestion, she shooed me off to check my horse or on some other pointless errand. All I did was to be there with the horses like she told me to." He raised his eyes in sarcasm and I laughed quietly.

Sleep came easy as it always does to tired men. I dreamed of quieter days gone by and of my father. His face was a haze but his image was there. He was with his friends, talking and laughing while they shared a happy moment around a campfire. He lifted his head and illuminated by the flames, I saw his face, just for a moment, but I saw his face as clear as if he was there with us.

SEVENTEEN

Sault Ste Marie

For the next ten days we travelled hard. Always moving and stopping only to rest the horses. Our destination was Sault Ste Marie, a small town on the shores of Saint Marys River. We could have made the journey in one week, but Larsen led us in a wide circle, keeping to dense woodlands so we would be unlikely to meet anyone. He feared that search parties could have been organised from Toronto and Ottawa, and he was taking no chances.

Food was scarce, although game was plentiful. Hunting meant staying in the one location for too long and that would increase our chances of capture. After seven days, we reached the shore of Lake Huron and from there we followed the shoreline west. That gave us the opportunity to fish when we stopped for night camp. I had no luck in catching fish. I watched Larsen cast his line and despite copying his every action, I failed to emulate his results. My humiliation was exasperated when Katherine cast a line and within just fifteen minutes had managed to hook two bloater fish.

I found the journey particularly tough. The constant travelling, although exhausting, I could cope with. The meagre rations were a hardship that I was prepared to endure. What I did find difficult was the feeling of been a hunted man. My neck developed an ache from looking over my shoulder. I continuously scanned the hills and trails behind us, expecting to see hordes of riders coming into view. Now and again, my eye would catch a distant movement, a deer or perhaps a wild goat. My heart rate would rapidly increase and my whole

body would tense. Even after I realised it was just a harm-
less animal, both my mind and body could take an hour before returning to a sense of normality. I noticed that Larsen
and Katherine never looked back or flinched at an unexpected movement. I envied them their calmness, but I could
not achieve the same level of confidence they seemed to
possess.

It had been on our second night that Larsen explained his
plan to me. As night closed in, we camped at the top of a
small hill, deep in the heart of a maple and oak forest.

It was an ancient wood and the old trees, while standing
tall, did not stand straight. They leaned over from the burden
of supporting heavy branches that reached out in every direction, as they drooped under their own weight. Some hung
so low that they were just inches from the ground. It made
riding through the wood a slow affair. We had weaved a path
all day as we had negotiated the maze of old wood blocking
our route. The deeper we penetrated the quieter it became.
Even the usual chirping of birds had vanished. It was as if
the woods were abandoned and its wildlife gone to seek out
a new life in one of the newer pine or spruce forests. Whatever the reason, the result created a surreal feeling to our
surroundings. Every twig that snapped under the horses'
hooves had a thunderous sound that broke the deafening
silence and only added to the eeriness of our world.

Katherine and I sat on a low hanging branch that skirted
the ground before sweeping back up, as if to try and correct
its deformed growth. We listened to Larsen as he explained
the situation in his usual casual manner.

"Sault Ste Marie is where we are headin'. It's on Saint
Marys River. It's an important town because the river links
the two lakes, Huron and Superior. Every week, the ferry
from Buffalo stops there as it makes its way west to Duluth
in Northern Minnesota. That's where we're goin'. From Duluth, it's two weeks to the ranch. We can fit out there for the
trip north."

"But the ferry?" I said, only continuing after I first formed
my question in my own head. "I thought we were avoiding it

because of Wilson's men?"

Katherine sat quietly, turning her head as each one of us spoke.

"There is that risk, but they would have been expectin' us to board in Buffalo, it's the best way to travel west, after the train. I don't reckon they'll figure on us boardin' halfway. Wilson ain't got enough men to cover everythin'. I don't think we'll have any trouble from him until we reach the high country. He knows where we're goin' and all he has to do is wait." He paused for a moment while he sucked on his pipe. "Nope, our problem is the police. You're a wanted man, Tom. There's sure to be posters in every town by now."

I felt my stomach churn again. "What about Katherine? They'll be looking for her, too?"

She took on a rather mischievous smile before answering me, and I wondered if she realised how much trouble she was in. "They're on the lookout for—" She sat up straight, took on an innocent look as she moved her head back to point her nose upwards, and used one hand to hold up her hair— "Miss...Arabella...Woodhall." Her voice had taken on an eastern tone and her accent retuned to that of a refined and educated lady. She let go of her hair, letting it fall back down behind her shoulders, and she looked at me while grinning.

Larsen broke into a rapturous fit of laughter and Katherine, struggling as she attempted to remain dignified, could contain it no longer. Her face changed as she began to giggle. Surrounded with such humour, I found myself taken in by the moment and the silence of the ancient wood was shattered by the three of us laughing as if we did not have a care in the world.

"Well, I'm goin' to get me some sleep," Larsen said. He lay down close to the fire and pulled his blanket over him.

"Walk with me, Tom," Katherine said as she began to stand.

We did not go far as it was hard to see where our feet were treading in the dark. There was a full moon and unhindered with a clear sky, shafts of moonlight shone through whatever gap they could find between the trees.

"I want to thank you, Tom."

"Thank me? It should be the other way around. But I don't understand. Bill said my escape was your idea. Why did you risk yourself for me?"

Before answering, she brushed loose pieces of bark off an old tree that had fallen long ago. Broken branches lay all around, their own weight ensuring they had shattered on impact when the tree had come crashing down. A stump remained and showed where it had split when the old oak's weight worked against it, causing it to topple. We sat down together on the fallen trunk.

"When Bill told me about you, I just had to go to the police station. I don't think I can explain it in a way you would understand. Maybe it was because I saw a chance to help him. He's done so much for me that I could never repay him. I suppose he's told you I'm not really his daughter?"

"Well, yes, he told me." I was uncomfortable at knowing something so personal.

"That's alright, it's not a secret." She saw my embarrassment and sought to put me at ease. "When you refused to blame Bill or mention the Indian girl, I just knew I could not leave you to hang. Your loyalty to them told me more about your character than words ever could."

"You mean..." A thought was forming in my mind as I spoke. "If I had of implicated them, you would have left me there?"

She smiled and even in the half-light of the moon, I could see her whole face broaden with amusement.

"Tom, if I thought you were not worth saving...you'd be dangling from a rope by now."

"Well, I'm glad I made a good impression." I smiled. I could see the amusing side of the whole affair.

"Oh, you did, Tom. You certainly did." She nodded to emphasise her meaning and then she did something I was not expecting. She leaned forward and kissed me. I was taken aback. She moved her head back, but only by a few inches. It was my turn to respond, one way or the other. Her lips were soft and her breath so warm, I doubt I could have rejected her even if I wanted to. I wrapped my arm around her waist and pulled her towards me. Our lips met again and we held each other as we kissed. I felt her body against mine and her breasts pressing into my chest. I ran my fingers through her long hair and we stayed in each other's embrace for a long time before we let go and sat looking at each other for a while before speaking.

I was first to break the silence. "I never realised you felt that way about me."

"Oh, Tom, for a college educated man, you can be so slow sometimes." She patted me on the cheek, mocking me, but not in a hurtful way, more in affectionate jest. She stood and reached out for my hand. We walked back to camp, her hand in my hand. At one point, she stumbled and would have fallen had I not caught her. There was no embarrassment – a barrier between us had been set aside. I felt I could say or do anything and never feel awkward or discomfort with her again. Between the trees, we saw the flickering light from the fire and as we got close, Katherine stopped and turned to me.

"Better not mention anything to Bill...not just yet."

I nodded. I did not feel I was betraying his trust. I just thought that there was a time and place for everything and this was neither. Katherine stretched up, standing on her toes to kiss me on the cheek before letting go of my hand to walk into camp. I slept soundly that night, more soundly than I had in a long time.

We entered Sault Ste Marie in the middle of a heavy rainstorm. The main street had turned to mud and few people ventured out into the deluge. Rainwater ran off the sloping roofs and splashed up from the ground before forming wide pools of dirty water that lined both sides of the street. We were saturated right through and despite holding rainproof blankets over our heads, the rain had penetrated all of our clothing. We turned a corner and found ourselves outside a hotel.

"You two go in, I'll find a livery stable to put up the horses. Then I'll find out about the ferry." Larsen had to raise his voice for us to hear him above the roar of heavy rain.

We dismounted and handed the reins to him. He nodded for us to come closer and he leaned down to talk. "Check in as Mr and Mrs Marshall, and get a joinin' room for your uncle. We're travellin' to Duluth to visit your father-in-law as he's gravely ill, understand?"

"I understand," I said. "Mr and Mrs Marshall."

A bell tinkled as I pushed open the door. We walked to

the reception counter and waited for someone to show. It was a small hotel. Behind the counter there were nails hammered into the side of a shelf with the room numbers written above them. There were eighteen rooms in all. A small woman emerged from a backroom. She was hunched forward and gripping the ends of a white laced shawl that she held tight around her shoulders. Without uttering a word, she walked past and around the counter to face us.

"Voulez-vous une salle?" As she spoke, she lifted herself up onto her toes to get a good look at our saturated clothing. We were dripping water all over the carpet and she shook her head in disapproval.

"Yes, a room please. And a joining one for my wife's uncle. He's tending to our horses."

"How long?" She switched to English with ease but retained her French accent.

"I don't know..." I looked to Katherine for help.

"Until the ferry comes in from Buffalo," she said.

I nodded in agreement.

"One night. The ferry comes tomorrow," the woman said as she slid the hotel register around for me to sign.

I picked up the pen and dipped it into an open jar of ink. I paused for a moment before signing. It was an unnatural action to sign a false name and I had to concentrate as I wrote our assumed names onto the page.

"Room six." The woman looked up the staircase. "Your uncle can have room seven. I'll give him the key when he arrives."

Our room, while basic, was cosy, although after a cell in Toronto's police station and sleeping outdoors, it did not take much for me to feel I was living in luxury. It was a corner room on the first floor. There were two windows. One overlooked the main street while the other looked out onto the adjoining side street. A door led to the next room and I tried to open it, but it was locked from the other side. A double bed dominated the room and a large wardrobe stood in the corner, the top of it almost touching the ceiling.

We were saturated and we both shivered with the cold. For this reason, the highpoint of the room was a small stone fireplace set into the sidewall. Stacked beside it was a generous pile of wooden logs. I set about building a fire while Katherine lit three gas lamps that were fixed to the walls. It was early afternoon, but the rain clouds outside cast a dark shadow over Sault Ste Marie that made it seem like late evening.

The fire took hold and the flames shot upwards into the chimney.

"We have to get out of these wet clothes," Katherine said while twisting the end of her jacket with both hands. A steady stream of water drained out and down onto the carpet. There were some towels next to the washbasin and she picked up two and threw one to me. I looked around, wondering where we could change, but she was not waiting. She turned her back and took off her jacket before pulling her shirt over her head. Her slim figure was silhouetted against the warm red glow of the fire. She turned around and lifted the open towel up to cover herself. She smiled at me, that mischievous smile that she could not seem to help as she wrapped the towel around herself and tied it at the front. After kicking off her shoes, she used one hand to pull off her trousers, the other hand making sure the towel did not fall. I hung her clothes over the backs of three chairs that were tucked in under a table in the centre of the room while she sat down in front of the fire, folding her legs as she did so.

I changed and wrapped myself in the other towel before sitting beside her. The heat from the fire slowly warmed the room and us with it. Larsen had still not returned and I was beginning to get worried, but Katherine laughed it off and put my mind at rest. We moved our clothes closer to the fire and wisps of steam escaped from the drying fabrics.

We talked for hours. We were different in so many ways that it surprised me how natural our mutual attraction felt, and how comfortable we both were in each other's company. It was as if our feelings for were predetermined by some unseen force as it patiently bided its time, waiting for fate to contrive a situation that would allow our paths to cross.

Katherine was different. I could not say she hungered for danger, but when it came, she swept along on the tidal wave of adventure as if it were an everyday occurrence. I assumed her carefree nature was moulded by the influence of Larsen. Whether he knew it or not, his fearless attitude to life formed and sculptured Katherine into the woman she had become. I thought about my own childhood. How different would I have been if my father had guided me through those impressible years that determine the character of an adult? And my mother – what if she had not devoted her life to shielding me from the uglier side of humanity? Maybe I was the way I was because that is the way fate decided it would be. My mother's influence and my father's nature blended together to shape me into the man I became. And who was I to question fate? After all, it was fate that brought me to Katherine.

I was intrigued when she told me she had met my father. It was many years ago and she summoned up memories of him sitting in their kitchen on several occasions. He had told her about his son back in Boston who was only a few years older than her.

She related a story to me about a neighbour of theirs. It was an old woman that had been relieved of her rent money by a devious conman. The old woman was distraught. She remembered Larsen and my father galloping away from the house in a cloud of dust to take up pursuit. It was several days before they returned, but when they did, they had her money. She could not remember what had happened to the conman.

EIGHTEEN

Dead Man's Hand

We did our best to assume the appearance of travellers waiting until the ferry from Buffalo called in. The hotel's breakfast room, which also doubled as a dining room in the evenings, was full of such people. We sat beside a window that looked out across the town's main street. The rainstorm that had accompanied us into town had passed, although the street was still muddy and dotted with puddles of rainwater that would take time to dissipate. People crossing did so in a zigzag fashion as they tried to avoid such pools. Hopping over them was not an option as the ground was thick with slippery mud and the slightest misstep meant falling over.

Katherine poured coffee for the three of us. Larsen and I had ham and eggs while she was content with the French bread that was placed on every table. There were about thirty people in the room and the noise of conversation coupled with the rattle of dishware from the kitchen allowed us to talk without fear of being overheard.

"The ferry gets in around noon, but it could be early or late by a few hours either way," Larsen said.

"That's good, we'll only have to wait a few hours," I replied. The truth was I was relived. I was eager to get out of Canada. "Did you find out anything else?"

"Well, the good news is there ain't any wanted posters of you, but there is a police station and about a half dozen constables in town. Best you stay in the room until the ferry arrives." He turned to Katherine. "How much money we got left?"

"I've got a hundred dollars and you should have about the same," she told him.

Larsen began to look embarrassed and peered down into his coffee mug before mumbling something incoherent.

"What was that, Pa?" Katherine said.

"I said I ain't got it no more." He spoke low, so low it seemed he was hoping we would not hear him.

"Not cards again?" Katherine's tone was one of frustration rather than anger.

"Oh hell, Kate, it weren't my fault."

Katherine's eyebrows raised as her eyes widened.

"I had a dead man's hand," he said, shrugging his shoulders before continuing. "How was I to know the other fella had three queens?"

"That's the whole point of poker, you don't know what the other fella has." She mocked him with her tone and his eyes pointed back down into the cup with shame.

"What's a dead man's hand?" I asked. The phrase caught my curiosity. I had never played poker, but I did know the basic rules. Larsen did not reply. He did not want to compound the shame of losing his money.

"Two pairs," Katherine told me. "Aces and eights. It was the hand Bill Hiccup held when he was shot during a poker game, so that's what they call it now." She looked back to Larsen. "Well, we have enough for the ferry, the hotel bill and some left over to get new clothes."

"Clothes!" Larsen looked up and almost choked on a gulp of coffee that was halfway down his throat.

"That's right, I need a dress."

"You're going to spend the last of our money on a dress?" His tone mirrored his look of astonishment.

"That's right. I may not have attended finishing school, but I saw enough of high society in Ottawa to know I am not travelling on that ferry dressed like a ranch hand. You spent your money on cards...I'm spending mine on a dress, any objection?"

There was silence at the table. I looked at their faces. It was a battle of wills. Katherine stared without blinking, her eyebrows raised and daring him to object. He did not dare. He bit his lower lip and after a few moments, grunted, unable to utter any words. I remained silent during the exchange, but I had to bite my own lip in an attempt not to laugh.

Having won the verbal exchange, she produced a wide grin. It was not a grin of triumph, rather a smile reflecting her happiness with the thought of being able to go shopping. I had learned a lot about Katherine over the last two weeks and this head-to-head confrontation with Larsen confirmed my thoughts. While not actually his daughter, their relationship bore all the hallmarks of a father and daughter bond. She knew how to get her own way. If the situation called for tears, they would be summoned. If a more forceful approach was required then that came just as easily. I found it amusing that Larsen, as tough as he might be, could be manipulated so easily by his daughter. Although I would never dare to voice my thoughts.

Katherine touched my arm. "I might have enough to get you something decent to wear."

I kept my eyes down – I could feel the intense stare from Larsen.

"Anyway," he spoke, changing the mood with his raised voice. "Tom, you wait upstairs. Kate, you take care of the hotel bill and get your blasted dress. I'll see to the horses. When you hear the ferry's whistle, make your way down to the river and I'll meet you on-board."

We all agreed and after finishing the last of our coffee, went our separate ways.

For the next hour, I sat in the room looking down at life passing by below me.

There were various stores along the main street selling food, clothing, and hardware supplies. Noise from the street filled my room. The town had become busy, despite the earliness of the hour. Each store had a steady flow of customers entering and leaving their doorways. People jostled as they tried to pass one another on the raised planked walkways that ran along the side of the muddy road. Business picked up whenever the ferry was due as the town's population swelled with travellers such as us. The muddy road was busy with goods wagons, delivering and collecting stock. Heavier reinforced wagons trudged along at a slow pace. They were hauling logs that had been floated downriver, to local timber yards. Their wide wooden wheels sank into the soft mud, leaving long trails along the road that slowly filled up as dirty brown water seeped into the fissures. These particular wagons used extra horses to help pull the heavy weight stacked onto the carts. Men walked alongside the wagons, yelling furiously and waving whips that snapped sharply as their cracks urged the burdened horses forward.

I glimpsed Katherine several times, standing and looking through store windows. She would walk away, only to appear back a few minutes later to study whatever was on display in the window. Eventually she disappeared among the throngs of people that were congesting the narrow walkways.

I leaned back in my chair and put my feet up onto the window sill. My eyes felt heavy and the street's noise faded into the distance as I slowly fell asleep.

The key rattling in the lock woke me. I dropped my feet to the floor and sat up as my chair straightened.

"Katherine?" My voice was hoarse as I tried to shake off the grogginess.

There was no answer as my voice was drowned out by the rattle of the key turning in the lock. The door opened and she stepped in. She only took one step into the room and then stood still, holding wrapped paper bundles under each arm. There was something wrong in her expression. She did not smile and a look of subdued panic was in her eyes.

"Are you alright?" I stood up and there was a mixture of tiredness and confusion in my voice.

She attempted to say something, but events overtook her. The bundles fell to the floor as her body pushed forward without warning. She stumbled towards me and I threw out my arms to catch her. From behind, a big man with broad shoulders came into the room. I recognised him as soon as he turned his face towards me. It was John Thornton. He held a gun and pointed it straight at us. Without looking around, he used his other hand to push the door shut behind him.

"Well well, if it isn't Tom Anderson and his legal representative." The tone of his voice was a mixture of sarcasm and joy.

Neither of us spoke. The surprise and disappointment of our capture left us lost for words.

"Sit down, both of you," he said, his voice becoming sterner.

We did as we were told, sitting at the table and waiting to see what was going to happen next.

"Keep your hands where I can see them," he said.

We rested our elbows on the table with our hands near its centre.

"So Miss Woodhall, what's your real name?"

"Anderson...Elizabeth Anderson." Katherine looked down at the floor, sobbing as she did so.

Thornton looked surprised and then nodded as what he believed to be the truth was coming out.

"Alright Mr and Mrs Anderson, you did a good job making fools of me and my deputies, but I warn you, any more clever stuff and there'll be a double funeral."

"How did you find us?" I asked, resignation filling my voice.

"Well, I won't say it was clever detective work, cause it wasn't. I happened to be in town on business and by chance, I saw Miss Wood...I mean Mrs Anderson." He smiled, amused at his intentional slip of the tongue. "I followed her into the hotel. I guessed she might lead me to you."

"So what happens now?" I asked.

A sickening feeling was beginning to build-up in my stomach. My own predicament never occurred to me, but the thought of Katherine going to jail was too much to bear.

"Now? What happens now is that we take a walk down to the station house. You stand trial for murder. And your little lady here, she stands trial, too. I'm not sure about the charges yet, but you can be sure it will be five or six years' worth."

Katherine's sobbing intensified and tears streamed down her cheeks and onto the room's faded carpet.

He took two steps to one side and flicked his wrist twice. The gun's barrel nudged us towards the door. We stood. A strange feeling of calm overcame me. I had to do something and I had to do it fast. Concern for my own safety never entered my mind. I paid no thoughts to the possibility of being injured or killed. I was scared. I could feel the blood surging around my body, pumped by my heart that felt as if it had swollen to twice its normal size as it pounded against my ribs. Had there been time to think, I would probably have gotten sick, but Katherine's fate spurred me into action.

There was no preconceived plan, there was no time to weigh up or analyse the situation. I knew what I was doing, but it resembled a dream where events occur without thought. For the first time in my life, my actions were driven by instinct and instinct alone. I held Katherine's arm as I helped her off the chair. She was crying, but I suspected it was an act, although I was not certain. I led her forward, placing her between Thornton and me. My right arm was out of view to him and without turning my head, I reached back to grab the heavy candlestick holder that was in the centre of the table. As we passed him, I prodded her in the small of her back. She reacted perfectly. She let out a wail of despair before raising her hands to her face. It was enough to distract him for that vital second.

He turned his face towards her and his arm relaxed, letting the gun droop slightly with the tip of the barrel pointing towards the floor. I lunged forward and swung my arm around in a wide circular motion with the solid base of the candlestick holder careering towards him. He realised the danger and began to hunch his body down while raising his gun up towards me. At the same time, he lifted his left arm in an attempt to block the impending blow. But he was not fast enough. The round flat bottom of the holder impacted on the side of his head. His face showed the effects immediately. His head lolled away from the blow and his eyes rolled in their sockets. The weight of his upper body seemed to be too much for his legs, which bent at the knees. Thornton's mouth fell open in an apparent involuntary motion as his body collapsed onto his bending legs. The gun fell from his hand and bounced before coming to a rest beside his crumpled body.

Katherine turned the door's key and then pulled on the handle to make sure it was locked. Her cheeks were red and bloated, but her eyes were wide and alert. It had been an act and it was a good enough one to fool Thornton. I knelt beside him. His chest rose and fell and I breathed a sharp sigh of relief that he was alive. There was a small indent and an open gash where he had been struck. A small pool of blood welled up to fill the wound and began to trickle down behind his ear.

"What will we do with him?" I asked Katherine.

A moment ago, I had acted without thinking and my actions were driven purely by instinct, an instinct that I never knew was within me. Now that I had time to think, I became confused as to the best course of action.

"Tie him up. I don't think anyone knows he came here. It was chance that he saw me walk into the hotel."

I pulled the curtains down from their rails and used the cord to bind his hands and feet. He was starting to come around, moaning and grunting as he slowly regained consciousness. Katherine pulled off one of the bed sheets and tore a strip from one end. We used it to gag him and tied a double knot at the back of his head. His eyes had opened and he was mumbling, but his muffled words were inaudible. I had no doubt he was cursing us.

Luck was on our side. A ship's horn sounded a long shriek to announce its arrival at the dock. It sounded four times. It was early, two hours early. We both looked at each other. Neither of us spoke, but the look of relief on our faces was self-evident as we realised our good fortune. The ferry would only stay for an hour at most, just long enough for passengers to embark or disembark. All we had to do was get to the boat and hope that Thornton would not be discovered until after we left. We gathered our belongings and locked the door behind us. As we left the room, Thornton was still uttering a tirade of muffled curses and struggling to free his hands, but I was confident he was bound securely. I could only pray it would be a while before the room was opened for cleaning.

The hotel's lobby was full of people. Most of the guests, like us, had been waiting for the ferry. There was a crowd cluttered around the reception desk. The small French woman was visibly flustered. Guests anxious to make the ferry were jostling for position at the counter. The woman was grabbing keys and throwing them into a drawer, and not taking the time to hang them on their assigned nails.

I waited by the staircase as Katherine joined the crowd. After forcing her way to the front, she returned the key, paid the bill, and came back to me. I felt a little more confident as the mass evacuation would mean a lot of vacant rooms. It increased my hope that our room would be left undisturbed for a while.

NINETEEN

Mr and Mrs Marshall

The Canadian Rose was as modern a ferry as one would find on any lake. She was 300 feet in length and each of the three levels above deck were lined with cabin windows.

As we stepped onto the sloping gangplank, I looked towards the rear of the ferry. Livestock and horses were being loaded at the rear. It was Eclipse that I first noticed – his black and white patches made him stand out from the other horses. I slowed for a moment to watch and when there was a break in the cattle, I saw Larsen walking on-board. He was pulling our three horses behind him. The animals were jostling for space among a compact herd of cows.

Katherine had booked us a cabin and I remained on deck while she went down to stow our bags. I stood gripping the side rail as I watched the last of the passengers boarding. My heart was thumping and my knuckles turned white as my grip tightened. I was mentally willing the last stragglers to hurry on-board. Should one of them stop for any reason, I was on the verge of screaming down at them to keep moving.

The dusty road leading back towards the town was empty except for the odd carriage returning after delivering passengers to the wharf. A ship's officer was directing two men whom were removing the walkway. Thankfully, the officer seemed eager to be underway and wasted little time in his work. Two short but loud blasts of the ship's horn signalled that we were about to depart.

I thought I felt some movement. It was hard to be certain because of the gentle motion of the boat on the river. I studied the gap between the hull and the dockside. I was relieved to see the space slowly widen. I watched each expanding inch with more and more relief as inches became feet and in a very short time, we had drifted halfway across the river. The power of the ship's engines sent out a shuddering vibration that could be felt by one's feet on the deck below them. Huge plumes of billowing black smoke were forced out of the boilers and up through chimneystack to be released into the air. The ship pushed forward and a widening wake of disturbed water opened up behind us, leaving a long trail on the river's surface as we surged forward.

Crowds of men, women, and children stood at the rail to watch Sault Ste Marie fade into the distance. None, I imagined were as relieved as me to see the town disappear behind us. We had escaped the clutches of the Police by a mixture of luck and bold actions. I thought about what I had done, reliving every moment in my mind. I still found it hard to believe I had knocked down Thornton. Had I failed, we would have been shot. Of that, I had no doubt, and with that thought, I felt ill. I leaned over the rail to wretch, much to the amusement of other travellers whom assumed I was seasick.

Our cabin was small. There were four beds, each one a bunk that folded up conveniently against the sidewalls. A porthole allowed a bright shaft of light to shine across the room where it produced a tawny circle of illumination on the bottom of the door. Beneath the porthole was a small table top, which just like the beds, folded up flat. There were no chairs as the lower bunks were intended to double as seating.

I looked out through the circular glass. The lake was calm with only the tiniest ripples visible. The afternoon sun shone off its surface and caused a glint that hurt my eyes if I stared straight at it. The Canadian coastline was a few miles off and becoming hazier all the time as we steamed further across the lake. We settled in, making ourselves comfortable despite the soft thud thud of the room, which was vibrating in rhythmic harmony to the ship's steam engines.

"Pity we couldn't afford a cabin higher up," Larsen said as

he looked around the small room that was already beginning to feel claustrophobic.

"We could have, if you hadn't lost your money playing poker." Katherine was quick to remind him of their earlier conversation. Larsen grunted just as he had that morning, probably regretting he had spoken.

"It'll only be for one night." I intervened without taking sides.

Katherine jumped to her feet. "There will be music in the upper saloon tonight. I can wear my new dress. And Tom, look what I got you." She pulled a large paper wrapped parcel from under the bunk. She tore the paper open with all the excitement of a child revealing a surprise gift. A white shirt was held up in one hand and a black velvet jacket in the other. She glanced down into the remainder of the wrappings. "I got trousers for you as well."

"Thank you, that's wonderful." I lied, doing my best to display gratitude. I did not have the heart to tell her I hated the soft feel of velvet, and the shirt looked a bit too fancy for my liking. It had gold thread embroidery in the fabric, which ran down the front in two wavy lines.

"Come on, Tom, let's go on deck and get some air." Larsen invitation saved me from having to try on the garments.

We left Katherine to pack away our belongings and made our way through the boat's dim passageways and up the narrow spiral staircases. We emerged into the bright sunshine of the early spring sun and sat on one of the many benches near the rear of the boat. A line of dense smoke was trailing behind the ferry. It rose from the chimneystack, its drift determined by the wind. It hung low over the water and trailed for half a mile behind the vessel.

The decks were pandemonium. Children ran wild from one end of the ferry to the other while their parents strolled at a more leisurely pace. The diversity of people was great – trappers, businessmen, and families seeking a new life in the Northwest. I heard many foreign languages spoken, mostly by the immigrants who had made the long journey from Europe. I could hear German, Russian, and Swedish, but there were other European dialects that I could not place.

"You did good back at the hotel. Kate told me what happened." He was nodding in approval of my actions.

"I still can't believe it," I replied. "A month ago I would never have had the courage to hit someone. It all happened so fast. Had I time to think about it, I think I would have done nothing."

"Well, you did good. You got Kate out of there and I'm grateful."

There was a few moments silence as we thought about how our present situation could be a whole lot worse.

"You know she likes you, Tom?" he said.

"I like her, too."

"No, I mean she really likes you." His voice had a slight tremble. It was hardly noticeable and had I not know him so well, it would have been undetectable. For me, it was an insight into his character that I never dreamed existed.

"Bill, I can assure you that I have nothing but respect for Katherine. I'd never hurt her in any way."

He sat up straight and let out a roar of laughter that caused other passengers to look around. He placed his heavy hand on my shoulder. "It's your welfare I'm worried about."

I laughed with him. We did not discuss the matter further. Little had been said, but I understood what he wanted me to know without him having to explain. He looked on her as his daughter and despite his manly persona, had all the worries and fears that came naturally to a parent.

"What will we do after we reach Duluth?" I changed the subject, much to the relief of us both.

"That's where it starts to get dangerous." He pulled out his pipe and tobacco pouch before continuing. "My place is two week's ride west of town. Wilson don't know about it, but there's a chance news will get to him that we got off the ferry. He'll have put the word out and I'm well known around those parts. Like I said before, he knows where we're goin' and the closer we get, the quicker word will reach him of our whereabouts."

"How far is the gold from the ranch?" I asked.

"About two hundred miles. And there ain't no rail and no roads. It's a four week journey on horseback... mountain country the whole way. If we can avoid people and steer clear of minin' camps, we just might get there and back without havin' to tangle with Wilson."

I nodded with the hopeful anticipation that we could find my father's gold without further violence.

Night-time aboard the ferry was quite a social affair. I linked Katherine's arm as we entered the dining room. We were still using the name, Marshall, and she giggled when the usher addressed us as Mr and Mrs when taking our coats. As for myself, I felt a strange twinge in my stomach when I heard it. It was pretence, but the feeling of having a wife excited me, especially as it was with one so beautiful.

Long rows of tables, covered with white linen cloths filled one side of the room. Men and women, all dressed very respectfully, sat while eating and drinking. Waiters carrying silver trays rushed about as they fussed over the diners. The other side of the room had a raised stage where a small orchestra of musicians in matching black and white attire played. The mellow sound made by bows gracefully sliding across violin strings sounded angelic and in perfect harmony with one another. The low plucking of cello strings reverberated around the room, their echoes held captive by the iron walls of the ship. An open area between the tables and the stage lay empty. Its polished wooden floor shined as it reflected the glow from a gas fed chandelier that dominated the centre of the room.

Our tickets gained us access to this grand affair, but a dress code ensured that the lower class passengers had to seek enjoyment below decks. As a couple, we had passed the inspecting glances of the door attendant without any hindrance. Katherine wore her new dress with a glowing pride. Its red satin fabric gracefully swished around her ankles whenever she turned. A matching hair ribbon complimented the garment. To say she looked beautiful was a momentous understatement. She was stunning and her beauty was admired by many a male's roving eye, usually when their partner was not looking.

While I passed as a gentleman, I felt very uncomfortable in my new clothes. My velvet jacket had the air of respectability, but over the last two months, I had gotten used to wearing casual if sometimes raggedy clothes. The matching black trousers were too tight around the waist and I found myself stopping short of fully exhaling for fear they would bust a button. I caught a glimpse of myself as we passed a mirror and I felt like I was looking at another man's reflection.

"This way Mr and Mrs Marshall," the usher said as he led us to a table.

His speedy pace reflected the pressure of his workload. I squeezed Katherine's hand when he addressed us and she responded with her characteristic giggle. The usher reached the table long before us and he stood waiting as he held a chair out for the lady. I had begun to walk faster, but Katherine tactfully pulled my arm back and covered her mouth with her fan.

"Privileged folk never rush," she whispered from behind the fan.

We ate oysters dipped in caviar and washed them down with red wine that had been ice chilled. We sipped from our glasses with all the elegance of a sophisticated couple whom apparently never knew any different.

I was in another world and it was far removed from the one in which I had been living. In the elegance of our surroundings, the cruel world dominated by violence and by men that put little if any value on the sanctity of human life felt as if it had been a bad dream – a nightmare, where greed and the moral disintegration of all things decent was rife.

Katherine reached out to place her fingers in my hand. It was like a jolt, disturbing me from my dark thoughts. It reminded me that life did not have to be like that. It could be like it was before ever I heard of the name Wilson. I closed my fingers around hers as we sat there, looking into each other's eyes without speaking. There was no need to talk at that moment. Our eyes spoke silent thoughts and those thoughts were complimented by the soft melody of the ship's orchestra.

"This is nice." She smiled, and her smile was as beautiful as a warm orange sun dipping below a clear horizon. It was a never-ending field of colourful flowers whose scent once inhaled would remain with one for an eternity. I knew at that precise moment that for the first time in my life, I was truly and hopelessly in love.

"Nice?" I replied. "No, it's beautiful." Her smile grew even more captivating, although I would not have thought it possible. I tightened my grip on her hand, ever so slightly. "Katherine—"

"Yes?" She interrupted, hanging on my every word.

"Do you think...when this is over, I mean... Do you think that maybe—"

"Maybe what, Tom?" She leaned forward, eagerly awaiting me to finish my question.

"That maybe there is a life for us? Together I mean?"

"Oh, Tom." A tear welled up in the corner of her eye and she used a napkin to wipe it away. "I love you, Tom Anderson. I think I loved you since Bill told me about your journey together from Boston. When I met you in the jail, heard your voice, saw the type of man you were, your honesty, your loyalty to my father and that Indian girl... then I knew it for sure."

Her words filled my heart with a happiness I had never experienced before.

The background music quickened. Its level intensified as the orchestra broke into a French waltz. Couples began to stand at their tables and from all corners of the room, well dressed men led elegantly dressed ladies towards the dance floor.

"Shall we dance, Mrs Marshall?" I said.

"Yes, I would love to, Mr Marshall."

For the next hour, we glided around the centre of the room, surrounded by captivating music that filled our very souls. Perhaps the floor was congested with other waltzing couples, perhaps it was not. We were unaware of anyone else. At that moment, we were the only two people in the world, locked in each other's embrace, with neither of our thoughts extending past the other's eyes. And at that moment, I was happier than I had ever been in my entire life.

TWENTY

Duluth and Westward

The Buffalo ferry slowed as it closed the gap with the wharf at Duluth. The whole boat shuddered as the powerful steam engines were thrust into reverse. Behind us, the calm surface water transformed into a foaming mayhem as the boat's propeller forced water back under the hull. The wharf was thronged with people. Most of those waiting were waving to relatives that had lined the deck to look out for familiar faces.

The excitement was fantastic and passengers spilled down the gangplank to be overwhelmed by waiting family members. I had never witnessed so many crying in one place at the same time and the air was alive with the wails of joy. Some travellers, those that had no one waiting to meet them, stood on the wharf, looking around in a bewildered fashion, unsure of what to do next.

I linked Katherine's arm and pushed our way through the crowd. We walked along the planked jetty to look for Larsen at the rear. We did not have to wait long. The ship's officer in charge of cargo let the horses off first before unloading the less disciplined cattle. We wasted no time. Ahead of us was a long ride to the ranch. We had no money, no food, and few supplies. A pound of coffee and a pouch of tobacco was all we had to see us through the journey.

We made our way through the busy streets of Duluth. The town was booming and the ferry was bringing in people faster than the town could grow. Even as the dusk darkened the sky, the sound of saws cutting timber and hammers pounding nails filled the air. For every building I saw under construction, there were at least a dozen tents providing temporary shelter.

As we rode into the surrounding countryside, the flickering lights from candle lit rooms dimmed into the distance. We thread carefully across fields and ditches. It was pitch black, without even the light of a moon to guide us.

"We'll camp here and move on at dawn." Larsen spoke as he lowered himself down from his horse.

"I'll get a fire going," I said.

"No fire," he quickly replied.

"What's wrong, Bill?" Katherine asked.

He did not answer straight away. He stood still, staring back into the darkness. "I don't know. Maybe nothin', but—"

"But what? What's wrong?" Katherine said as she looked back in the direction he was looking.

I looked too, but all I could see was a wall of darkness. There wasn't a sound. It was dead quiet, too quiet.

"I just got this uneasy feelin'," Larsen said. "I felt it the moment we got off the boat. Like someone was watchin' us."

"Can't we keep going?" I had lowered my voice to a whisper.

"No, too dark," he answered in a low voice also. "We'd risk injurin' one of the horses if they put a hoof wrong."

So there we spent our first night in Minnesota, sitting close together for warmth and waiting for dawn. It was impossible to sleep other than brief moments when exhaustion would win out over discomfort. The drift into slumber never lasted long. We would wake with a jerk and a moment of panic as we wondered had something or someone caused us to wake.

Dawn broke slowly. The early morning rays of light lacked the heat to rid the light coating of frost that blanketed everything, including our clothes. We walked around and stamped our feet to warm ourselves before saddling the horses. We all felt as wretched as we looked – a night without a campfire was a truly miserable affair. Our stomachs ached from hunger and no fire had meant no coffee. We rode on in silence. Nobody felt like engaging in conversation.

It was midday before our lot improved. We reached high ground and from a rocky hill slope, we had a good view of the surrounding countryside. It was green country. Forests grew up hills and gracefully swept over them to cover the opposing sides. Fenced fields lay to the south and were only occasionally broken by the brown colour of ploughed earth. The midday sun climbed to its zenith and cast its heat across the land. Its warmth rejuvenating both our bodies and our minds.

We gathered wood and lit a small fire to boil water for coffee. From our vantage point, there was little chance of anyone surprising us. I held my hand up to block the sun's glare and scanned the countryside. Small farmhouses lay dotted here and there, but other than scattered cattle grazing in distant fields, there was no sign of life. But Larsen couldn't relax. He sat and stared back in the direction of Duluth. His eyes flicked from left to right as he investigated every bush, every cluster of trees. There was nothing to be seen, but he was unable to shake off his uneasy feeling.

The hot coffee did its work well and we bucked up. Katherine started to smile again and we talked and even joked.

"Tom." Larsen called me back up to his high point where he had remained to keep watch.

I clambered up to him.

"I'm going to ride down to one of those farms and see if I can get us somethin' to eat," he said.

"Do you think we are being followed?" I asked while casting my eye across the peaceful fields.

"I don't know. There ain't no sign of anyone, but I got this bad feelin' in my bones." He took a deep breath while rubbing his chin. "They could have watched us gettin' off the ferry and are trailin' a few miles behind."

"But, you don't see anyone?" I said.

"No, but that don't mean they ain't there...just means they know their business."

"How many do you think?" I asked.

"Not many, two or three maybe. We're safe for the moment. If they plan on jumpin' us, it'll be dark, while we're sleepin'." He started to slide back down the rock. "Keep your eyes and ears open just in case. I'll be back in a few hours."

I nodded and slid down behind him. I routed out my gun from Eclipse's saddle and loaded it.

Larsen rode down the hill and we watched him disappear behind the trees. I decided to stay at the position he had taken to watch out. There was nothing stirring. A peace hung over the landscape, but I had seen his suspicions proved right too many times to dismiss any strange feelings he might have. Katherine sat beside me and rested her head against my chest.

"Tom, what are you going to do when you find the gold?"

"I don't know. To be honest, I haven't thought that far ahead." I ran my fingers through her hair. I knew she was thinking of something and I waited for her to come out with it.

"Forget the gold, Tom. Why don't you forget the whole thing? We can go somewhere, just you and me. That's what you want, isn't it, for us to be together?"

"Yes, that's what I want," I said.

She lifted her head to look at me. I put my hand around the back of her neck and pulled her towards me. Our lips met and we kissed. It was a loving kiss, soft and with meaning. She buried her head into my chest again and her arms slipped around my waist. She held on to me as tightly as she could, as if she never wanted to let go.

"But I can't let Bill go on alone," I said.

"He'd understand." She spoke without looking up.

"Maybe he would...I don't know how to put it into words, but I just can't leave him."

"You're just like him." She wasn't angry, but her voice had an air of resignation about it.

I had a strange feeling at that moment. Was I just like him? Eight weeks ago, I thought myself to be the exact opposite of Bill Larsen. He was the type of man my father was – wild and fearless. Could I have changed that much in so little time? Maybe I was more like my father than I thought. Maybe I'd just needed a man like Larsen to bring out my true nature.

"It's just something I have to do. I have to see it through. I don't think I could ever rest easy if I didn't finish what we started."

"Like I said, just like him." She sat up to face me. "And when it's over, there'll be something else. Something to find, someone else to kill. There's no end to it."

I reached out to hold her soft cheek in my hand. "Katherine, I swear to you, when this is over, that's it. Do you think I could stomach this any longer than I have to? When it's done, we'll go away, far away, just the two of us. I swear it on the lives of our unborn children."

Her mouth opened with astonishment at what I had just said. I was shocked myself. I had not being thinking about children and I didn't know why it came out.

"Children?" Her face lit up with happiness. Her eyes widened, wider than I'd ever seen them before. And her smile...her smile was that of unhindered joy.

"Isn't that what you want?" I said, and continued before she could answer. "It's what I want. With you, I mean."

"Oh, Tom. Yes, it is what I want, more than anything else."

Her head fell against my chest again and I wrapped my arm around her while stroking her hair with my other hand.

It was a while before we spoke again. She, like me, had let her thoughts drift away to another way of life, and like me, was lost in a world of happy daydreams.

TWENTY-ONE

The Killing

Larsen did well and we watched with delight as he emptied the contents of his saddlebag onto the ground. There were six eggs, two pound of fresh pork, and two dozen dried biscuits. We ate the eggs raw as we had no pan to fry them and not enough water to spare for boiling. We tore off thin strips of pork and skewered them with sticks. Sitting around the fire, we held the strips above the tip of the flames. The meat crackled and sizzled as the meat slowly darkened. Tiny spurts of flame jumped into the air as grease dripped down onto the burning wood. I watched their faces as they chewed on the tender meat. There are few things in life to rival the pleasure of food feeding a hungry belly.

It was our third night when they struck. Larsen was right, we were followed. Three men had trailed us from Duluth and just as he had predicted, it was late when they made their move. The ghastly events of that night are something that will stay with me forever. Over the past two months, I had seen several men killed, but not like this. It was necessary for us to kill, but there was an added degree of savagery involved, and to my shame, I played my part in the brutality.

Katherine slept soundly and I lay down to watch her face while she slept. She looked happy even while sleeping. I tried to close my eyes, but Larsen kept disturbing me by sitting up to stare out into the surrounding night. I began to get a bad feeling in my stomach. I also sat up and the two of us looked across the flames at one another.

"Did you hear somethin'?" he asked.

"No, I just got a feeling something is wrong, like something is about to happen."

"Put out the fire," he whispered.

I nodded and poured the contents of the coffeepot over it. The fire hissed and sputtered as the coffee dampened the smouldering sticks. Katherine never stirred and the two of us sat upright with our rifles laid across our laps.

A twig snapping in the distance caused us to exchange looks. Larsen pointed in the direction of the noise. "Over there. I thought I heard somethin' ten minutes ago, I just wasn't sure," he said, again keeping his voice low.

He pulled out his handgun and cocked it before laying it down next to him. I pushed aside my blanket and got to my feet. I backed up slowly and concealed myself in the entanglements of a bush. Larsen stayed where he was and we remained silent as we waited for them to come to us. It was almost impossible to see anything. There was a moon, but a thin cloak of clouds dulled its light. The noise of twigs being crushed underfoot and the rustling of leaves became almost constant.

I pushed the safety catch down on my rifle and then held out my hand on front of me. I squinted in the darkness trying to see it. I could make out its outline, but visible or not, one thing was noticeable, I was not trembling. Yes, I was scared. My mouth was dry and my heart was pounding, but I felt in control. It was a peculiar feeling, one that I was not used to in dangerous situations. Naturally, I would have preferred to be anywhere else but there, but I was there, and whatever had to be done, I felt capable of it. I had changed. I was not the man that left Boston two months ago.

Something caught my eye – a shadow among the shadows. Only because it moved, it was noticeable. Another one, there were two. Two men were creeping into our camp. They wanted one of us alive; otherwise, they would have opened fire from the safety of the trees. They were hampered by the darkness just as we were. But a break in the clouds just at that moment gave them away. One of them opened his mouth and I saw the glint of a gold tooth along with the gleam from the tip of a knife. He was within four feet of Katherine and creeping in a hunched like fashion towards her.

The blackness lit up in an eruption of gunfire. Larsen shot the second man, and as the intruder reeled in pain, he fired his gun into the ground several times, unable to control his movements. Katherine sat up screaming. I stepped forward and shot the man holding the knife. He jerked with the impact, but did not fall. I fired again and kept stepping forward towards him, firing with every step as I advanced. His knife fell and he twisted and contorted as every bullet tore into his body. I shot him six times, every bullet finding its mark. He dropped to his knees and stared blankly at me, before falling to one side. There was a moment of silence and the air was thick with the smell of burnt gunpowder.

"Tom!" Katherine shouted as she pointed behind me.

I knew my gun was empty. I gripped the barrel with two hands and spun around, swinging the rifle out in a circular motion. There was a crack as it made contact with the man's jaw. He grunted in pain and fell to the ground, dropping a handgun as he did. He was lying face down and his arm reached out to grab the gun, which was no more than two feet away from him. I picked up the first man's knife and jumped down onto his back, my knee pushing down hard onto his spine.

"No, Tom. No!" Katherine screamed, but it was too late. I could not stop myself. I plunged the blade into his back, just below his neck and midway between his shoulders. His head lifted up and he gasped in agony, blood spurting from his open mouth. I twisted the knife and pulled it out. He wheezed as his lungs pushed out trapped air and his head fell down into the dirt, and into his own blood.

I stood and looked around to see Larsen kneeling beside the man he had shot. Katherine was sitting with her knees tucked up under her chin and her hands were clasped together holding them tightly against her chest. The man was still alive. He was clutching his stomach and his shirt was wet from seeping blood.

"What's your name?" Larsen spoke in a soft voice.

"B...Be...Ben Tucker." He struggled to speak through clenched teeth. His body trembled and despite the cold, beads of sweat ran down his face.

"Who sent you?" Larsen asked.

"I... I don't know."

"Someone sent you, why were you followin' us?"

"Pri...price."

"What price? What do you mean?"

"Price on..." He paused and took two slow breaths as he tried to compose himself. "Price on Anderson and you."

"How much?"

"Two hundred dollars dead...one thousand alive."

"Did Wilson put the price on us?"

"Don't know no Wilson. Oh Lord in heaven help me!" His face twisted as he let out another pitiful whimper.

"Who's offerin' the money?"

"Word is...bring you to him...to...collect. That's all I know...I swear."

"There ain't nothin' we can do for you. You're gut shot," Larsen told him.

"Water...please, some...water." His bloody hand reached out to grasp Larsen's arm.

"Katie, throw me that canteen," Larsen called out, but she did not answer.

"Katie!" he yelled again.

Her body jerked at hearing his raised voice and she began to look around as if she had just woken from a deep sleep. She became aware and reached out for the canteen, but she shook with fright and then froze as the injured man let out an unmerciful cry. He clutched his stomach all the harder and his whole body tightened. We watched his eyes roll upwards until they showed mostly white. His body relaxed for a moment before going limp as his head rolled to one side. He was dead.

For once, I did not welcome the dawn light. The dark receded to reveal the true horror of the previous night. Three men lay dead, men I did not know and had borne no malice towards. The ground was sodden with blood and dark footprints crisscrossed one another from where we had stood in pools of blood before spreading it around the damp morning soil.

We buried the dead. We had no shovel so we spent the morning gathering stones and larger rocks. The three men were laid down together and we piled the rocks around and above them. It would be their only protection against scavenging animals. Larsen lashed two broken branches together and made a crude cross.

It was midday before we finished. All morning I had been unable to make eye contact with Katherine and she had avoided any conversation with me. We stood in silence for a few moments around the pile of rubble. It seemed the Christian thing to do; a moments silence, a moment of regret and reflection for our sins.

"Our Father, which art in heaven—" The words came from Katherine and our heads bowed in respect. "Hallowed be thy Name."

I've heard the Lord's Prayer many times, but this was my first time to truly hear it, to really understand its power and its meaning. Her voice was soft and she spoke slow with each word resonating in my head.

"Thy Kingdom come. Thy will be done in earth, as it is in heaven. Give us this day our daily bread. And forgive us our trespasses, as we forgive them that trespass against us. And lead us not into temptation, but deliver us from evil. For thine is the kingdom, The power, and the glory, For ever and ever. Amen."

Katherine looked up to see tears streaming down my cheeks. I was ashamed and I could not hide it. She reached out to hold my arm.

"It's all right, Tom." Her eyes were wide and forgiving.

"I don't know what's wrong with me," I said, my voice shaking.

"Ain't nothin' wrong with you," Larsen said. "At Gettysburg, I saw men fightin' and killin' all day long, only to cry themselves to sleep at night. No, there ain't nothin' wrong with you at all, not a damn thing."

The air had been cleared. I still carried the guilt, the shame, but nothing was hidden, and I felt the better for it.

TWENTY-TWO

Larsen's Ranch

I was not quite sure what to expect. Neither Larsen nor Katherine had described their ranch to me, which meant that my only expectations were whatever my own imagination had envisaged. Montana itself was a beautiful state. Rolling hills covered in dense green forests gracefully crisscrossed one another as they made their way northwest towards the Rockies. Pure water, rich in iron flowed down from higher ground far off. Age-old rivers meandered their way across the landscape, ensuring the existence of both grazing land and flourishing woodlands alike. The wondrous image of Northern Montana transferred its splendour into my mental image of the ranch. I pictured endless green valleys, where hundreds, if not thousands of cattle grazed freely. An image of a grand and spacious ranch house came into my mind. It stood on a hill, proudly looking out over its vast property.

What I found was quite different. Larsen's ranch was nothing more than a scattering of shabby cabins and sheds spread around fifty acres of unfenced fields. There were cattle, I counted around fifty and stubborn brutes they were too. After stabling the horses, I found myself face to face with a large heifer. We were crossing the open area between the barn and the main cabin. I clapped my hands and waved the beast away, but she refused to move, choosing instead to stand her ground and stare me down.

"Yup there!" Katherine shouted from behind me and waved her arm outwards. The cow jolted and wandered off towards some other nearby cattle. "Cattle are like horses," she explained as we walked. "If you show fear or indecision, they will sense it."

The cabin had a weathered look about it. The horizontal logs were mostly peeled of bark and had a soft appearance, as if having absorbed a lot of rain over the years. Inside was a surprise and did not reflect the building's exterior. It had an open plan design except for a door leading to bedrooms at the back. It was immaculately clean and several wool floor rugs along with cushioned chairs made it quite cosy. This was thanks to Mrs Dolan who took pride in her house. She was a heavyset woman in her late fifties, but her face was younger than her age would suggest. She had soft fresh skin, void of wrinkles that took years off her age. Katherine told me later that she washed her face daily with a cream she made herself – a mixture of goat's milk, crushed herbs, and other ingredients that Katherine could not readily recall.

Mrs Dolan welcomed Katherine as lovingly as a mother would welcome a returning daughter. She flung her arms around her, almost crushing her with the strength of her embrace. Larsen also received a warm-hearted welcome, and I noticed a tear well up in her eye as she hugged him. I believe it was the relief of seeing him return unharmed. I found Mrs Dolan to be a wonderful woman, always happy and a true optimist. Her husband, she told us, was out hunting and unlikely to return for a several days. She sat us at the table and fussed around us like a mother hen. Her warm personality was a joy and it did not take long before I felt as if I had known her all my life.

"Eat up, Tom," Larsen said as he peeled the skin from a baked potato.

"Why, what's the hurry?" asked Katherine, taking the words out of my mouth.

"Tom will need a good night's sleep. We got an early start tomorrow."

"Tomorrow?" My voice mirrored my surprise. I assumed we would rest up for a while and I had a hankering for Mrs Dolans cooking.

"Yep, we got a two week journey ahead of us and the quicker we get there and back the better our chances."

"Can't it wait a few days?" Katherine reached out to touch his arm as she spoke. "Tom is exhausted and you need rest, too. And there are the horses—"

"No," he interrupted. "I think we best get goin'. The long-er we wait the more time Wilson will have to spread the word of our arrival." Larsen was unyielding with his plan.

Mrs Dolan remained silent, but I could see a look of con-cern on her face. I got the feeling she knew it was pointless trying to talk Larsen out of a plan.

"You will be careful, won't you, Tom?" Katherine placed her hand on mine as she spoke.

"Don't worry about him. He's Johnny's son, he'll be just fine," Larsen said.

His words echoed it my head. He was comparing me fa-vourably to my father. For the first time in my life, I felt a surge of pride to be compared to him. However, the atmos-phere changed when Katherine spoke.

"Yes," Katherine said. "But Johnny is dead and I don't want the same to happen to Tom."

There was an awkward silence and none of us seemed to know what to say, but Mrs Dolan tactfully broke the hush. "More coffee, anyone?"

I held up my cup and she duly refilled it.

"Well, I'm off," Larsen said as he pushed back his chair and got to his feet.

"Where are you going?" As I asked, I noticed Katherine and Mrs Dolan exchange glances – apparently they knew.

"Town. It's five miles west of here. I'm going to get my-self a decent drink and maybe try my hand at cards. Do you want to come along?"

"No thanks." I was weary of travelling and wanted to take it easy, even if it was just for one night.

As he walked out the door, I felt a brief twinge of awk-wardness. I had chosen to stay with the women instead of going into town, but my embarrassment soon passed. I was much too tired to really care.

Katherine and Mrs Dolan seemed content to sit talking at the table. Ontario was the main subject of conversation and Katherine spoke at length about the lavishly stocked stores and the exotic clothing that was on display there.

I excused myself and decided to go for a walk. I quickly became impressed with the setup of the ranch. It appeared to me that the Dolan's were probably self-sufficient. At the rear of the main cabin was a vegetable garden. Neatly laid rows of turnip, carrots, cabbage, and numerous other vegetables stretched towards a hay field that presented itself as a solid wall of golden sheaves. I made my way around the side to find clusters of grape trees growing alongside raspberry and strawberry bushes. Next to a chicken coop there was a large shed. I pulled open the door to look inside. There were piles of lumber neatly stacked. Birch trees stripped of their branches and all cut to the same length. It appeared they were awaiting collection and I assumed Mr Dolan made money by selling them to local sawmills.

I checked on the horses. They were resting and paid little attention to my presence. After refilling some of the water troughs, I made my way back to the cabin.

Mrs Dolan met me as I approached the door.

"I have some errands to run. I'll be back this evening," she said.

"Take care and thank you for the wonderful meal." I rubbed my belly to show my satisfaction.

"Goodbye, Tom." She made her way to a horse and trap that was next to the barn.

I went into the cabin. It was quiet and there was no sign of Katherine.

"Katherine," I called out, but there was no reply.

I called her name again.

"In here, Tom." Her voice came from one of the back rooms.

I went through to find her sitting on the edge of the bed. She was not crying, but her eyes were red and I thought she might start at any moment.

"What's the matter?" She didn't answer, just shrugged her shoulders.

"Katherine, what's wrong?" I sat down and put my arm around her.

"Everything," she said, her voice trembling.

She could hold it in no longer. Her face crunched up and trickles of tears began to roll down her cheeks. I held her as she laid her head across my chest. We did not talk for a while and I comforted her as she let the tears flow. She continued to sob, her body jerking with each snuffle. It was quite a while before she stopped crying. She sat up straight and looked me straight in the eye, but without speaking.

"Will you tell me what's wrong?" I squeezed her hand.

She took a long breath and gently bit her lower lip before

speaking. I noticed it was a habit that Larsen often displayed.

"I don't want to lose you," she finally said.

"You're not going to," I replied.

"You can't promise me that, not if you leave tomorrow."

"I have to go, I told you that before. Anyway, there probably won't be any trouble. We'll dig up the gold and come straight back."

"There's always trouble," she said. "It follows Bill like a bad stench. Wherever he goes, people die. It's not his doing, he's a good man, but people die all the same. If you go with him, you won't come back. It was the same with your father."

I remained silent for a moment. She was right, there were some things I could not promise.

"I'm sorry, Katherine." I squeezed her hand again. "I have no right to promise such things. But, I can't explain it, for some reason I just know that nothing bad is going to happen to me. It was different a few weeks ago, but something has happened. Something has changed within me. I can't explain it, not even to myself. I've come a long way since that night when Bill came knocking at my door. I know it's nearly over, I can feel it, sense it. I'm not like Bill, no matter what you think. When this is over, I want to live a quiet life, a happy life, with you."

She smiled a little, her eyes beginning to shed their sadness. "I love you, Tom Anderson. And I'll be waiting when you come back."

We sat still for a moment, content to hold hands and look into each other's eyes. After a while, she let go of my hand and stood facing me. Neither of us spoke. She placed her hand on my cheek and caressed it. Her fingers slowly moved across my lips until her soft fingertips reached my other cheek. I felt the warmth of her palm press against my face. Her eyes widened. They looked happy and sad at the same time. The corners of her mouth turned up as an inner joy began to show. She took a step back and gazed at me for a moment.

I remained silent, not feeling any pressure to say or do anything. Her two hands came up and she began to open the top button of her shirt. Her movements were slow and deliberate, adding to my growing sense of arousal. When the top button was undone, her fingers traced a path downwards, stopping to open each button in turn. Still I said nothing, my eyes and attention transfixed on her every movement.

She stretched her arms back to pull the shirt off. It fell behind her to the floor, exposing her breasts to me. They were proud and firm and I desperately wanted to reach out and touch them, but I did not. I waited and watched.

She opened her trousers button and they slid down to her feet. She moved towards me as she stepped out of them. She was beautiful, the most beautiful woman I had ever seen. Her skin was soft and pure, and so perfect. Her body was illuminated by the orangey glow from the dusk sun through the window. I reached out and placed my hands on her sides. She shuddered a little when I touched her. I stood and pulled her close to me. She began to undo my clothing and within a minute, we were both naked, our bodies pressed together. We lay on the bed and I realised the most beautiful and intimate moment I had ever experienced. We fell asleep in each other's arms and that night I felt closer to her than any person I ever had before.

TWENTY-THREE

The Journey North

We left early, departing during that eerie half-light that exists just before the breaking of dawn. I looked back at the cabin, which was in darkness. I was thinking about Katherine and my heart ached at the thought of leaving her. We rode northwest and made for a trail that led into the mountains. Larsen took the lead and I followed, pulling two packhorses behind me. I patted Eclipse's neck. He was eager to go forward and I had to pull on the reins several times to hold him back.

The sun rose high into the sky and its blistering heat spread across the countryside. Other than the noise of our horses, the only sounds were the squawks of birds flying above and the occasional clicking from crickets. By afternoon we were beginning to climb. It was a slow and steady uphill trek, but in the distance the mountains rose sharply. I could see our journey was going to become a lot more demanding over the coming days. We kept going until darkness hampered further progress. We set our camp in a hollow on the side of a small knoll, and for the first time I began to think seriously about the implications of becoming a rich man.

"Tell me, Bill, what are you going to do with your share?"

He sucked hard on his pipe before answering. "Well, my plan was always to set Kate up so she didn't have to worry about money. After that, I was going to give somethin' to the Dolans, make their life a little easier. As long as I've enough to keep myself in tobacco and coffee, I ain't really bothered." There was a moment of silence before he spoke again. "What about you? Back to Boston?"

"Boston?" I said, almost as if I had forgotten the city existed. It seemed a faraway place now, not just in distance, but in memory, too. "No, I don't think I could ever settle in Boston again. Katherine and I have been talking about a place of our own. I don't know where, we haven't made any definite plans yet." I looked up at him and waited for his reply. In fact, I was waiting for his approval.

He nodded. "I'd like that. I know it's what Katie wants and I know you'll look after her."

"I will, you have my word on it," I said, relieved that he had no objections.

"Well, first we gotta find that gold!" he said as he got to his feet and began to lay out his bedroll.

There was no more talk. We slept as tired men do and did not wake until the first signs of the dawn light.

It was three days before we got into the mountains. I had thought we were in mountain country, but now, looking back at the landscape behind and below, I could see we had only been travelling through hills. We climbed higher and higher. Much of the time, we walked, pulling the horses behind us as they stumbled and slid, trying to get a foothold on the narrow steep trail. The mountains ahead seemed to get bigger all the time. The more distant ones were snow-capped, their white peaks glistening as they reflected the sun's light. Behind us, a long valley twisted and turned as it wended its way back to civilisation.

It was on this day that I shot an elk. Larsen spotted it first. It was grazing on a steep incline a half mile away. We tied the horses and took our rifles out. We split up; I was to try to get above while he would attempt to come up from behind and below the animal. If we got close enough then at least one of us would get a shot, depending on which way it ran. I climbed for ten minutes before turning in the elk's direction. I was above a crest and had good cover, but I tread lightly, careful not to dislodge any loose stones that would alert our prey. I wasn't in position when a shot shattered the silence. I rushed to the rim of the crest's overhang to see if Larsen had shot the animal. I couldn't see any sign of the elk, but I could see Larsen standing out in the open and using his hand to block the sun as he looked up the hill. I shouted and waved my arms until he saw me. He began to point up and waved at me to go back. I ran back and stopped to listen. It was quiet at first, but then I began to hear bushes rustling and twigs snapping. The noise got louder and more consistent. I held my rifle up and waited, trying to determine the direction of the noise.

It happened in an instant. The bushes parted and the elk came charging out. The beast was huge, and although I do not believe he was intentionally charging me, I still had to jump backwards to avoid his antlers, which almost tore my stomach out. He ran straight past at full speed and in the direction I had come from. I had only a few seconds to act. I regained my balance, lifted my rifle, took aim, and fired. The animal continued for a few strides and then began to lean to one side. His front legs started to give from under him and he went tumbling forward. He hit the ground hard and his body slid for another few feet before coming to a halt. One of his antlers snapped off the ground and shards of the brownish bone were hurled into the air. I hurried to him. I had shot him through the back of the neck. There wasn't much blood, just a small patch of red covering the wound. He wasn't dead. His rib cage rose and fell as his lungs still functioned. His eyes were open and I saw his pupils move. I had no wish to see him suffer any more so I placed the gun against his head and squeezed the trigger.

I sat on a rock and waited for Larsen to make his way up the hill. I waited with pride. I was under no illusion that the elk had fallen to a skilfully aimed bullet, for my marksmanship was seriously lacking. It was a lucky shot. However, it did not diminish my sense of achievement.

"That was a fine shot, Tom." He stood over my kill as he inspected the two bullet holes.

"I was lucky," I said.

"All good shots have their share of luck." He smiled, appreciative of my honesty.

"What happened?" I asked. "I heard you shoot, but I wasn't in position when you fired."

"Damn elk heard me blunderin' through the undergrowth. He took off up the hill. I fired off a round, but he was movin' too fast. I guess I didn't have your luck."

He smiled again. It was a sarcastic smirk and I could not resist some sarcasm of my own.

"If you want, I can check your rifle. Maybe the sight is bent?"

"It'll be bent if I crack it across your head." He broke into a fit of laughter at his own comment.

Finding his laugh infectious, I joined in, and the calm silence of the mountain was broken by two travellers laughing while standing over a dead elk.

The sun rose early in the clear Canadian sky. For once, we did not break camp at dawn and I was glad to have the opportunity to rest. We spent most of the morning cooking our bounty. Larsen skinned the animal and cut long thin strips that we skewered and roasted above the flames of our campfire. The meat was tasty and to our liking. We ate each piece as soon as it was done. The succulent juices of the animal's meat tasted so good that we both displayed immense facial expressions of pleasure as our taste buds were satisfied.

The shooting of the elk had come at a good time. We had exhausted our supply of fresh food, although we still had a plentiful stock of dried biscuits and canned beans. Our plan from this point had been to supplement our supplies with wild game, and we could not have had a better start than killing such a large beast. Living off the land meant we could avoid mining camps and trading posts. The less people that knew about our presence, the better chance we had of completing our adventure unhindered. The only drawback to hunting was that it slowed us down, but it was a price we had to pay.

As the midday sun scorched us from above, we sought shelter under the dense overhang of some spruce trees. Our bellies full, we sat without talking while we waited for the food to digest. Before leaving, we cut pieces of meat from the dead animal. We treated the uncooked flesh with salt we had brought along for this very purpose of preserving food. The strips, we rolled up and wrapped in clean cloth. We would be feasting on our success for many days to come.

It was mid-afternoon and the sun was at its highest when we broke camp. I looked back past the two packhorses trailing behind me to see scavenger birds descending on the carcass. They had waited half the day and now their patience was being rewarded. There was little talk as the hours passed. There was only so much lonely men can talk about while travelling. We sat in silence as our horses took us up the steep hill slopes and down the sharp inclines of the opposite sides. Although we were continuously going both up and down, we were mostly going up – climbing higher and higher into the mountains.

I marvelled at the panoramic view surrounding me. Bright green forestry blanketed the rolling hills that resembled waves making their way north. Long valleys lay behind us, twisting and turning as they meandered their way back down to the lowlands. Before us, the mountain peaks rose high into the clear blue sky, their white caps coated in snow that covered them all year round. The icy appearance of snow-capped mountains was a sight that amazed me as we sweated and baked beneath the burning sun.

Our journey continued in this fashion for the next four days, but it was then that our luck ran out. We were getting close to our goal. Larsen had just told me we were less than two days away from the valley where he and my father had buried their gold.

The morning had passed normally, but we rounded a bend in the trail and came face to face with a dozen men and twice as many horses and mules. The horses and mules without riders were heavily laden with boxes. The men were miners bringing supplies to a mining camp further down the slope. They seemed friendly and some of them offered us tobacco and coffee from their supplies. However, two of the men knew Larsen and their glances to each other made it obvious that they realised the significance of his presence. None of the miners appeared to be armed. If they had weapons, they were packed away on the string of mules.

Larsen conversed with the men with small talk and the conversation was like a game of cat and mouse.

"How do, Bill. Ain't seen ye for manys a year." The man that spoke was a scruffily dressed character, his clothes riddled with holes and torn lining. His teeth did not fare much better. Three teeth were all that I could count and they were stained a dirty shade of yellow.

"Oh, I've been around," Larsen replied.

"Where ye headin'?" the man asked.

"Northwest. I got some tradin' to do in Calgary." Larsen packed tobacco into his pipe as he spoke and did not look up at the man.

"Who's yer friend?" the man asked, nodding in my direction.

"This is Mr Peters. He works for the railroad as a surveyor. We just happen to be travellin' in the same direction."

"How's that daughter of yours?" the man asked, but before Larsen could reply, the miner turned to his friend, whose gaunt appearance was that of a half-starved man, such was his thinness. "Pretty little thing she is." The other man snorted and chuckled in a childish manner at the mention of a pretty girl.

"Fine, just fine," Larsen said, ignoring the miner's remark. "She's in Ottawa attendin' school."

"Won't do her no good. She'll grow up just like her mother was." The miner's expression changed from one of friendliness to one of distain.

"You know, Doolin—" Larsen still did not look up from his pipe— "I've know you for ten, maybe fifteen years. You were trash when I first met you, and you're still trash." He lifted his head as he put the pipe to his lips. As he did, his elbow pushed aside one side of his coat, thus displaying a gun that was shouldered beneath it. The miner noticed it, as did I. "Take heed, speak ill of my kin and I'll put a bullet in you. Won't cause me a thought." Larsen's look was cold, his eyes wide and unyielding. I'd seen those wild eyes on a man before, back at Olaf's farm when Wilson's man tried to kill me. It was a sign, a sign that a man was a mere breath away from killing.

The toothless man made no reply other than a sneer at Larsen. He kicked his horse and yanked the reins sideways. The horse whinnied as it turned to gallop to the front of the line.

"Come on ye lazy bastards! Come on!" The toothless man shouted at his travelling companions.

The string of horses and men began to move and we waited, watching them until they went further down the trail and disappeared from sight.

"Come on, let's get movin'." Larsen coaxed his horse forward and made no remarks about our encounter with the miners.

I knew what it meant and he did not have to explain. The toothless one would pass on our whereabouts as soon as he reached their camp. Word would get to Wilson and he would have men looking for us on our return journey. There was no point in discussing it, as we both knew what lay ahead.

Two days passed. We were riding along the edge of a high ridge when Larsen stopped. He dismounted and stood looking up and down a gorge below us that ran parallel to the ridge.

"This is it." There was surprise in his voice and his tone lacked his normal confidence. It was as if he never really believed he would return.

"The gold?" I said, with a burst of excitement.

"Yep." He pointed to the far end of the gorge where it met the steep side of a cliff. "The other side of that cliff, there is a ravine and just beyond that is where we buried the gold, between two huge boulders that look out of place against the pine forest behind them."

"How do we get down into the gorge?" I asked, looking at the near vertical slope.

"A mile more, maybe two. The ridge dips further along. We'll be able to walk the horses down."

"Well, let's get going!" My excitement was hard to hide.

"Easy, Tom. We've come a long way. No sense in doing anythin' foolish at this stage." He looked west towards the setting sun. "It will be dark in an hour. Let's find somewhere to camp and we'll start fresh in the mornin'."

I had to curb my enthusiasm as we set up night camp. It was an exciting night. It reminded me of childhood days and the nights before a birthday or some other eagerly awaited event. We drank coffee and talked until the late hours. Larsen relived tales of lively times he had shared with my father and I listened intently, living every moment as he recalled them.

That night we slept close to the spot where my father had left the toil of many years safely hidden for his family. I lay awake for a long time, gazing at a billion stars twinkling across the night sky. My mind drifted back to childhood memories. I recalled moments I had spent with my father; moments that I had all but forgotten. I remembered my mother too, and pictured them together.

Three men slept in our camp that night. Bill Larsen, me, and my father, Johnny Anderson.

TWENTY-FOUR

Gladstone

I hardly slept at all. My excitement was such that although tired, slumber was almost impossible. The few occasions my eyes did close, I instantly began to dream about gold and the rich lifestyle that it might bring. I saw myself and Katherine, dressed in fine clothes and sipping tea from delicate china cups in the grand gardens of a sprawling estate. A large house stood behind us. Its white facade was adorned by red and green ivy clinging to the walls as the climbing plant crept upwards towards the roof.

I was awake to see the first rays of light brighten the morning sky and I watched the last lingering stars fade until they vanished from view. I did not wake Larsen. He slept soundly as he always did. It was early and he would not have thanked me for disturbing him before the dawn light had taken a firm grip on the day. I walked the short distance to the rim of the ridge and sat with my legs dangling free over the side. The shadows below receded before the morning light, as they crept along the ground like an ebbing tide. The blur of trees on the opposite side of the gorge became less obscure as their outlines sharpened and their rich green coats blossomed in the rising sun's glory. It was the dawning of a new day, a day I had been striving towards since leaving Boston.

Larsen woke midmorning. Despite my eagerness to finish

the last stage of our journey, he was in no great hurry to start travelling. After working the stiffness out of his body, he sat down to smoke his pipe and drink coffee. It took three cups to satisfy him. While he drank, I sat drumming my fingers off my leg.

We ate arrowroots for breakfast and the last of the Elk meat. The meat's tenderness had being diminishing over the past few days and now it was hard, its moisture dried out from the preserving salt. Even though we had no more food, I was not sorry to see the last of it disappear.

It was noon when we found a safe path down into the gorge. It was too steep a descent for us to ride so we inched our way on foot, each of us leading two horses behind us. I slipped countless times on the loose dirt, but Eclipse stood firm and by holding onto his lead rope, I was able to prevent myself from sliding down in an undignified manner. The bottom of the gorge was a cluttered mass of weed and small trees that had more branches than leaves. Clumps of grass dotted the ground, faded brown from the scorching sun. A narrow stream ran along the centre of the gorge. Clear water trickled down from the mountains as it wended its way towards lower ground. We filled our canteens and drank our fill, as did the horses. I was surprised at how cold and clear the stream was. Every stone, every pebble beneath the surface was vividly clear in its clarity, such was the purity of the liquid. The mountains far off in the distance had filtered the water of all impurities, leaving it pure in both substance and taste.

We trampled our way along the gorge and soon found a track leading up the other side. Although an easy climb, it took the best part of an hour to reach the top. My legs ached from the exertion and when I suggested we rest, Larsen readily agreed. I lay down exhausted to let my body recuperate, but the calling of my name had me struggling to my feet again.

"Over there, see it?" Larsen said, his arm outstretched and pointing.

"See what?" I scanned the countryside before us. The land sloped down to meet a mile of open ground carpeted in yellow grass that stretched out towards a solid line of trees that seemed to wrap themselves around the side of a hill. Then I saw it.

"I see it. Bill, I see it!" My vision focused on two large

boulders, as wide as they were tall. Their grey stony surfaces butted out of the treeline like two great eyes observing all that lay before them. "Two boulders that look like they don't belong." I repeated his words from yesterday.

"That's where me and your father buried the gold from our mine. Right in the middle of them. All we gotta do is go dig it up."

The thoughts of rest vanished from our minds. Our bodies were refreshed from renewed enthusiasm. My mental euphoria was stronger than my tired bones.

"Thanks, Bill." I reached out my hand and he grasped it with a firm handshake. "Partners," I said him and he nodded with a smile. My mind cast back to that night in Harper's Hotel when he reached out for my hand with the same single word, partners.

We remounted and made our way down the slope. We did not gallop, although the urge to was strong. The mile of yellow grass between us and the boulders reached the bellies of our horses and we did not want to risk injuring a horse by stumbling into an obscure crack or hole in the ground.

We were about half way across when Larsen lurched forward in his saddle. He had a strange look on his face, a mixture of pain and surprise. As I watched his face contort, the delayed echo of a gunshot broke the silence. It seemed to last for a couple of seconds as the noise of it waned while being carried away in the air. He slid sideways before falling off his horse and down into the soft grass beneath us.

"Bill, are you alright?" I jumped off Eclipse and knelt over him.

"I...I don't know." He struggled to speak. His eyes were darting around as he tried to comprehend the situation.

"I heard a shot." As I spoke, I noticed some red streaks of blood on the grass. I rolled him to one side and saw a hole in the back of his coat. Around the hole, it was damp and when I put my finger in to look inside, I saw blood oozing out of a gaping wound in his back.

"Jesus, Bill, you've been shot!" I said.

"I know that," he said sarcastically through gritted teeth.

"I heard a shot, but it was after you were hit." I started to lift my head above the top of the grass.

"Get your damn fool head down!" He grabbed my shoulder and pulled me back. "Whoever fired that shot must be quite a ways off." He took a deep breath as he tried to cope with the pain. "Have a look back in the direction we came and try not to stick your head up too far."

I parted the tall grass as I looked. At first, I saw nothing, but then I saw the dark figure of a man leading a horse down the same hill we had just come from.

"I see him, Bill. He's making his way down the hill. That's close on half a mile away. I didn't think a gun could shoot that far."

"Listen, Tom, we don't have much time." He squeezed my arm, ensuring he had my full attention. "Take the horses and ride like hell for the trees."

"I'm not leaving you," I insisted.

"Damn it, Kid, just do as I say. I reckon I might know who that is back there."

"Who?"

"Ain't many that can make a shot like that. There is one man, a fella called Gladstone, came out here from England."

"What makes you think it's him?"

"I don't know for sure, but it could be. He's a hunter and I know he's worked for Wilson before."

"A hunter?"

"Yea...a hunter of men. Look, Kid, just take the horses and ride for those boulders. Find yourself good cover and wait for him to come to you."

"But, what about you? I can't leave you."

"I'll be alright. When he sees you ride off, he'll reckon I'm dead. If we play it right we'll get him in between us."

"I don't know..." There was a pool of blood spreading under his shoulder, faster than the grass could soak it up.

"I'll be alright. You're wastin' time, get goin'! You can tend to me after."

I climbed onto Eclipse, leaning forward and trying to keep low. I hated the thought of leaving him behind, but there was no time to argue and I thought it best to do as he said. Crouched forward with my head pressed against Eclipse's neck, I galloped towards the safety of the trees. The other horses ran behind me and I hoped if anyone was trying to line up a shot, their panicked run would help cause confusion.

I entered the line of trees with such speed that a wall of branches met me like a thousand whips lashing my body. I covered my face with my arm and closed my eyes. Riding blindly, I heard the sharp snapping and crunching as the wall of wood gave way. A heavy branch, thicker than the others, caught me across the chest. My ribs felt as if they had been crushed. Eclipse ran on, his forward momentum making it impossible for him to stop. I was suspended in the air for a few seconds before falling to the ground. I opened my eyes and stared upwards through the trees.

The blue sky shimmered as the tree tops swayed back and forth. I lay still. My whole body ached and I was afraid to move in case the pain increased. But move I had to. I tried to sit up, but the pain was excruciating. I rolled to one side and clambered to my feet. My back felt as if it was broken, but I assumed it was not, for how else would I be able to stand? There was no time to lose. Eclipse had stopped only a few feet away and I made my way towards him. I put pain to the back of my mind as I pushed leaf covered branches aside. I pulled out my rifle and two boxes of cartridges. As fast as I could, I ran towards the back of one of the boulders. My feet slid as I scrambled up the stony surface. The rear of the giant boulder was not smoothly rounded like the front. It would have been an easy climb had its fissures not been filled with loose stones and slippery moss. Upon reaching the top, I had a clear view of all before me. I could not see Larsen, but the trail of trampled grass showed our route and a wider patch indicated where he fell. The man following us was halfway between the far hill and Larsen. He rode slow, taking his time and riding parallel to our track.

I loaded my rifle, pushing in each bullet one at a time. I paused for a moment. The sensations I had become used to in such situations were not present. My mouth was not over-ly dry. My heart beat faster, yes, but for once it did not feel as if it was about to explode out of my chest. All I could do was wait. He was too far away for me to shoot. I decided to do nothing until he passed Larsen. That was his intention when he urged me to ride on. If we could get him between us, the rider would stand little chance.

The sun above scorched me. Sweat rolled down my face and into my eyes, stinging them. My hands also became sticky in the heat. I wiped them dry on my trouser leg. The rider continued his cautious pace, his outline shimmering in the sunshine. Finally, he got level with Larsen. He stopped about thirty feet to the right of him. He sat still, turning his head from my direction to where Larsen lay.

"Come on...come on!" I urged him forward under my breath. He was thinking, thinking whether to check on Larsen or whether to ride on. I prayed he would choose the latter.

My prayers were not answered. I saw the horse's head turn as the rider tugged on the reins. He trotted towards Larsen. He was still out of range, but nevertheless, I fired. I knew I would distract him and it worked. He spun his body around in the saddle to face me, pulling his rifle out as he turned. He did not return fire. He knew he was beyond my range as he scanned the treeline for my position.

Now it was Larsen's turn. He sprung up and out of the grass like a mountain lion surprising its prey. He fired off two shots even before the man had time to move. But when he did move, he moved fast. The rifle fell to the ground and a handgun came out from beneath his coat. His gun flashed as he returned fire. The scene was surreal and all I could do was watch. Larsen stood while Gladstone sat. Barely twenty feet separated them. Puffs of gun smoke obscured the two men as they continued to blast bullets at each other. Larsen's gun emptied first, and the mounted rider paused for a moment before leaning forward, stretching out his arm to its utmost as he fired his last shot.

The thunderous echoes waned as their reverberations dispersed into the air. The two men remained motionless, neither one moved even to reload their weapons. I stood watching, waiting to see what happened. A few seconds passed although it seemed like longer, and then in the same moment, both men fell. Gladstone slumped forward and slid off his horse. Larsen fell backwards, his body remaining straight and stiff like as the tall grass swallowed him from view. After they fell, all I could see was a solitary horse that began to wander off in a casual manner.

I scrambled down the rock face and emerged out of the trees and into the open. Neither man had gotten up. I ran into the grass and towards them. By the time I got close, sweat streamed down my face. I checked Gladstone first, aiming my rifle as I approached him. The silence, which was only broken by the noise of tall grass swaying in the light breeze only added to the unreal atmosphere. Gladstone, if that was his name, was dead. He lay on his back, his eyes wide open and staring blankly into the cloudless sky. I tried to count the bullet holes, maybe five or six. At that distance, Larsen had not wasted a single shot. Confident he was dead, I turned to check on Larsen. My heart sank when I found him. He was dead, his body peppered with holes. It seemed neither man had wasted their shots.

I did not know what to do. My friend was dead and his last act was to save me. I fell into despair and sat close to him. For how long, I do not know, maybe hours. The sun continued its westward drift as the afternoon passed.

It was getting dark when I got to my feet. There was work to be done and as low as I was, I had to carry on. I rounded up our horses. They had not strayed far and had stayed close to Eclipse. Gladstone's horse had gone. He had wandered back towards the hill and was nowhere to be seen.

I laid the two bodies across the packhorses and brought them back to the edge of the woods. We had packed a spade with us and I used it to dig two graves. The digging was not easy. The ground was hard and compacted with small stones that hindered the spade. I worked until the darkness obscured everything. I only reached half the depth I had hoped for, but I planned to cover them with larger stones the next day. I covered the two men with blankets and refilled the graves with the dirt I had dug out. I was exhausted and could do no more. My arms ached from using the spade.

My camp was a sad affair. I sat alone and dwelled on the day's events. Had I not heard the howling of distant wolves, I would not have bothered to light a fire. I tried to sleep, but my troubled mind kept me awake.

When morning broke, I forced myself to work. I spent half the day covering the graves. It was backbreaking labour. Small stones were of no use, as they could be dislodged by scavenging animals. Larger rocks lay scattered around, but the more I needed, the further I had to walk. I marked the stranger's grave with two branches lashed together in the shape of a cross. I carved the name Gladstone and a question mark into the wood, as I was not certain if that was his name.

I left Larsen's grave unmarked for the moment. He deserved something more fitting than a hastily constructed cross. I located a decent sized rock about a quarter of a mile from camp. Studying its size and shape, I decided it would be a suitable marker to place at Bill's grave. It was relatively flat on two sides and rounded on the others. It was too heavy to lift so I manhandled it back by tilting it over and rolling it a few feet, whereas, I would have to tilt it over again to get a rounded side touching the ground. It took two long hours of rolling, tilting, and rolling again before I got it into position. My arms were sore and my back ached from stooping down to push the heavy rock. I gathered a few suitable stones and began to scratch an inscription into its surface. By the time I finished, my fingers were bleeding and my knuckles rubbed raw. I stood back to study my work.

Bill Larsen
Died March 1878
A Friend to those in need
RIP

Sadness overwhelmed me as I stood remembering my friend. I had only known him a few months, but in that short space of time, he had had a profound effect on my life. I felt it poignant that he had been my father's friend as well as mine, although at different times. While I did not truly know my father, Larsen was like a link that had brought us closer together. It comforted me in some unexplainable way that they had been friends. Because Bill had thought so highly of him, I knew he must truly have been a good man, a man that a son could have looked up to, and be proud of. It was natural for boys to try to emulate their fathers as they grew. As I stood over Larsen's grave, I made a promise to myself. I would try to live as Larsen had done; a friend to those who needed one, and an enemy to those who inflicted their badness upon others. I believed my father lived that way and how better could I honour his memory?

TWENTY-FIVE

Anderson's Gold

The two boulders resembled a mystical gateway from Greek mythology as memories of college and Hercules's fabled pillars came into mind. How they ever came to rest in their present position intrigued me. I recalled Larsen's words, two boulders that look like they don't belong. He was right, if ever something did not belong, it was those two rocks. There were no mountains within twenty miles and they did look out of place, bulging forth from the green forest like giant grey eyeballs. I pondered on the mystery for a while before concluding that an ancient river had once flowed through the valley, and had carried the enormous boulders down from further north.

I stood with the spade in my hand and studied the ground between them. Right in the middle, Larsen had said. But where was the middle? The front faces had smooth rounded surfaces, but the sides resembled weather-beaten mountainsides, and the base of both sides jutted out at various points. One boulder stretched back into the woods twice as far as the other and had become overgrown with moss and scrub. I paced the distance between them. The distance varied at different points. At the widest gap, I paced out thirty steps and at the narrowest, just fourteen. Thick green grass that reached above my knees grew between them, unlike the yellow grass that we crossed to get here. The rich greenness was a result of the tall pine trees shading the ground from the full strength of the sun.

I climbed up the side of one boulder. Loose gravel rolled

down as my hands and feet searched for cracks in the stone. I stood the height of three men and looked down upon the area. At first, the view shed no light on my problem, but then a small patch of grass caught my attention. It covered an area similar to the circumference of a wagon wheel. There was a notable difference. The grass was a shade darker and denser than that which surrounded it. I wondered if it was the result of the earth dug and refilled when they buried their gold. I slid down the rock face and looked for the patch. From the ground, it was almost impossible to see. I eventually located the area, but only because I had seen it from above.

I began to dig. I tried to pull clumps of grass from the ground, but a handful of twisted grass proved to have the strength of a rope. Larsen's knife solved the problem. Grabbing the strands in my fist, I pulled them tight while I hacked low down. The digging was no easier than it had been for the graves. I persisted and dug down to twice the depth of the spade's head. I found nothing. I widened the hole out to one side and then the other. Finding nothing, I began to question my theory on the darkened patch of grass. As late evening cast a shadow across the land, I decided to give up, at least until the next day.

I slept soundly. I was tired and slept well past dawn as my body recuperated. There was only coffee for breakfast and my stomach rumbled in protest. The day was cold. The wind had changed direction during the night and blew from the north. My hands hurt when I rubbed them together over the fire. Welts from handling the spade covered the skin of both palms. I needed food and water and I decided to spend the day hunting and put off my search for gold until the following day.

My rifle needed cleaning if I was to hunt. I sat close to the warm flames to dismantle it. I laid each piece out on the ground. As I reassembled it, I cleaned and oiled every part. A lone hawk swooped down far across the prairie and the gun's sight followed his descent as I tested the rifle on an empty chamber.

Half a mile into the woods, there was a clearing. I brought the horses there and tied them to trees. Eclipse and I were the only ones going on the hunting trip.

We followed the edge of the woods and headed east. There were plenty of birds flying near the forest's edge and I thought about shooting one, but they seemed so small and not worth the effort. I was hopeful of finding larger game as the journey progressed.

We continued due east and the open grasslands began to diminish as rocky outcrops became more numerous. Likewise, the forests to my left became less dense as we travelled up-hill. The going became tougher for Eclipse. No longer was there grass underfoot. It was almost all rock and loose stones that littered the ground. It was safer for me to dismount and lead him. The light began to darken as a line of black clouds crept across the sky, driven south by the northern winds.

I had travelled a third of the day without seeing any game. I was about to turn around when I heard something. I stood still and listened. There was a low rumbling sound and at first I thought it to be distant thunder, but there was no break in the sound. It had to a fast flowing river or perhaps a waterfall. I continued towards the sound, which I determined was further east. Assuming it was a river, at least I could cast a line to catch fish.

The roar became louder the closer I got. A steep hill rose before me and I believed the river would be on the other side. It was a tough climb. Small trees dotted the hillside and I moved from one to the other, gripping each one for support. Eclipse struggled behind me, his hooves slipping as they tried to grip the stony surface. He was not going to make it to the top. I found a spot where the ground levelled out a little and tied him to a tree. I took out the rifle and the knife, and continued on alone. When I reached the top, I could look for an easier route for him. I moved faster on my own and reached the top without much difficulty.

The scene was breath taking. I stood looking down into a deep winding gorge. A river flowed along the bottom and the rumbling roar came from six sharp drops where the water cascaded as the river worked its way downhill. Between each drop, the water slowed and appeared almost stagnant. The river was forty to fifty feet wide and black boulders broke the surface in so many places that a man could easily find a path across by hopping from one to another. The water was only fifty feet below me, but the other side of the ravine rose up almost vertical to twice that height. Its sheer walls caused the noise of rushing water to amplify as it echoed back, producing the constant roar that guided me here.

I studied the river, looking for a suitable place to fish, but something upstream caught my attention. A black bear sat on a rock and was peering down into the water. It remained perfectly still and had it been a man, I would have said he was in deep thought. I sat down and watched in fascination. There was some movement on the bank behind the bear, bushes twitched and shook, but the bear was indifferent to the commotion behind it. From the bushes, two bear cubs fell out. They were wrestling and playing, no different from small children. I continued to watch the scene play out. The mother leaned forward and with a graceful sweep of her claw, scooped out a fish and sent it spinning through the air to land on the bank. A trail of falling water followed the fish, leaving a broken line upon the water's surface and causing ripples that spread in a circular fashion to my side of the river. The cubs charged the fish, which from its size, I thought might be a salmon. The fish wriggled and hopped into the air in convulsive spasms as it tried to fight off death. The cubs leapt off the ground, mimicking the fish's movements. Then they took turns in charging the salmon in mock attacks. It appeared dead, but just as one of them stretched out a paw to touch it, the fish gave a last involuntary jerk and the two cubs fell backwards in a frantic bid to escape. Their mother was oblivious to the playful antics of her young. She resumed her statue like stance and waited for the water to settle.

A thought came to mind. I should shoot the bear for food. I wondered why it had not been my first thought on seeing them. Had they been elk or moose, there would have been no hesitation, but because the bears seemed almost humanlike in their activity, the thought seemed cruel and did not come naturally. Nevertheless, I was hungry and the bears were game. I grabbed my rifle and decided to kill.

I made my way down the gorge and towards the black bear. Bushes provided me with cover as I closed the distance. The roar of the water covered any noise I made as I pushed branches aside. I thought as I crept along. Which one should I shoot? The mother seemed the obvious choice, but there would be more meat than I could use. I had no salt to preserve the meat and I would be only able to carry so much back to camp. A feeling of guilt also made me reconsider. If the mother died, then both cubs would soon perish. I decided it made more sense to shoot one of the cubs. They were small, but more than big enough for my needs. I would only shoot the mother if she attacked me. My mind made up, I continued to move closer and it was not long before I stood at the base of the hill and opposite the bears. They were unaware of my presence. The cubs had tired of the fish and wandered along the bank, swiping at insects that followed them and buzzed annoyingly around their heads. The mother had focused all her attention on the fish passing below her.

I lifted my rifle and took aim. The larger of the cubs was about the size of a medium sized dog and my gun sight followed him as I wrapped my finger around the trigger. I took a breath, held it, and fired. The cub collapsed and the other one jumped sideways with fright. The mother stood up on her hind legs and let out an instinctive roar. Her size was immense. She stood the height of a tall man and must have weighed the equivalent of three. I pulled back on the chamber's lever and the spend cartridge spun into the air as another one moved forward to take its place. The surviving cub had run back into the safety of the bushes and the mother seeing her dead cub, let out another roar. It was as loud as her first, but this time it seemed to be a wail of grief. I felt bad, but the deed was done. I held the rifle in readiness for what might happen next. I thought she might charge towards me, but she did not. The bear went back down onto all fours before lowering herself into the water. She made for the far bank and climbed out beside the cub's body. She shook the water from her fur and a momentary cloud of wet mist surrounded her. I watched from the safety of my position as she sniffed and pawed the body for a few minutes. She turned and walked towards the spot where the other cub had entered the scrub, and continued to snort repeatedly as she vanished from sight.

I sat and waited. I knew nothing about the habits of bears and was unsure if they were gone. An hour passed before I felt confident enough to cross the river. Leaping from one stone to another, I made my way to the far bank. The cub was heavier than I thought and I needed both hands to hoist him up and over my shoulder. The bear in its grief had left the salmon behind, so I picked it up and shoved it into my coat. I did not feel safe until I returned to my side of the river.

The sky darkened as black clouds from the north swept south, tumbling along like a dark blanket being pulled across the heavens. I wasted no time and Eclipse hurried without encouragement from me. He sensed the changing weather and my eagerness in returning to camp. Evening began to resemble night and I listened to the low rumbling noise that accompanied us. There was no mistaking the source of the noise this time. Distant flashes along the horizon heralded the impending storm. Rain began to fall. Light drizzle at first, but it quickly turned more persistent. Rain blew into my face and I had to keep rubbing my eyes in an effort to see. I lost sense of direction. The heavy downfall made it difficult to see more than a short distance. It became impossible to determine west, but Eclipse surged ahead, so I relaxed the reins and put my trust in his instinct.

It was pitch black when I found the boulders. They would have been invisible had it not been for the lightning, which lit up the landscape with every flash. Thunderous explosions that sounded like a thousand cannons accompanied them and deafened me with their violent booming. I entered the woods to find that the ground had become a pool of mud. Eclipse struggled to keep his footing as we looked for the clearing. The packhorses were straining at their lines, terrified by the ferocity of the storm. There was little I could do, other than talk and hope the sound of my voice would have a calming effect. It did not settle them as my voice was drowned out by the thunder and the noise of rain falling.

Camp was truly miserable. I stretched out a sheet of canvas and tied it between two trees. Even with the covering of treetops above, water still dripped through to ensure that everything became saturated. Attempting to light a fire was pointless. I pulled out some bear meat and bit into the raw flesh. The bloody taste of uncooked meat made me gag, but I stopped short of vomiting. Sleep was impossible and I sat in the dark with my knees tucked up under my chin, shivering with the cold. There was nothing more to be done except wait for dawn and hope the rain would abate by then.

It was a horrendous night and passed more slowly than any night I had previously experienced. Dawn did come eventually, but in the gloomy half-light there seemed little change from night. The rain continued to fall without any sign of easing, but thankfully, the thunder had passed on further south.

I broke camp and made for the boulders. What I found was disheartening. Between the two rocks lay half a foot of water. The muddy pool stretched out into the long grass of the prairie. Floodwaters from swollen rivers further north were emptying their excess into the valley. Digging was impossible as the ground was turning into a sea of mud. We were in danger of becoming trapped and the need to get to higher ground was paramount.

I tied the horses in a line and set off for the other side of the valley. I walked ahead, pulling them behind me. The ground had softened and my feet sank every time I put a foot down. It took all my strength to pull my boots out of the sticky mud. I took a last look back – Larsen's gravestone was almost submerged with just the tip of the rock visible above the rising water.

The distance across the valley was about a mile, but it felt more like ten. Every step was an effort. Eclipse and the stallion coped better than the two packhorses, which were smaller and lacked the strength of the bigger horses. We kept stopping as I went back to help them push on. The floodwaters continued to rise at an alarming rate and had reached my knees before we were halfway across. I began to feel the force of the water as a current developed. The situation was worsening every minute and I began to fear for my life. I was about to cut the packhorses loose when I decided to try a different method. If it did not work, I would have to leave them behind. I cut the main line and tied one packhorse to the stallion and the other to Eclipse. Grabbing the two lead horses' reins, one in each hand, I marched forward as forcefully as I could. Lifting my legs high out of the mud, I took long and forceful steps in an effort to make progress. It worked. The two strong horses pulled the weaker ones along and I watched as the hill got larger the closer we got.

The water reached my waist when at last we started to climb up and out of the river. I collapsed with exhaustion and lay in the rain as I recovered from the ordeal. When I felt strong enough to stand, I stood looking back across the plain. The yellow grass was gone, hidden beneath the flowing torrent. The boulders stood jutting out of the water with the flooded woods behind them. I felt an immense sense of failure. It could take weeks, maybe even months for the valley to drain. It would be pointless to wait. I made a silent promise to myself to return when I could, even if I had to wait until next season.

A glint of sun caught my eye and I looked to the north. The line of black clouds had broken along the horizon and rays of sunlight were beginning to shine through. The storm was ending. The rain had at last begun to ease off as blue skies replaced the gloomy clouds that were moving south. I sat down to reflect on my situation. I had failed to find my father's gold, but I had escaped with my life, and with that thought, I dropped to my knees and offered a prayer of thanks.

TWENTY-SIX

A Heavy Heart

I was alone and could rely on nothing but my own instincts. Larsen had taught me much and it was time to put his teachings into practice. I was confident I could find my way back to the ranch. However, the return journey was not a matter to take lightly, for a man could wander this vast wilderness from one month to the next without meeting another soul.

I checked my supplies. Before fleeing the valley, I had packed the bear meat and fish into a sack, and tied it to one of the packhorses, but the sack was gone. It must have worked loose while crossing the prairie and washed away in the river. The spare canteens had also suffered the same fate, leaving me with just one. I did not dwell on my bad luck. As a boy, my mother used to say, *What's done is done, time to move on.* I had forgotten her advice for a long time, but I decided now to draw strength from her words.

I had a plan. It was a simple one as my travels with Larsen had taught me that it was best not to complicate things. To ensure I would be travelling south was straightforward. All I had to do was keep the snow-capped peaks behind me and remember that the sun rose in the east and set in the west. I had marvelled at the wondrous mountain scenery enough throughout our journey to remember many notable landmarks. A fast flowing stream, an oddly shaped hill, and a giant boulder perched on a ridge were just some of the landmarks that I hoped would aid me in my journey. Food was the critical factor. Without sufficient nutrition, a man would grow weak both in body and mind. Traversing the high country without a clear and sharp line of thought was equal to any other danger the mountains might hold.

I pushed on for one and a half days before I camped. I felt it important to make distance in case Wilson's men were still hunting me. A full moon and a clear sky allowed me to keep going throughout the night. Leading three horses slowed my pace, but as the hours passed, so did the miles. A mixture of hunger and exhaustion eventually forced me to stop. My eyes hung heavy and I had almost fallen off Eclipse on more than one occasion. I made camp in dense woodland where the closeness of the trees made it impossible to see more than twenty feet in any direction. It was ideal for my purpose. Two men on horseback could pass within calling distance and never catch sight of each other. Before entering the woods, I had crossed a small brook that ran south. I kept a close distance to the stream as it would provide me with water and possibly fish.

The horses were my first concern. It was a lot of work for one man and the absence of a companion to share the work-load was a burden I had to endure. I unpacked and unbridled each horse in turn before wiping them down and tying them to a rope that I strung between two trees. Moss and clumps of thick grass covered the ground and I left plenty of slack on the lines to allow them room to graze.

Although tired, I spent several hours setting traps close to camp. If luck was on my side, I would snare some small game while I slept. And sleep I did, all night and half the next day. The past week had been an exhausting ordeal and my body was in need of rest. I slept soundly, without stir-ring, and when I woke, I felt the better for it.

I made a decision to stay for a day or two at most. While I knew it would be safer to keeping moving, the fact was, I needed more rest and I was hungry. The horses were like-wise exhausted and I had to think of them also. I concluded that it would be better to rest and eat, assuming I could trap food. If all went well, I could build a small supply of food that would see me through the next few days, allowing me to travel fast and make up for lost time.

I led the horses back to drink at the stream. It would have been more convenient to camp closer to water, but I decided it was wise to keep distance and hide myself deep in the woods. I had no idea if men still hunted me so I considered my choice the more prudent one. The horses drank the moment they reached water and needed no encouragement. I felt exposed out in the open and as soon as they drank their fill, I wasted no time in returning to the safety of the trees. I would return later, but not until the cloak of darkness would help to conceal our presence.

I went to check on the traps laid the day before. Of the six that were set, I was hoping that one or two would yield game. However, my hopes were dashed upon finding four untouched and the remaining two disturbed, and although sprung, they had not snared anything. Judging by the broken sticks and tangled wire, I assumed a large animal such as a wild boar had robbed them of their bait.

There was nothing for it, but to reset them. I spent some time strengthening them by selecting new and thicker sticks. Each stick had to be cut, and stripped of its bark before notched and set in position. I made another two and set them quite a distance from the others. For bait, I used a chunk of rotten meat that I had cut from the mangled carcass of a dead beaver.

Hunger drove my actions now and I decided to try fishing. I equipped myself with wire and hooks, and made my way back to the stream. I found a sheltered spot on a bend where the overhanging trees cast a soothing shadow across the water's surface. The stream widened at this point and the water seemed almost stagnant, unlike the fast flow further upstream. I sat in silence and with as little movement as I could manage for one hour, and then two. I was starting to become despondent when a slight jerk on the wire signalled success. A brown river bass had become hooked and I pulled him in as he wriggled feverishly in a futile attempt to break free. My luck held and after a short time more, I caught another bass, almost twice the size of the first.

My stomach rumbled in apparent protest at two days neglect. The fish cooked quickly over the flickering flames, far quicker than it had taken me to gut and descale them. The bass tasted better than any fish I have ever tasted before. There was a sweetness to the white flesh, the like of which, I had never experienced. I knew I should keep some of my food for the following day, but hunger got the better of me and I gorged every piece, even sucking the bones clean.

Under the safety of darkness, I made my second trip to the stream with the horses. The woods had a different atmosphere at night. Every sound seemed amplified disproportionately to the action that caused it. Twigs cracking and crunching beneath horses' hooves sounded like nearby gunshots. I cringed with every sound, convinced it could be heard for miles. Every few minutes I would stop and listen in dread for the noises of other men who might be searching the forest for me. Nothing but the eerie sounds that haunt all forests at night would answer me. An unseen owl, perched somewhere high above hooted slowly, his cry drifting through the trees as it faded into the distance. There were rustles in the undergrowth from small animals that only came out at night, using the cloak of darkness to hide them from predators. There was the never-ending clacking of branches as the tree tops swayed in the wind.

Dawn broke cold. The temperature had dropped and a light coating of frost covered all that was exposed. I rubbed my hands together to rid them of numbness. The tips of my fingers stung as warm blood began to circulate. The fire had burnt itself out and I rebuilt it, eager to get water boiling for coffee. I waited for what seemed like an eternity for the water's surface to start bubbling. I was beginning to crave coffee just as Larsen had, and as the black liquid scorched my insides, I smiled as I thought of him and his love of the drink.

Success welcomed me upon checking my traps. Six were untouched and two destroyed in much the same manner as the previous night. However, much to my joy the last two yielded game. A mountain hare and a medium sized grey squirrel had fallen foul to my efforts. I returned to camp with a feeling of pride in my achievement.

I stoked the embers of the dwindling fire and threw on fresh wood. The damp wood crackled and hissed as the heat drove out its moisture. While the meat roasted above the flames, I readied the horses. They stomped the ground and pulled at their lines. They, like me were keen to be on the move again. I believed I'd made the right decision in stopping. My body was refreshed and my thoughts no longer hampered by drowsiness. I was still hungry, but far from starving.

I only ate a small piece of the rabbit. The temptation to gorge myself was strong, but I had to be sensible. Careful rationing of my food would allow me to travel four or five days without having to stop and trap more food. I waited for the meat to cool before wrapping it in cloth and shoving it down deep into one of the saddlebags. I broke camp before noon and left the woods by way of the stream, allowing me to fill my canteen while the horses quenched their thirst.

For two days, I travelled south and the beauty of the country I traversed was staggering. Rolling hills blanketed in green forests surrounded me and the sight was breath taking. The sweet smell of pine and spruce never left my nostrils, and the scent seemed to invigorate every part of my body. Whenever I reached high ground I would stop and study the landscape behind me. I saw neither man nor any sign of men trailing me. It was at those times, standing high on a hilltop and looking at the hills and trees stretching out as far as the eye could see, that I felt as if I was the only man alive. The dark cloak of loneliness would begin to gnaw at my heart and I would have to remind myself that I was returning to Katherine, and she was waiting for me.

Sitting alone in the flickering light of my campfire was when the weight of isolation would be at its worst. Sometimes I would talk to Larsen as if he was sitting opposite me. I would ask him questions or try to discuss the day's events. Silence would answer me for I was truly alone. On occasion, I would forget that he was dead. I would turn to say something only to stop mid-sentence when I realised he was not there. It was then that I was at my lowest and the feeling of despair would weigh heavy upon me.

I passed the time by drinking coffee and studying the heavens. The night sky was clear and billions of stars peppered the heavens like sparkling diamonds strewn across a dark blanket. Sleep came easy with the fresh mountain air filling my lungs and a hard day's travel behind me.

I woke in the dead of night. The horses whinnying and pulling at their lines disturbed me. I sat up feeling groggy and rubbed my tired eyes as I tried to adjust my vision to the dim light created by the dying fire. Other than the horses stirring, it seemed quiet, but then a rustling noise from the surrounding undergrowth caught my attention. I waited and listened as hard as I could. I heard it again. My rifle was next to my bedroll and without turning my head, I reached out for it. Shining eyes began to appear in the darkness, glinting off the weak flames of the campfire.

"Damn wolves!" I yelled and let off three shots in rapid succession.

The thunderous explosions shattered the mountain's silence. I peered through the cloud of white smoke, which quickly cleared, carried off on a light breeze along with the fading echoes of the gunshots. The scrutinising eyes scattered in various directions, only to crisscross one another and reappear elsewhere. Vicious growling began to surround the camp and one of the pack horses started to buck. The horses were panicking, neighing and tugging at their lines. The horse that was bucking managed to snap his line. I jumped to my feet and tried to grab the trailing rope as he charged past me, but the frightened horse was moving too fast. My fingers were only beginning to close around the fibres of the rope when it was pulled from my grasp, leaving me with a rope burn across my palm. He disappeared into the night, running at full speed. Almost at once, I heard the ferocious pack take up chase and after no more than thirty seconds, it was obvious they had cornered the poor beast. Snarling, growling, and yelping echoed in the night as the horde fought each other for the right to tear into the doomed animal's flesh.

With the pack of wolves occupied, I took the opportunity to ready myself in case of their return. I reloaded my rifle and gathered every scrap of loose wood that I could find to build up the fire. I took out Larsen's hunting knife. The blade was long with one edge serrated. I stabbed its sharp point into the closest tree trunk where I could reach it with ease. I could think of nothing else to do so I sat down next to the fire and laid the rifle across my lap.

"There'll be no more sleep tonight," I told the horses, whom had still not settled down. I continued to talk in the hope that my voice might help to calm them. "Easy there, they'll probably not return now." No sooner had I spoken, when some movement caught my attention. Eclipse's ears pricked up, also aware of the returning pack. They were circling the camp, moving into position before they would enter the light that radiated from the now blazing fire. Every now and then, one of them would turn his head and the light would reflect off his eyes giving away their position.

I held the gun up but did not fire. I wanted to wait for a clear shot and avoid wasting ammunition. There was a low growl from behind and then more snarling from the front as they worked themselves up for the attack. I stood and turned to meet each new noise, unsure of which direction the first attack would come from.

And then it came. Three wolves dived out of the darkness, attacking the horses, biting and snapping at their legs. I roared at the camps invaders and aimed my rifle, but the petrified horses were turning and kicking wildly, preventing me from getting a clean shot. Hearing something behind me, I spun around to see two of the vicious predators in full charge towards me. I pulled on the gun's trigger, blasting off a shot and hitting the closest one in the head. The force of the bullet caused the wolf's body to jerk up and twist sideways before falling to the ground. The second wolf leapt into the air, launching himself at me. Without enough time to aim, I spun the rifle sideways, striking the beast across the face with its butt. The animal howled in pain and crashed to the ground. It staggered to its feet, only to find the gun's muzzle aimed straight at him. I fired two bullets into his side and the wolf crumpled into a heap next to his dead companion.

Another beast, larger than any of the others had entered the melee. He was approaching cautiously from the side with his head hunched low and fierce teeth exposed. Again, I aimed and fired, but the gun jammed. I frantically tried to free a spent casing from the chamber, but the wolf, detecting an opportunity, broke into a run and leapt into the air, knocking me to the ground. His teeth sunk into my arm. While trying to keep my torn limb from being ripped off, I reached back with my free hand to grasp the handle of the hunting knife. Pulling it free from the tree, I plunged it into the wild animal's neck. Blood spurted out like an erupting geyser as I pulled it out to stab him again in the stomach. The wolf's body went limp and collapsed on top of me, and I rolled to one side to push the bloody beast off.

I staggered to my feet. The attack had ended and I had fought them off. I turned to find the second packhorse lying on his side and drenched in blood, a gaping gash across his neck. Two dead wolves lay beside him with their heads caved in. The horse's eyes were wide open as he stared pitifully at me. I picked up the rifle and struggled with one hand to free the jammed cartridge from the chamber. I walked over to the mortally injured horse and stood over him. With a heavy heart, I aimed the gun at his head and pulled the trigger.

Dawn started to show itself, and as the rising sun shone, it gave the pine forests and rolling hills a completely new appearance. The country's staggering beauty was revealed as the dark cloak of death receded to expose the camp, which was a scene of carnage, littered with dead bodies and blood-splattered soil. I tended to my mangled arm. A feeling of queasiness came over me as I studied the wound. The wolf had sunk his teeth deep into my flesh and torn back the skin to expose the bone. My arm needed stitching, but I could not face doing it as I would probably faint. I wrapped a spare shirt around it and tied it as tight as I could. The gaping wound still seeped blood and it soaked through the cloth. I could only hope the blood would congeal and stop bleeding.

TWENTY-SEVEN

The Hennessy Place

Infection gripped me. My arm continued to bleed and no matter how tightly I bound the wound, blood still seeped from the torn flesh. My clothes, saddle, and even Eclipse were soon stained with dark streaks of sticky blood that dried and flaked in the warm air. I was weak and as each day passed, I grew weaker. Sweat saturated my body even on the coldest of nights. At night camp, I raved like a drunk fuelled by bouts of delirium. By day, I sat swaying on my horse as if in a drunken stupor.

Any sense of direction I possessed disappeared. The distant snow-capped peaks lay hidden behind tree-covered hills. The sky clouded over and the sun was of no benefit in guiding me. I was lost and death would soon have sought me out if it were not for Eclipse's instinct. He continued to trudge south, mile after mile and day after day. I was useless. I knew what needed doing – I knew I had to hunt, rest, and dictate the way home.

Although I knew these things, I could not do them. My mind was preoccupied with the nonsensical considerations of an idiot. My body lacked the will to do anything other than slouch forward upon my horse. For many days and nights, I continued in the same fashion. For how long I did not know. Time was lost to me. The sun's brightness and the darkness of night were the only two characteristics of time that governed my actions. When it was bright, I would sit helplessly and leave myself at the will of Eclipse. When darkness crept over the landscape, I would fall to the ground and sleep where I fell.

"Tom. Tom Anderson." The words whirled around in my head as if in a dream.

"Are you Tom Anderson?" The voice seemed distant and kept repeating my name over and over again.

"Bill, is that you, Bill?" I said.

A shadow moved, but it was just a blur and I could not focus on the person or the voice.

"Are you Tom Anderson? The words continued to echo inside my head.

I screamed at it to leave me be, but the voice continued to torment me. I yelled again, begging it to leave me alone, but it would not stop, no matter how hard I pleaded.

"Anderson. Tom Anderson." I repeated the shadow's words. I do not know what I said next or even if I said anything. I know I wanted to speak, but words failed to form in my brain. I was delirious and words, shadows, and thoughts blended as my mind reeled in the confusion of a disorientated mind. The sound of the voice faded away into the blackness that came over me.

Rays of warm sunlight upon my face woke me, and I opened my eyes. Two oak rafters stretched across the ceiling above me. I lay without moving, studying the beams. My vision followed the dark groves that ran lengthways along the run of the timber. I studied the lines as they compacted to go around the many knots in the wood.

I felt warm, and I felt clean. I sat up. The white bed sheets were folded neatly around me. I wondered for a moment if I was dreaming. Voices drifted in the open window. I pulled back the sheets and swung my legs out of the bed. A pile of folded clothes lay on a wooden chair next to me. I did not recognize them. They were not mine, but I assumed they had been left for me. I dressed as quickly as I could for fear a stranger would enter.

The sun blinded me for a moment as I looked out the window. Ploughed fields stretched into the distance and a dozen women walked the tilled channels. They carried large wicker baskets hanging from straps around their shoulders.

Each woman preformed the same action of reaching into the basket and throwing a handful of seeds onto the dirt. I stood watching the peaceful scene. Beyond the fields, the dark silhouetted outline of mountains stretched along the horizon. I recognized the snow-capped peaks far off in the distance, their blurry outlines seeming familiar to me.

The door's handle rattled as it was turned from the other side. I turned and was surprised when Mrs Dolan walked in. Her face brightened at seeing me up and about.

"Tom, it's good to see you recovered." She crossed the room to embrace me and my sides hurt from the power of her arms.

"Where's Katherine? Where am I?" I had so many questions and I kept blurting them out faster than she could answer.

"Oh, Tom, so much has happened, I hardly know where to begin," she said and then started to sob, fumbling in her apron pocket for a hankie.

"Katherine...where is Katherine?" I began to panic.

"Come out to the kitchen." She led me along a hallway and down a staircase to the kitchen.

I had no idea whose house I was in, or what Mrs Dolan was doing here. I was anxious to find out what was going on, and sat nervously at the table as she poured coffee for me.

"For God's sake, Mrs Dolan, what's happened?" I could wait no longer. Fear and dread filled me. "Has something happened to Katherine?"

"Men came to the ranch. They took her," she said, her face displaying the anguish of her voice.

"Took her? Who took her? Where?"

"Into town. They said Wilson sent them. They told us Bill was dead and you were to bring the gold to them. They said if you do that, they will let Katherine go."

"When? I mean when did this happen?"

"Five days ago."

"Five days!" My chair fell backwards as I stood. The thought of Katherine in the hands of Wilson's men for five days sent a sickening surge through my stomach.

"My husband tried to stop them, but...but they..." Her head fell into her hands as she wept and her shoulders jerked up and down with involuntary motions as she continued to sob into her hankie.

I walked around the table to comfort her. I said nothing. What could I say that would ease her pain?

Mrs Dolan sat up straight and fought hard to hold back further tears. "They killed him and set fire to the cabin." She continued to snuffle as she tried to be brave.

"Whose house is this?" I asked.

"Our neighbours, the Hennessey's. They've been so good. When Bill's horse came back alone, he and two others went out to look for you. They found you just one day's ride away. They brought you in two nights ago, you were so ill we put you straight to bed."

"Eclipse?" I said, remembering nothing since my delirious state.

"They brought him in, too. The horses are in the barn."

I lifted my chair back up and sat down to finish my coffee. I had to think straight. I was alone and I sorely missed Bill.

"Can I have something to eat?" I did not feel like eating, but I was weak and felt light headed after standing up. My body needed food and whether I liked it or not, I had to eat to restore some of my strength.

Mrs Dolan prepared a bowel of thick turnip soup for me and put a half loaf of bread next to it. I had not eaten in days and the sensation of soup working its way down into my stomach felt good.

"Tell me about town. Did they say where they would be?"

"They said you are to go to the hotel."

"Isn't there any law there?"

"Yes, there is a marshal, but he's gone away on business. Mr Hennessey said Wilson probably paid him to leave town." She sat down again, facing me. "What are you going to do, Tom?"

I straightened up. "I'm going to see Wilson and end it once and for all."

"Now?" she said.

"No, not now. Tonight when it's late, better that way." I was thinking clearly now and drawing on experience I had gained from my time in Larsen's company.

"Feeling better?" A voice came from behind me. I turned to see a man standing in the kitchen doorway.

"Yes...yes, thank you. Mr Hennessy, I presume?" I stood and reached out my hand.

"Yes, that's right." He shook my hand with a firm grasp.

He was older than I had expected, although I had not given it much thought. He was in his seventies and a stocky man of medium height. His face was hard, his skin almost leather-like, as you might expect of a sailor who had spent his life battling into the wind. He was bald except for two clumps of white hair either side of his head. Despite his years, he had the physique of a man half his age. His shirt bulged with a strong chest and his upper arms sported muscles that made his hands seem small and out of proportion.

"We need to take a look at that arm." He looked at my injured arm as he spoke.

I looked down. I had forgotten about my arm. A fresh bandage covered the wound, but a damp patch of blood marked the extent of the gash.

Mrs Dolan cleared the dishes from the table as I retook my seat. Mr Hennessy pulled out a chair to sit next to me.

"I want to thank you, Mr Hennessy, for finding me."

"That's alright. We thought you were probably dead, but Mary convinced us to go and look for you."

"Well, thanks to both of you." It had been the first time I had heard Mrs Dolan called by her Christian name. She nodded in recognition of my thanks.

Mr Hennessy unravelled the bandage while Mrs Dolan began to place items on the table – a bottle of whiskey, a knife, white cloths, and a pot of steaming hot water. They have done this before, I thought. As the wound became exposed, I looked away. One glance at the ripped flesh was enough to make my stomach churn and my head feel light. I focused on a French Dresser that had plates and dishes displayed along its shelves. I cringed with pain as they wiped the skin around the wound, probably with the whiskey. My arm felt as if it was on fire and I would have pulled it away had Mr Hennessy not gotten such a firm grip of it. I studied the china on the dresser, anything to divert my attention. The plates were remarkably thin and appeared quite fragile. Light blue images of Chinese women working in rice fields were painted on them, each piece displaying a different scene. There was another surge of pain. It felt as if flesh was being cut away. The pain was too much to bear and I slumped back in my chair as I passed out for a few seconds.

"You all alright, Tom?" Mr Hennessy said.

"Yea...I'm alright." I lied. I wanted to scream, but somehow I held it in.

"Finished now, just stitchin' it up," he said.

I passed out again only to come around after a few seconds. They continued to knit the skin together. There seemed to be no end to the pain, but finally I felt my arm released. A pool of blood had formed on the table's surface and was trickling over the edge, dripping down to the floor. A new bandage was wrapped around my arm and the familiar red patch did not show through. It still hurt more than ever, but the job was done. Mr Hennessy slid a glass of whiskey towards me. I lifted the glass and without hesitation drank its contents in three large gulps. My windpipe felt as if a lighted torch had been shoved down it, but at least it took my mind off my arm.

"Eclipse?" My arm tented to, I began to regain a line of thought again.

"In the barn," he said.

"The stallion, too?" I asked.

"Yes, we found Larson's stallion and one of the packhorses close to your camp. They was loose, must have followed you down from the mountains."

"Not me," I replied.

"What do you mean?" He looked confused.

"They followed Eclipse, not me."

He nodded, waiting for me to say something else. I decided not to explain. How could anyone understand the actions and loyalty of Eclipse? He continued south, always south, for days on end when I was of no help. He saved my life. Of that, I had no doubt.

"Can I see them?" I asked.

"Sure, Tom. They're your horses."

"Thank you, I owe so much to you and Mrs Dolan."

"Hell, you owe nothing. Bill Larsen was a good friend to me when I needed one. I don't forget things like that."

Eclipse pushed against the stall gate when I entered the barn. The sliding lock rattled and looked as if it was about to break away from the door. The other horses pricked up their ears when they heard his whinnying. Larsen's big stallion looked out from the next stall. I pulled back the gate's latch and Eclipse shoved the gate open with such force, it pushed me backwards. Hennessy laughed as Eclipse pushed past and ran out into the yard. I began to follow, but his hand on my shoulder stopped me.

"Mary told us about the gold, but there was no sign of it when we found you."

"I know. We never got it."

"Never got it, or couldn't find it?"

I explained to Mr Hennessy what happened. He expressed no surprise when I described the flash flood that in the space of a few hours turned a serene valley into a raging river.

"That's wild country up there," he said, nodding as if at some time in the past in which he'd personally endured the hardships of the high country. "You could wake up to find the sun scorching the ground, and by noon, find yourself fighting a snow blizzard."

"I realise that now," I said. "Next time, I'll be prepared."

"Next time...you're going back?"

"Yes, but I think I'll have to wait until next spring."

He nodded. "Yes, that would make sense. Ain't nothing but wolves and mountain goats able to travel up there in winter."

"I might need some help, next time..."

"You got it." He reached out to shake my hand. I remembered back to the time I shook hands with Bill in Harper's Hotel. Nothing was said then, just as nothing more was said now.

"Right now, I've got more important business to attend to." I reached out to grab Eclipse's rein.

"Going after Wilson?"

"Just as soon as it's dark."

"Want some help?"

"No, but thanks for the offer."

"You'd be crazy to go in alone. I heard he has half a dozen men at the hotel."

"Maybe, but this is something I have to do by myself."

Hennessy's grip on my shoulder tightened. "I knew your father, Tom. He'd be right proud of you."

A few months ago, his comment would have meant nothing. I might have even treated it with distain. But something had changed...I had changed. I was not the same man that left Boston. I believe my father would have been glad I had grown into a man, and I would like to think that Larsen would have also looked kindly on me now. I could only hope my mother would have understood. She devoted her life to ensuring that I grew up to have a normal life, but what was normal? When the evilness of others comes calling it is not normal to turn one's back. My mind wandered back to the time I cried on the road to Boston. I had cursed my lack of courage, but what was courage? I had not known then. The odds were against me and that was my excuse not to act. But I knew now what courage was. It didn't mean you were not scared. It was when you knew you could not prevail, but the knowledge of that did not deter you from trying. I understood the courage of men like my father and Larsen now. They never let the prospect of defeat hinder them in any way.

We walked out into the sunshine. Eclipse ran in continuous circles around me, leaving a track in the dirt.

"That's a fine horse, if you ever want to sell him—"

"No, never," I interrupted.

"Well, I can understand that. Sure is a fine horse," he said.

"What do you know about the men that took Katherine?"

"Only what Mary told me. Five men, one had the dark skin of a Mexican."

"Mexican?"

"Yes, that's what she said. Do you know him?"

"We've met," I replied.

Mr Hennessy pulled a pipe from his side pocket. I followed him over to the fence, where he began to tap the old tobacco out. He continued to offer his help, but I was steadfast in my conviction to go after Wilson alone.

TWENTY-EIGHT

The Lion's Den

The sun was dipping behind the hills as I rode along a dirt path leading to the main gate. A magnificent orange glow dominated the western sky, its splendour fuelled by the receding sun. But the peaceful scene did not reflect the violent purpose of my journey. Any qualms I may have held about killing had long since been lost to me. My mind flashed back to Emma's treatment at the hands of Wilson's men. A sickening thought filled me with dread. I swore a solemn oath to myself. If any harm has befallen Katherine, God help the man that has laid a hand upon her. I tried to clear such thoughts from my mind, forcing myself to remain clear-headed and focused.

I rode on and watched the sky darken as night took hold. I could not have travelled more than three miles when I heard galloping hooves pounding the ground. I pulled on Eclipse's reins and turned to face the direction of the approaching sound. I sat still and listened into the night. They were coming fast and from the direction of Hennessy's place. I reached back to pull out my rifle. I laid it across the saddle and waited. Through the darkness, shapes began to emerge. As the shadows got closer, the outline of three riders began to appear. I wrapped my finger around the trigger, but eased off when I heard a familiar voice calling out to me.

"Tom!"

"Mr Hennessy, what's wrong?" I shouted.

"Ain't nothin' wrong, we're goin' with you."

They struggled to keep their horses still after reaching

me. The three horses, filled with adrenalin, paced around in circles. Streams of breath puffed out of their nostrils and formed whirling plumes of vapour in the cool night air.

"I appreciate the offer, but this is my business," I said.

"When somethin' happens to a neighbour, then that makes it our business. We're comin', whether you like it or not." He leaned forward to emphasize his words.

Even in the half-light, the determined look on his face was plain to see. I knew it would be pointless to argue the matter further.

"This here is Ben Long and Nathan Thomas, friends of mine," he said, looking around at his companions.

I nodded to both men and they nudged their horses closer to shake my hand. They reminded me of Hennessy. Both men were in their sixties and had tough leathery faces. However, those were the only similarities. Ben Long's name could not have been more apt. He was exceptionally tall. His horse was also tall, but Ben's wiry legs looked as if they might reach the ground should he straighten them out. Nathan was quite different. While of average height, he was a burly character. His shirt buttons strained with the pressure of holding in his chest. His upper arms were similar to the thickness of most men's legs. He reminded me of a strongman I had once seen when a travelling carnival visited Boston.

After the introductions were complete, we continued along the main trail. It had been my firm conviction not to involve anyone else in this filthy business, but now that it had happened, I was grateful. I had no idea what I was going up against and their appearance was that of men with experience.

Oakcreek was a prosperous town – its thriving economy fuelled by the profits of the copper mines that lay to the south. We stopped just outside the main streets and tied our horses at the rear of a lumberyard. From there we walked through a maze of planed wood that was stacked in huge piles up to three times a man's height. As we crossed the yard, I began to hear the noise from busy saloons. Drunken men laughing and women shrieking against the backdrop of music hall pianos created a rowdy racket that grew louder the closer we got.

Nathan grabbed my arm. "Best you wait here while we see what we can find out."

"Alright, I'll wait," I told him.

We remained in the shadows while Ben and Nathan walked towards the main street.

"They're good men," Hennessy reassured me. "They know everyone in town. Better we know what we're facin'."

I nodded. I felt the familiar signs of fear returning. My mouth was dry and my stomach felt as if it was turning over in my body. Despite my fear, I was eager to get going. Katherine was close and my body ached to see her.

"Mr Hennessy, whatever happens, leave Wilson to me," I said.

He looked at me for a few moments before answering. "Alright Tom, he's all yours."

Nothing else was said and we sat in silence. An hour passed and they had still not returned. The boisterous din from the town continued. I began to think that something had gone wrong, but then I saw the dark outline of a man approaching us. The burley shape of Nathan Thomas was unmistakeable. He hunched down as he pushed his sturdy frame between the horizontal fence planks. He sat on the ground and leaned back against the fence, which creaked from the weight of his upper body.

"What's happening?" I asked.

"Took us a while." Nathan was breathing heavily as he spoke. "Wilson has eight men in town and we had to locate each one."

"What about Katherine?"

"Ain't heard anything about her. We reckon she's in the hotel with Wilson and a Mexican that works for him."

"Mex?" I said.

"You know him?" Nathan asked.

"Yes, we've met. What about the other men?"

"They are spread around town enjoying Saturday night. Three are in one of the saloons, two are in the steak house, and two are holed up in a whore house in the Chinese Quarter."

"So it's just Wilson and this Mexican fella in the hotel," Hennessy suggested.

"And Katherine," I added.

Hennessy turned to me. "Alright, Tom, it's your show. What do you want us to do?"

A strange feeling came over me. It was a sensation I had

never experienced before. I remembered the countless times I asked Larsen such questions. Now men were asking me. I was no longer the apprentice.

"Where's Ben?" I said.

"I left him watching the hotel," Nathan replied.

"Do you know what room Wilson is in?" I asked.

"No, but he has taken the whole second floor. That's all we heard."

"Alright." My mind was clear. "Nathan, you and Ben cover the hotel from across the street. Me and Mr Hennessey will go in the front door. If it's just Wilson and the Mexican, now's our best chance."

"If any of his men return?" Nathan asked.

I paused for a few seconds before answering. "Kill them."

He stared at me for a moment, studying the cold and emotionless look on my face. "Alright, give us a few minutes to get in position."

I nodded and watched him clamber back through the fence and walk back into the town.

Hennessy guided me along the main street and towards the hotel, which he had told me was at the far end of the street. We passed several drunken men that staggered from one establishment to another. They paid us no heed, more concerned with the task of remaining upright. The roads were dark. There was no street lighting. Lanterns hanging outside doors of saloons and eating-houses were the only source of lighting.

Oakcreek Hotel was a three-story building on the corner of Main Street and Copper Lane. All the front windows were in darkness except the last three on the far end of the second floor. As we approached the hotel's entrance, I glanced across the street and saw Hank and Nathan partially obscured by the shadows. Both men had rifles in their hands.

The lobby was quiet. The desk was unattended and the only noise I could hear was the deep breathing of a man asleep and sprawled across a leather couch. He was facing the other way with his arms and legs sticking out awkwardly. I guessed he was sleeping off a bout of heavy drinking.

We went up the staircase. On the first floor landing, we heard muffled voices from a room further down the hall. We continued up to the second floor. My heart was pounding as we walked along the corridor. It was well lit with lamps on both walls. We stopped three doors from the end. I turned to look at Hennessey. He appeared calm and his confident manner reminded me of Larsen. I put my ear to the door facing me and hearing nothing, moved on to the next one. I heard something. It sounded like someone moving in a chair or maybe stretching out on a bed, but there were no voices. The last door was quiet, just like the first, so I moved back to the middle one. I pointed at the door, afraid to make noise by talking. Hennessy nodded and stood back to indicate that he was going to watch the other two doors while I went in. I nodded in reply, and as slow and as gently as I could, I put my hand on the round doorknob and turned it.

It turned halfway and stopped. The door was locked. I stepped back and pulled out my revolver from beneath my coat. I took a deep breath before stepping forward and lifting my leg to the level of the lock. My foot made contact with the door and I surged forward, putting all my weight behind my leg. The door burst inwards and splinters of wood torn away from the frame spun through the air. A man stood at the opposite window. He spun around and I recognized the tanned skin of the Mexican. His face displayed his surprise. He was not armed and held out his arms to show me.

"Where is she?" I said.

"No comprendo, Señor." He shrugged his shoulders.

"You better comprendo or I'll blow your damn head off." I lifted my pistol to point at his face.

"Tom!" Hennessy cried out and as I turned to look around, a succession of gunshots erupted. Hennessy crouched and began firing towards the last bedroom door. Above him, chunks of wall were exploding in small dust clouds as bullets tore into the plaster.

The Mexican saw his chance. He ran to the wardrobe where a gun hung from a holstered belt. I fired but missed. My bullet shattered the windowpane and caused the net curtain to flutter. He pulled out the gun and fired, but I dived to the floor and fired again as I landed. This time my bullet found its mark. It ripped through his chest and he stumbled backwards against the wardrobe. After a moment, the Mexican fell sideways, and his body hit the floor with a loud thump. I stood up without taking my eyes off him. His arm started to rise into the air, although it shook as he struggled with the weight of his weapon. I walked over to him and put my foot on his wrist. He moaned in pain and the gun fell from his hand.

"Where is she?" I demanded.

"No...no...comprendo." His voice was weak.

"You Mexican bastard." I aimed at his chest and fired three bullets into his body. He moaned with the impact of the first shot, but uttered nothing after the other two.

I ran back to the corridor. Hennessy was standing again, his face dripping with sweat. He did not look at me. His eyes and gun were fixed on the last door.

"I think it's Wilson, and I heard a woman cry out," he said.

"Katherine?" I asked.

"I reckon so."

I stood to one side of the door and called out. "Wilson?" There was no reply and I called out again.

"Yea, it's me," he answered.

"If you have hurt her, I swear—"

"Back off, Anderson, she ain't hurt. Not yet anyways."

"I'm coming in," I said.

"Sure, come right ahead...it's open."

I reached down to turn the handle. It was unlocked and I pushed the door in, but stayed to one side and out of sight. After a few moments, I moved forward as slow as I could. I began to look around the door's frame, my gun following my line of sight. Wilson stood with his back to the window. He held one arm around Katherine's neck and the other held a gun, its barrel dug into her side.

"Let her go," I said as I stepped forward into the room.

"You've impressed me, Anderson." He spoke with an air of confidence and seemed unperturbed by his predicament. "You've come a long way since Boston."

"Let her go, she's got nothing to do with this," I said to him.

"And then what? You'll stand aside while I walk out of here?"

"Shoot him, Tom, shoot him," Katherine urged me, her voice distorted by the tightness of his grip.

"Little lady has guts, not like some I've known. Remember that cute little thing back in Boston? Hell, she cried so much, we had to gag her."

"Did they—" I spoke to Katherine without taking my eyes of Wilson.

"No, Tom, I'm alright," she answered, anticipated my question.

"He's trying to rattle you, Tom." Hennessy's voice came from behind me.

I took a deep breath. Hennessy was right. Wilson was trying to throw me off. I was calm and he was needling me any way he could. I looked into Katherine's eyes. Her face was red from Wilson's chocking hold on her, but I could see the honesty in her expression. She was telling me the truth.

"I reckon you've got about one minute before my men get here. What are you going to do?" Wilson said.

His voice took my attention back from Katherine. Before I could answer, the sharp crack of gunfire erupted from the street outside. Wilson sidestepped away from the window and tried to look out, but he was hesitant to turn his head too much.

"I don't think your men are coming," I said, and threw his own question back at him. "What are you going to do now?"

He did not reply. We stood, continuing our standoff while listening to the gun battle rage outside. Anger began to spread across his face, and he looked around the room, desperately trying to think of a way out of his situation.

"Shoot him, Tom!" Katherine cried out again.

I watched his face. The look of anger had giving way to fear.

"Don't do it, Tom. He'll kill her, and you if he can!" Hennessy shouted.

The gunfire from the street finally abated and after a moment's silence, there was a high-pitched whistle. It was short and sharp and Hennessy immediately commented on it. "That's Hank. It's all over out there."

"Well, what's it going to be?" Wilson said. "I walk out, or she dies along with us...it's your call."

"Put your gun away, Mr Hennessey." I spoke without looking around.

"Are you crazy?" Hennessy said.

"I said put it away."

"Don't, Tom. He'll kill you." Katherine's voice was break-ing under the emotional strain.

"Don't cry, Mrs Marshall, everything is going to work out just fine." I smiled as I spoke and her eyes began to widen.

My remark meant nothing to Wilson and my calling her Mrs Marshall was something he did not comprehend. But she began to understand, and it was as if she could read my mind from that moment on. I pushed my gun into its holster beneath my coat and a grin began to show on Wilson's face. His gun arm relaxed and he began to remove his other arm from around her neck.

Katherine, feeling his arm move away, reached down and grabbed his gun. She pushed his arm to point the weapon into the corner of the room. Although his strength would have far exceeded hers, the speed of her action took him by surprise. A look of disbelief and helplessness showed in his expression. At that very instant, I drew my revolver, aimed, and fired, all in one swift movement. His shoulder jerked back as the speeding bullet shattered the bone. His body twisted and he fell back against the wall. He still clutched his gun, which was now pointing down to the floor. Katherine ran to my side, throwing her arms around my waist and bur-ying her head into my chest.

"It's over now," I reassured her without taking my eyes off Wilson.

"Well, finish me, what are you waiting for?" Wilson said, his voice trembling from the pain.

My finger began to tighten around the trigger.

Well, Anderson? I'd of killed you. Come on!" he yelled.

"Tom, don't," Katherine pleaded to me.

My mind was in turmoil. I wanted to kill him and I had no qualms about spilling his blood. Larsen's face flashed into my mind, and the memory of my father. There were other imag-es, too. All the people killed or hurt because of him. My fin-ger continued to increase the pressure on the trigger.

"Don't you see...if you kill him like this, you'll be just like him." Katherine's words brought me crashing back to reality. But it was more than her words, it was her voice, too. Any-one else's words would have had no impact, but her loving tone reminded me of the line that defined good from evil.

"Drop the gun," I said, my voice calm and steady.

He thought about my demand for a moment, but as he

looked into my wild eyes, he knew I would not hesitate. He let go of the gun and it fell to the floor. Hennessy pushed past me and kicked the weapon, causing it to spin across the floor where in came to a stop against the far wall. He stood back keeping his own pistol aimed squarely at Wilson's stomach.

"Let's go." I looked into Katherine's eyes. They were moist with happiness and she nodded back to me while smiling.

"Don't worry about this vermin. We'll bring him to the army post west of town. They'll see he faces justice," Hennessy said as he grabbed Wilson by the scruff of his neck.

Outside the hotel, a large crowd had gathered, drawn by the noise of gunfire. Four men lay dead, their bodies lying in the street with people standing over them and prodding them with their boots as if to confirm their deadness. Hank and Nathan were sitting on the hotel steps, each smoking a cigarette. I shook both their hands. I did not speak for I did not know where to begin in expressing my gratitude. They smiled and I think my expression and my firm grasp of Katherine's hand spoke for itself. The crowd of onlookers parted as Katherine and I walked through them. It was as if Moses himself was waving his staff to part the Red Sea.

The End

ABOUT THE AUTHOR

Stephen O'Sullivan lives in Dublin City, Ireland. He works as a service technician for an international security company.

He first put pen to paper three years ago when his young daughter asked him to write a story for her. After just a few sentences, he was addicted to writing and hasn't paused since.

Anderson's Gold is Stephen's first novel, but many of his short stories have been published in various magazines and newspapers.